Shining City

Shining City

Tom Rosenstiel

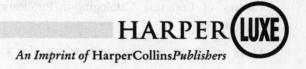

An Imprint of HarperCollinsPublishers

HarperCollins
PUBLISHERS
Since 1817

HarperCollins books may be purchased for educational, business, or sales promotional use. For information please e-mail the Special Markets Department at SPsales@harpercollins.com.

FIRST HARPERLUXE EDITION

ISBN: 978-0-06-264443-5

HarperLuxe™ is a trademark of HarperCollins Publishers.

Library of Congress Cataloging-in-Publication Data is available upon request.

17 18 19 20 21   ID/LSC   10 9 8 7 6 5 4 3 2 1

For Rima, Leah, and Kira, always

Let us resolve tonight that young Americans will always . . . find there a city of hope in a country that is free. . . . And let us resolve they will say of our day and our generation, we did act worthy of ourselves, that we did protect and pass on lovingly that shining city on a hill.

—RONALD REAGAN, Election Eve speech, November 3, 1980

Time, which is said to be the father of every truth, uncovers all.

—NICCOLÒ MACHIAVELLI, *The Prince*

Life being what it is, one dreams of revenge.

—PAUL GAUGUIN

Prologue

N
o one survives long in the city counting on it to be better than it is. That doesn't mean, Peter Rena thought, you should make it worse.

In Rena's mind this attitude was more practical than moral. Maybe Martin Luther King was right and the long arc of history did bend toward justice. It was pretty clear to Rena you shouldn't expect to recognize the curve in your lifetime. You just tug in the right direction, because if you do, others might, too. And if you don't, the arc might bend the other way.

Rena didn't ponder such questions often. These meditations, when they came, tended to visit him at night, in his den, sometimes induced by John Coltrane and Grey Goose and Dolin vermouth. They usually appeared at the apex of some mess he and his partner had been hired to help wash up. Often after he had told some client to come clean and there was an argument about it. Even when the trouble was bad and the options limited, many clients still wanted assurance they would be rewarded for doing the right thing. Rena would tell them no: Do the right thing, because the alternative is the wrong thing.

Rena and his partner were sometimes called fixers, but the term didn't fit. They never fixed problems—they just ended them. Clients came to them because they were good at getting to the bottom of things, finding what others missed, and they didn't mince their words. They also tended to calm people down; whatever the trouble, Rena and Brooks had usually seen worse.

At night Rena would listen to his music and try to empty his mind. He would take another cauterizing sip of martini, and he would read. Inevitably his thoughts would wander back to his day. Many clients at some point would talk about destiny. They would wonder whether what was happening to them was fair. The most successful and powerful often struggled the most; they had more to lose. But those conversations didn't interest Rena much. He didn't believe in destiny, or fate, or anything else that suggested people hadn't made choices.

Rena believed in history. And preparation. He believed in will, and in the value of understanding the psychology of your opponents. And your allies, if you had to depend on them.

Above all Rena believed in facts. Facts were real and had a habit of sticking around. And when there were a sufficient number of them, you could know the truth about something. Maybe not all of it, but enough.

Plenty of people in town peddled something else. They promised they could create "new narratives" and control the cycle and guarantee the outcome. And they believed it, too, because of how the machinery of the city was arranged. It was positioned so the status quo mostly remained intact. Change was expensive and unpredictable. Failing to change, on the other hand, had subtle benefits. It generated more outrage, more fund-raising, and repeat business. It was even a kind of insurance: If everyone lost, all involved could claim victory in their enemy's defeat.

Washington is a city of promises. Some great and some sinful. Some so moving they are etched on monuments. From time to time Rena thinks about the city's promises. His favorites are those the young come to town with; those promises are clean and hopeful. The most common promises are the ones made in public that offer big things for nothing and are not really promises at all. And then there are the promises no one is meant to hear, paid for in money or favor. When they go beyond what the city can abide, people call Rena and ask him to untangle what has been paid and to whom. There, in the hidden city, Rena makes his way.

PART ONE

Death and Beginning

April 12

One

The key point in any interrogation is the moment of capitulation. The instant when the subject, exhausted of all other hope, concludes the interrogator is no longer someone to fear but a friend—maybe the only one.

Peter Rena senses that Congresswoman Belinda Cartwright, freshman, R-Utah, is nearly there.

"I don't think you understand," she says again with a beseeching look. "I was the victim here."

Rena stares back at her without expression.

They are alone in an empty room of the Cannon House Office Building, on a Sunday afternoon, chairs pulled close together at one end of a long mahogany conference table.

"Well, that makes all the difference," she adds. "I was the one defrauded."

The man who'd taught Rena interrogation in the army, Tommy Kee, called it the power of silence. "People get terrified when there are gaps, Pete, and you don't fill them up. They take it as a sign of personal failure." Tommy didn't believe in intimidation or fire ants, sleep deprivation or water techniques—"all the enhanced interrogation bullshit." He believed in what he called "fine listening"—looking for the parts that didn't fit, "taking time and taking notes," asking a few right questions, then letting people expose the parts of themselves they don't mean to. "Learn to control silence, and you can control almost anyone."

Rena has been listening now for more than an hour. He had begun sympathetically: "Explain it to me from the beginning." The congresswoman talked in the practiced way of someone who as a child was socially awkward, who under stress still talks too much—and who knows it. So he has let her go on, and she has tried to explain all of it—the missing money, how her husband had deceived her, how she was trapped. There is a lot to get through.

Her formal service in the House of Representatives amounted to four months, one week, and six days. An account in the *New Republican* tallied her list of accomplishments in that brief time as misappropriation of public funds, criminal conspiracy, several House ethics violations, and breach of various campaign finance statutes. "Matching the list to length of service," the magazine speculated, "it may set a record in the annals of public malfeasance."

Rena has spent most of the last two days learning every detail about Cartwright. She, on the other hand, knew little about her visitor. "He can help you with your problem," Phyllis Martinson, the senior female member of the House, had said—which meant the meeting wasn't optional. Drew Allman, the Capitol Hill veteran who had organized her office, had been more chillingly candid. "He's a crisis consultant." Some kind of PR expert, she asked? "No," Allman had said. "The guy who comes in when PR won't work."

A Web search revealed he was ex-military, Special Forces, one of those crazy guys who swim across alligator-infested waters to slit your throat and then swim back. He became some kind of military investigator, and spent time as a Senate aide. Now he runs a "consulting" company. "Research and Security"—whatever that is—the website doesn't list clients. "What do you mean, 'he comes in when PR won't work'?" she'd pressed Allman. "I mean when things are really bad, Belinda," he'd answered.

In the empty meeting room, they make a contrasting pair. Rena has black hair, olive skin, and large melancholy brown eyes. He is dressed in the supplicant hues of a Washington aide—charcoal pinstripe and blue tie. Underneath the suit, however, she can see a lean muscularity. There is a quiet and vaguely menacing quality about him, like a black jaguar. She, by comparison, is pale and has a round face with a deceptively sweet and guileless set to it. And unlike her visitor, she is dressed to be noticed, in a made-for-TV pink-rose suit, picked to suggest innocence.

"Mr. Rena, I was told you could help me," she says, careful to say his name the way he'd pronounced it for her—"Rehn-nah." "Can you help me?"

When he doesn't answer she finally utters what he considers her first honest remark. "Why are you really here?"

In a way she *is* a victim, Rena thinks. The daughter of a prominent Provo Mormon family and a promising young attorney, Cartwright represented in her maiden campaign youth and conservatism. In the middle of the race, she married her family's financial advisor, a doughy-looking character named Derek Knox. The wedding was a Latter-day Saints society event and a campaign public relations triumph.

It was also her undoing. Knox turned out to be a con man. Cartwright and her family's money were the mark. When the family money was gone, he tapped her campaign funds. Once in office, nearly destitute, she put Knox on her payroll as chief of staff to keep her personal finances afloat.

The leadership, however, had noticed her. Cartwright was a member of the Common Sense movement, that surge of Americans alarmed the nation is declining and convinced that government is the reason. When she arrived in Washington, the Speaker of the House saw in her an eager but pliant political novice and an opportunity to connect with the conservative Common Sensers that didn't run through his calculating majority leader. He made Cartwright a freshman member of the leadership team. National media began to profile her. Someone found a loose string about Derek Knox and pulled.

"We need this to be over, Peter," the Speaker's chief of staff had said when he'd called two days ago. "She's hurting the party. We need someone who can level with her and not lose their nerve. You're good at that, Peter, at being blunt."

If he were answering her honestly, then, he'd say bluntness was one reason he's here. That's fine with Rena. Candor isn't the worst reputation to have in a town where it's in short supply.

But it wasn't the only reason they'd called him. The Speaker's office also wanted distance from this—from cleaving a member of the Common Sense movement from the House. And Rena and his partner, Randi Brooks, offer that, too, if for no other reason than that they do something many consider immoral in modern Washington: work for people in both parties. Not anyone. But those they consider decent.

That makes them a rarity in the city now—and somewhat ideologically suspect. Even lobbying firms now keep separate Democrat and Republican staffs.

But the taint of bipartisanship that is attached to the consulting firm of Rena, Brooks & Toppin is also not entirely un-useful. Messages still need to be delivered. Frank talks had. Deals struck. It can be hard to make the first move. If possible, the go-betweens should be trusted by both sides.

Most of their work isn't political: corporations wanting background checks on potential CEOs or troubled executives, law firms with big cases, sports teams with stars in a fix or draft prospects surrounded by rumors. Not the profession he expected when he enrolled at

West Point. He once tracked down criminals, traitors, and terrorists for the army. But that had ended more than seven years ago.

Cartwright dabs her eyes with the remnants of the tissue and slowly shakes her head back and forth.

"I'm here, Belinda," Rena says finally in a voice just above a whisper, "because your career in the House is over."

Two

11:23 A.M.
Bethesda, Maryland

The seventeenth green on the Blue Course at the Congressional Country Club sits atop a gently rising hill guarded on both sides by a series of enormous bunkers. Elliott Hoffman sees his father, Julius, standing between the two sand traps on the right side of the green studying his next shot, a slippery chip of about thirty feet.

The old man, dapper in an elderly kind of way in his white Ben Hogan–style cap, is holding his sand wedge in one hand, dangling it back and forth, lost in thought. Elliott can see his father's mind working, studying the contours of the green, the elevation change, the way the ball is sitting on the grass, concentrating, thoroughly caught up in this one moment, pondering the many variables affecting the shot.

Elliott feels a wave of affection. There was a time he and his father barely spoke. Then somewhere in his forties—after the children were gone and the divorce from Ellen was final—they rediscovered each other. They let go old grievances, what his father called "the forgotten business," and just came to appreciate each other. Sundays with his dad were the best part of his week.

The moment of reverie passes, and Elliott looks at his father. Julius Hoffman is six months past eighty-five now. Everyone marvels at his vigor. He has become leaner with age, and the leanness makes him look brittle, the gray wisps of hair over his bald head adding to the effect, but all that is deceptive. Julius Hoffman is not only strikingly fit for a man of his age. He is still working, still handling his case load, still admired, even feared. "A steely tower of conviction," as the *Economist* had put it last year, catching that mixture of intimidation and integrity that Julius Hoffman now seems to represent in the public mind.

For all that, his father's greatest pride might be that he occasionally shoots his age in golf. He no longer hits the ball far—his drives go barely 150 yards—but his short game—the shots around the green—has actually improved.

Elliott begins to eye his own putt and doesn't watch his father swing. He can tell, however, that the shot is poor. Pop has either misjudged how hard to hit his chip or skulled the shot by hitting the ball with the lower edge of the club face. Either way, the ball flies too far, past the hole, and doesn't check up from backspin, but skids off the opposite side of the green.

The sound Elliott hears is also odd, not the usual amusing groan of mock agony his father makes after hitting a bad shot. The sound has come earlier—during the shot rather than afterward—and resembles a gurgling moan.

Elliott looks up. His father, a weird look on his face, is trying to climb the slope up to the green, but about halfway up he staggers and begins to make a brief, stiff-legged march backward down the hill. His momentum carries him down the slope, his legs start to cross, his knees separate, and he falls.

"El—" Julius Hoffman cries out to his son, failing to get out the full name.

By the time Elliott reaches him, Justice Julius Hoffman, the senior sitting justice of the Supreme Court of the United States of America, is dead.

Three

"A man would have survived this."

Cartwright's voice is lower and harder than before.

"A man falling romantically for a manipulative woman is a victim. But a woman duped by a man, that is unforgivable."

She may be right. It doesn't matter.

"You're past that now," Rena says.

She looks at him with an intelligence that was missing before.

"I thought everything in politics is perception," she says.

"Only the guilty argue that."

Cartwright shifts in her chair. Rena touches the top of her shoulder.

"If you go," he says, "I won't be able to help you."

"Don't patronize me, Mr. Rena."

"Do you know why you have to resign, Belinda?" He wants to reward her candor with his own. "Because you lied to your colleagues about when you knew about your husband. Then, when they vouched for you based on that, you made them liars, too. That is when you lost your claim of innocence."

She begins to cry silently.

The phone in Rena's jacket begins to vibrate and he can tell she's heard it. He lets it go.

"How you end this will determine how people remember it." She looks up at him. He has her attention now. "If you begin to tell the truth, people will know you are leveling with them. The press coverage will change instantly."

His phone is vibrating again with another call.

Rena gets up from his chair and walks over to the window to give her some time, and with his back to her he pulls the phone from his jacket and turns it off. He looks down into the empty interior courtyard below, one of Washington's secret spaces, a place only staffers and members of Congress could go. It is empty on a Sunday, but the flowers there, shaded by the building, are still in bloom.

When the crying stops, he goes back and sits down next to her.

"People want to forgive. They want a happy ending. If you give them one."

She smiles—a bitter, intelligent smile.

"How does all this happen?" she says.

He outlines the familiar contours of exiting a scandal—if she resigns, the party would back someone she would approve as a successor, a Common Sense supporter. The party would also help with her campaign debts.

Rena has already arranged the money.

"You will become sympathetic, almost overnight, because you'll have already paid the price of losing your job."

She nods, bent head raised, then sweeps away tears with the back of her hand.

"I will be with you, helping you," he says.

He also outlines the alternatives—that if she resists and keeps her House seat while facing legal charges, she will be shunned. Then he runs through the rest, the details of a resignation, how to do the press conference. Cartwright looks shrunken, sitting in the big conference room chair. They talk about how to tell staff. Colleagues. Who to talk to in the Speaker's office. Timing.

"And you become again the person you really are."

Cartwright cries awhile.

He reminds her to leave the back way, which will take her to the members' elevator, where she could get to the parking lot without being seen. She doesn't look up as he leaves.

Outside the door Rena shudders. When he did real interrogations, he often felt broken afterward. One time he slept for two days.

Eleanor O'Brien, his new assistant, is waiting in her car behind Cannon. He has found it useful lately to be driven to meetings by an assistant. It saves time, especially trying to park, and gives him the chance to talk on the phone without being overheard by cabbies or hired drivers. O'Brien doesn't seem to mind losing part of her Sunday. She is twenty-three, and the more she does, she says, the more she learns.

"How'd it go?" she asks.

"It's done."

She laughs. "So it was horrible?"

"Pretty much."

He yanks at his blue tie and unbuttons the top button of his white shirt. Though he wears a charcoal or navy pinstripe suit almost every day, this uniform he has never been comfortable in.

"May I ask you a personal question?" she says.

"I may not answer."

"Why did the Speaker call you to do this?"

"She asked the same question."

"What did you tell her?"

"Nothing."

"Is that what you're going to tell me?"

Rena takes a deep breath.

"I guess they thought she would hear it better coming from a stranger."

"You know what Smolonsky said about you?"

"I don't want to hear it." Walt Smolonsky is a hulking ex-cop who works for Rena and talks too much, especially if the person listening is young and pretty.

"He said people call you for jobs like this because you are not afraid of telling people the truth."

"He's a liar."

O'Brien says nothing for a minute and then asks, "Do you think she should resign? Cartwright I mean?"

"Of course."

"Because?"

"Because she stole—she used public money to cover her debts, and if that isn't a crime, it's close enough. On balance, I think it's better not to have liars and criminals in government."

"You know the other thing Smolonsky says?"

"Don't tell me."

"That your dirty little secret is idealism."

"He's screwing with the new kid's head."

She swings the car around the House office buildings and heads down Independence Avenue, which will take them past the Jefferson Memorial, the Washington Monument, toward the Lincoln, Roosevelt, and King memorials, and then along the Potomac past the Kennedy Center, where they will turn off toward Rena's home in the West End. Though he's driven it thousands of times in the decade he's lived in Washington, he always finds the drive past the monuments impressive.

O'Brien's phone rings.

"Oh, hi. He's right here." She hands the phone to Rena. "It's Randi."

"Your phone's off," his partner says. "I tried to call you."

"It's Sunday. Day of rest."

"How's that working for you?" Brooks asks.

Rena smiles. "What's up?"

"You hear the news?"

"About?"

"Geez, Peter. About Justice Hoffman."

"What about him?"

"He's dead."

"No."

"Heart attack. On the golf course. They say he was dead before he hit the ground."

"Where?" Rena says, trying to picture the scene.

"Some country club where he belongs. Burning Tree? No. Congressional. Fell into a sand trap or something."

Rena imagines worse ways to die than going fast, doing something you love.

"A lot of people thought Hoffman was a miserable asshole," says Brooks. "But he was the last real liberal of 'the Supremes.'"

Rena's partner is a lawyer who has done a lot of judicial appointments, pays close attention to who sits on the federal bench. An opening on the Court for Brooks is like a full solar eclipse for an astronomer. "His death leaves a huge hole on the left."

Brooks is also a liberal Democrat. Rena, who is a Republican and a soldier, isn't sure what label fits him.

He wants to go home and relax, and O'Brien deserves the rest of the day off.

"Nash won't have the balls to nominate anyone nearly as liberal," Brooks adds, speaking of the president, James Nash. "So this will set off a shit storm."

"Lovely."

"The 'Common Sensers and the Holy Rollers Wrath of God Squad' versus the 'Twentieth-Century New Deal Elitist Bleeding Heart Help the Homeless Gang,'" Brooks says. "And nobody will be able to tell when it's over which side was good and which was evil."

Rena's partner, a prep school and Ivy League girl, also likes to talk like a master sergeant.

"Let's hope we can stay out of it," he says.

Supreme Court nominations have taken on a particularly dishonest and jaded quality in recent years.

Rena looks out the passenger window. He's had enough of politics for one day.

"Amen to that," Brooks says.

He hangs up O'Brien's phone and returns it to her. Then he turns on his own. Almost instantly it begins ringing.

Rena looks down. No caller ID. He checks recent calls. There have been ten calls from Unknown Caller. He answers the call coming in.

"Mr. Rena, this is Spencer Carr."

Spencer Carr is the president's chief of staff.

"It's been too long, Peter."

Not long enough, Rena thinks. When Carr was a backbencher congressman he had lied to Rena about a deal being worked out with senators. Carr may not remember, but Rena hasn't forgotten.

"Yes, it has. How are you, sir?"

"Good. Peter, thanks. I hate to impose on your weekend. But the president would like to see you. Tonight."

Four

4:15 P.M.
Berkeley, California

S he will have to put the packages down to open the
door. He's sure of it.

When she gets to the top step of her apartment
building, she's going to stop, put some of those bundles
down, fumble with the lock, then hold the door. He'd
seen her make that mistake before; she forgets where
she puts her keys and then has this whole hassle with
the grocery bags.

If she does that now, he'll do it today.

The thought stops him. So it's really gonna happen.
After all the planning, all these months, all the hiding

and watching. He feels a surge of euphoria and fear mixed together, like a shot of syrup in his veins.

He watches her in the van's side mirror as she comes up the sidewalk. He needs her to get close enough to see him clearly but not feel threatened.

When she's twenty yards away he gets out of the van and shoves the door closed hard.

Embarrassed grin. "Sorry," he says. "Didn't mean to slam it."

She returns the smile. A shared secret. A little bond. How clumsy of him.

The woman is nearing middle age now. She looks smaller and rounder than she had back then. The frizzy hair, not dyed, is going gray. Something around her eyes suggests loneliness; something around her mouth suggests she has given up hoping that might change.

He moves around to the back of the van and opens the doors, takes out a tool kit in a canvas bag, and begins to head toward the entrance of the building basement. He wants her to get a good look at him. That will make her less suspicious. Phone company guy in overalls with a little hitch in his right leg, hat on backward.

He drops off the bag of tools. Then he turns as if he

were going back to the truck. He has the clipboard in his hand.

She hesitates at the bottom of the steps that lead up to the front door of the apartment.

She stopping? Forget something? Don't leave.

No. She's trying to remember where her keys are. She begins to move up the six steps to the front door. She is trying to figure out if there is a way she can manage the lock without stopping, without putting down all her things. She grimaces as she gropes for the keys in her purse, but she can't move her hand very much. Too many grocery bags. She is realizing it now, what he could see from the van. She ain't *that* smart.

Not hardly. If she had been, everything might have turned out differently. She wouldn't have ruined everyone's life.

Stay in the present, he thinks. This, right now.

He moves to the bottom of the steps.

"Ma'am? Let me lend you a hand. Here, I can open it for you."

Don't ask. Make her stop you.

Voice steady, friendly, like he had practiced in front of the mirror. He is moving up the steps. He has his pen out, as if he'd been writing something on his clipboard. He slips it back in the breast pocket of the overalls, with the name Jim on it, right below the phone company logo.

"That's okay," she says. She is hesitant but not fearful.

"Don't be silly," he says. "It's nothing. Just take a second."

She isn't sure. But she doesn't say no.

"Lemme open it for you."

"Well, I, I have to get my key."

"Lemme hold the groceries then."

She would be most worried about putting down the groceries. You put those plastic bags down and everything falls out. It would be a relief not to.

She hands the two grocery bags over. He takes them in his gloved hands.

"Thanks. Very nice of you," she says.

"My pleasure."

She opens the door and steps inside.

He begins to hand the bags back to her, leaning his arms through the open doorway.

She is smiling.

It only takes a second to push his way into the foyer and shove her farther inside. He shuts the door and drops the plastic bags, and the groceries spill out on the floor. A white thin trail begins to leak from a fallen milk container. He pulls a heavy plastic bag from his overalls, one he had in advance, one she cannot tear. He pulls it over her head.

His smile has turned upside down into the bad-man frown. Where he grew up, you practice that as a kid. And perfect it on the street.

She hasn't said a word. She is too surprised.

Now it's too late.

He can see her eyes through the plastic. They're huge. Shock melting into fear. He knows that look. He had seen it inside. Even strong men get it—when they realize it's the end. Her fear is so big it startles him for a second. She's gonna have an effing heart attack. The bag is inflating and deflating with her huge, gulping panicked breaths. His big, gloved hands are around her neck, sealing the bag. The bag is fogging up inside.

She is fighting him now. Thrashing to free her arms, which he has pinned across her chest. He lifts her off the ground. Eliminates her leverage.

She tries to call out, but it's all just gasping. She's too terrified to generate sound.

Good. She should be scared. Too bad it will only be a few seconds. Not scared for ten years. Not seeing her life chip away, like old fucking paint.

"You know who I am, you goddamn bitch?" he says in a loud whisper.

She thrashes, then stops, then thrashes again. She's losing energy. She thrashes again.

"This is for Peanut. You worthless piece of shit."

She loses consciousness. Then the bag stops inflating and deflating. She ain't huffing and puffing now.

She ain't anything.

He keeps his hands around the bag and her neck until he's sure.

He lays her down.

Then he opens the door. Picks up the clipboard he has left outside. He skips down the steps, as if he ain't got a thought in the world. He grabs the tool bag. Then he heads back to the van. He even looks down as if he were checking something on the clipboard. A work order or some shit.

He pops the driver's side door open and slips in, putting the tool bag beside him. Ignition. Side mirror. Check for traffic. He pulls out.

He breathes deeply to calm himself. It takes a few blocks to relax. He's done it. No more dreaming about it, doing it in his mind. He's no-shit-really-done-it.

It doesn't feel like he thought it would. And God knows he had thought about it. For months. For years. Seen it in his head, like he was watching a movie. Visualization, man. Dream it. See it. Make it happen.

It feels like he's still watching himself. He is calmer than he ever imagined. He feels serene.

So, it's begun. After all this time.

Be cool. Stay in the present. Think.

Because he's just getting started.

Five

7:50 P.M.
Washington, D.C.

Civilians rarely spot the sharpshooters. The camou-
flaging surrounding the White House is too expert.
The rifles, however—mostly Remington M24s—are
routinely sighted, safeties engaged, to keep the marks-
men sharp. The hardest part is fighting the boredom.

Rena glances at the rooftops around Lafayette Park
and spots subtle movement.

In the hours since the call, he has managed to relax,
run, and shower. Now he is back in the charcoal suit
and blue tie. He clears security at the white guardhouse
and crosses the driveway to the entrance to the West
Wing.

White House Chief of Staff Spencer Carr is waiting for him in the large eggshell-white lobby.

"Peter, thanks for coming."

Lifeless handshake.

Message delivered:

I'm not happy about your being here.

Carr, a former Internet executive and Silicon Valley congressman, is handsome in an arid way, like a Hollywood actor too good looking for character roles but not appealing enough for leads. So he plays villains.

He is famous in the Nash administration for three things: vast wealth, intense loyalty, and extreme ruthlessness.

"Is there anything more you can tell me about why I'm here, sir?" Rena asks.

"I'm in the dark, Peter," Carr lies. The lie is meant to be obvious, a sign of disrespect. Rena nods, holding Carr's gaze long enough to show he understands.

A few moments later the president's private secretary, Sally Swanson, rescues them to say the president will see them in the Residence. A meeting in the Residence, rather than the Oval Office, suggests the president wants this meeting unobserved.

Swanson leads them through her small office next to the president's and out a door to the West Colonnade, the breezeway overlooking the Rose Garden that links the West Wing to the living quarters. The West Wing was once the greenhouse. It was converted to offices under Theodore Roosevelt in 1902 when he needed the second-floor offices of the old mansion for his large family. It has kept expanding since.

They enter through French doors facing the back of the mansion and take an elevator to the second floor. Halfway down the large central hallway Swanson opens a door guarded by a Secret Service agent with an electronic earpiece and suit that bulges over a holster.

Inside, the president sits on a floral sofa, dressed in gray slacks and a crisp white dress shirt open at the collar, watching ESPN.

He turns and Rena looks into the most famous smile in the world. "Peter Rena," the president says warmly.

James Barlow Nash. The latest and most successful of the Nashes of Nebraska. The great-grandson of an-honest-to-god famous western lawman. Great-grandpa was suspiciously rich when he retired. Nash's grandfather expanded the fortune and moved into politics, not by running for office but arranging for other people to hold it on his behalf. Nash's father became a senator, and, even more remarkably, a Democrat, albeit one who denounced "communism, communalism, and most other isms that don't start with the word *capital*." Nash completed the transition—from regional figure to national one, and from conservative Democrat to something harder to define.

On a coffee table in front of Nash sits a small glass of whiskey, neat. Probably Labrot & Graham, Rena thinks, a Kentucky bourbon Nash doesn't like people to know he prefers. "It's bad politics to have favorites," Nash likes to tell aides. One of Nash's famous legal pads—supposedly he fills one each day—plus his beloved antique Parker pen, sit on the sofa beside him.

Nash summons everyone to sit and walks to a bookcase bar.

"Peter?"

"Whatever you're drinking, sir."

Nash looks at Carr, who nods, and the president brings over two whiskeys.

Nash looks at least a decade younger than his fifty-six years. He is tall, with piercing blue eyes and weathered craggy good looks that recall his cowboy ancestry. A political columnist once wrote that he looked like he was "marshal of the whole U.S.," and the phrase had stuck. Nash is also blessed with a physical grace that he uses to great effect in public. Perhaps the most striking quality about James Nash, though, is that he makes everything look fun—even the presidency. Which, given the state of things, makes some wonder if he is really trying.

"Peter, you heard about Julius Hoffman?" Nash says.

"Yes, sir."

"Glad you're keeping up."

"I try."

Nash grins mischievously and, having performed his bartending duties, slides back onto the sofa.

"Hoffman will be buried in three days. Even before he's in the ground this town will be wondering who I intend to pick to replace him."

Then, mocking a popular refrain in town, Nash adds, "What does Jim Nash want?"

Two and a half months into his second term, James Nash remains a frustrating enigma to much of establishment Washington. The Right considers him a cipher pulling the country toward oblivion by obstructing their efforts to cut stifling entitlements and regulations. The Left considers him a betrayer and coward for failing to press a progressive agenda once he gained power. A year before the election, virtually no one in town "who was serious" had given him much chance of a second term.

Nash, however, had built his career on being underestimated.

He'd started as a public defender in Lincoln—famous, wealthy, impossibly handsome, and working for the poor. He ran for the state legislature at thirty-three. When he sought the governorship eight years later, opponents scoffed at his lack of legislative achievement, but he won with the biggest margin of any Democrat in the state's history. When he hinted at a run for the White House, the website PoliPsyche called his two gubernatorial terms "diaphanous." "He stands for nothing," the *Weekly Review* declared, "other than hubris, a strong chin, and Paul Newman eyes." His signature phrase, "Let's get it done," sounded like a sneaker ad, a Democratic rival joked. The *Wall Street Journal* had called his run "pointless" and "vain." While his better-financed primary opponents focused on one another, Nash won Iowa and New Hampshire without registering in national polls. By March, through superior voter targeting and organization, his nomination had become a mathematical certainty.

Most people thought the incumbent president, Jackson Lee, lost the election during the first debate. "I knew your father," the president had said, implying Nash was riding on his famous name. "And he knew you," Nash countered simply. But something in Nash's tone made it plain that to know the real Jack Lee was to know he was a fraud. The remark captured a feeling the whole country seemed to be on the edge of accepting. The president's poll numbers began slipping that night.

The first term had proven . . . what? Pick your adjective. *Stalled? Broken? Polarized? Dysfunctional? Meandering?* The same words had been used to describe Lee. Old hands blamed the Common Sense radicals on the right for driving the government incoherently from crisis to crisis. Common Sense advocates countered that their no-compromise tactics might be the only thing that could break the pattern that had put the country on a downward course in the first place.

In the end, Nash won reelection because a majority of Americans disliked both parties more than they disliked Jim Nash. Whether Nash is a cause or a victim of the dysfunction, people agree on one thing: The government doesn't work. The same patterns keep playing out. When Nash manages to get anything done, it's by getting both sides to agree to deals they later regret—and for which their bases punish them.

The political press, or what is left of it, grants Nash his victories but mostly considers his presidency a series of muddled half-steps. His record, in the phrase now popular at dinner parties around the city, lacks any "clear theory of governance."

Whatever one thinks of him, James Nash now has forty-four months left in office—or about twenty-five months of governing time. After that, he enters the final awkward interval of his presidency when people will be waiting for him to leave.

Nash leans back into the sofa and takes a sip of his bourbon.

"So what *do* I want in a new Supreme Court justice, Peter?"

Rena doesn't know the president well. He is also the wrong party. His partner, Randi Brooks, is more political—and a Democrat. So why is he here?

"The Constitution says the president nominates justices and the Senate confirms them. The problem is that everyone else feels they should have a say in picking the next justice. That's as it should be, given that everyone should feel sovereign in a democratic republic."

Nash lifts his glass to toast the sovereign public.

"It's wonderful. Unless you happen to be the one responsible for actually picking these people," Nash says.

Rena smiles.

"And what do all my sovereigns want? My own party wants me to pick a true-blue bleeding liberal, someone who will push against all the decisions of a conservative court of the last thirty years."

The president nods to the invisible Left and continues.

"Many in the rival party, the honorable majority, feel that assenting to a liberal pick would be a failure of their leadership, given their control of the Senate and House. They have a constitutional obligation to assert their principles and I have a constitutional obligation to listen."

Nash is famous for "thinking aloud" like this, rehearsing ideas and clarifying calculations, frequently with people outside his White House circle. His hero FDR did the same thing.

"Then there is the realpolitik crowd," Nash says, "the city's permanent establishment—lobbyists, the press, and some of my own advisors—who say go for an easy confirmation. The last thing I need, they argue, is a bitter confirmation fight, or worse yet, to lose one. Not in a second term."

Nash is smiling. "It's really quite a fix to be in. When my grandfather was giving out raises during a bad year, he would say, 'You can either make some people happy and other people mad, or you can leave everyone disappointed.'"

Rena laughs.

"So what should I look for in a justice? The Founders said ignore political ideology. A justice has no power to create policy, anyway, no power to propose laws or make them. The only power judges have is their judgment. 'Merely judgment' is the phrase James Madison used in the Federalist Papers. So pick someone wise, someone of transcendent character, someone above politics."

Nash's blue eyes are shining.

"And through most of our history this has worked. Whatever presidents intended, our best jurists have been people of independent judgment and moderate pragmatism—former governors and acclaimed law professors—who often irritated their political sponsors."

Nash leans forward, as if to signal, Here comes my point.

"The problem is we've started to politicize the judiciary in a way we've never seen before. And it flows all the way down the system. Judges in lower courts, picked for their ideological purity, render partisan decisions and send them to the Supreme Court to be enshrined."

Nash picks up his whiskey, looks at it, and then puts it down.

"This is the great invisible crisis of our country, Peter. It's more corrosive than what's happening in Congress. Those fools we can vote out. This," Nash says, "this goes deeper and lasts for generations."

Nash is on his feet.

"If we are supposed to be a country of laws, not men, then people must believe in the independence of the judiciary that interprets those laws."

The president's movements are compelling. He is constantly breaking rope lines, moving toward people, being unpredictable, using his physical presence to draw your attention, like an actor whose little business with hands or objects steals scenes from other actors.

"If we want to begin to change things in Washington, Peter, we can start by doing it here, with a different kind of nominee for the one part of government that is not supposed to be political. We do it by doing something right that everyone recognizes. That people can rally to."

Nash wanders to the big windows overlooking the front lawn and gazes at a TV crew doing a stand-up. A lone figure, a woman correspondent, is bathed in the ghostly radiance of portable lights.

Rena looks at Carr but can't see the chief of staff's expression.

"Peter, our greatest vulnerability today is that we have forgotten the things that bind us. Through history our points of consensus have been our greatest asset. We weren't divided by tribal divisions or old national boundaries. We were bound by common ideas. Whenever we were threatened, this made us more unified than our enemies and better able to face our challenges. We are losing that. We are tearing ourselves apart from within. And the Supreme Court, which should be the one part of our government where we are reminded of the things we share, has become part of the division."

It's as impassioned a speech as Nash gives. Delivered for one.

Nash moves back toward where Rena and Carr are sitting.

"If I do nothing more as president than begin to change the dynamics of the Court, it would be an achievement. That is the opportunity we have, if we can find a way to do it," Nash says.

It's "we" now. Nash has already put him on the team.

"Now, if a president wants to do that, to break from this pattern and pick a different kind of judge, it would have to be one hell of a justice. Someone truly different. A paradigm-shifting kind of judicial character. And getting this person confirmed is going to be especially challenging. The nominee won't have the support of a conventional ideological base."

In other words, it's just the kind of political risk the city devours and spits back up so no one will dare take another risk like it for years.

"So, such a nominee must absolutely be bullet-proof. That means above reproach," Nash says. "It also means, he or she must have no secrets the White House doesn't know about beforehand."

In other words, this is a bucket of shit. And Nash is going to give it to you to carry around while wearing your nicest charcoal gray suit.

Nash sits down again and faces Rena.

"Peter, I want you to do more than scrub the nominee. I want you to get that person confirmed. Run the show. I want you at this person's side all the way through, you and Randi both. We'll give you all the support you need, of course."

This isn't what he expected. Rena thought he'd been summoned to help scrub potential nominees or maybe track down a specific rumor about someone. Not own the whole problem.

And this is a political job. Rena isn't qualified for it. Randi is. She's done a lot of court appointments. Why isn't she here?

"You'll work closely with the White House counsel's office. Spencer will coordinate. But you and Randi will pilot this. Handle the vetting. Prep for hearings. Steward the visits, handle strategy. We'll be with you the whole way. Peter, I need this person confirmed."

The moment Nash stops, Rena realizes he is trapped. For his firm this job would be a step up to a higher profile. Yet helping a president out with something this political isn't like what he and Brooks normally do with Washington clients—helping broker a deal in the House or getting a moderate senator out of a personal jam that a member from the other party might be in next time.

If he did this, it would create a breach with his Republican friends. Yet if they refused, it would amount to a similar breach with Brooks's Democrat allies. And that, in some ways, is just the least of it.

There is a cost to saying no to a president. If Rena and Brooks turn it down, they won't likely be asked by any president again. They weren't important enough to say no. In fact what Nash is proposing, hiring someone to steward a nomination this way, that kind of work is almost never delegated to outsiders.

That's the other alarm Rena is hearing. He and Brooks are such an unlikely pair to run this nomination, everything about it tells him something about this is off. Get a Republican to vet and steward a nominee. And if it all goes to hell, Rena and Brooks will take the blame.

An even more devious thought then enters Rena's mind. Is it possible Nash wants whoever he picks as a game-changing iconoclastic nominee to fail? Prove that the other side isn't serious about changing Washington? Use the loss for political advantage? His next choice would fly through. You always get the second nominee. The other side already has its victory. Nash can ram through a much more liberal nominee, and make the GOP like it.

Is Nash's White House that Machiavellian? And so theatrical that the president has to put on a show to convince Rena to play along?

Sure they are. It sounds just like Washington.

"I have a question, Mr. President. Why us?"

Nash seems caught off guard at the directness of the question, then smiles.

"Because, Peter, I cannot afford to have this screwed up. And without blowing sunshine up your ass, you guys—you and Randi and the team you have built— are better at scrubbing people than anyone in town. And because of who you are."

Yeah, you don't want to blow sunshine up my ass.

"A Republican?"

"Someone who has a history of taking risks to do the right thing."

So he's going to reference that, the martyred end of Rena's military career?

"My history includes paying a heavy price, Mr. President," Rena says. "I think it's called losing."

Nash smiles again.

"Yes, Peter, you being Republican helps, too. I need Republican votes to do this."

The president's story has some flaws, Rena thinks. There are plenty of firms in town that could scrub this nominee. Not many of them with a Republican principal would work for the White House. But if you have a nominee who is different enough . . .

Rena has other questions, but they're all some variation of the one he can't ask: Are you screwing me?

"I need to discuss this with Randi," Rena says.

Because everything about this makes me want to say no.

"Of course."

"When we're ready, we'll send you a list of names," Carr says, speaking for the first time. He's already assuming Rena is aboard. "We'd like your team to vet one of them. We will have different teams vetting the others. Then we will decide on one. When we have decided, then you will do a final vetting. And then we will go forward."

After Rena leaves, Carr sits back down and takes a drink. "You really want to do this?" he asks.

"I do."

"You know his past. He's hard to control."

"That, Spence, is why this works," Nash says.

Six

He had bought the row house, a redbrick Civil War–era home near Georgetown, to raise a family with Katie. The bedrooms they intended for children are now guest rooms, though there are rarely guests. Rena mostly lives—reading, working, and too often falling asleep—in the den.

He eases wearily into the brown leather Morris chair in the room's corner by the front window. The Arts and Crafts–style furniture that fills the den is about all that remains of the marriage, along with some pots and kitchen knives, and his regrets. Katie had never really liked the heavy angular oak pieces. She thought them too dark and masculine. But she went along with buying them because she knew they made him happy.

Maybe because he is more tired than usual or unsure where the events of the night will take him, Rena's eyes move to her photo, which still sits on the library desk. Freckled nose, dirty blond hair, shining eyes, taken four years ago during a visit to his grandmother's in Tuscany. His feelings about Katie haven't changed, he thinks, but he feels them less often.

They met, just for an evening, when he was a senior at West Point, though they both remembered it well. When they met again years later at a dinner party in Washington, it felt as if only days had passed. The differences between them were obvious. Katie had money on her mother's side and Old Virginia family lineage on her father's. Rena was an immigrant from Italy, with no family other than his father. She was poised and charmed people with her candor. He had the intense reserve of an outsider who'd learned to fit in by listening. From the moment they met, however, being together always felt like mind reading.

They never imagined not making it. They never imagined four miscarriages, his crisis in the army, or his pouring his energy into building the business to prove himself to her family. He never imagined his obliviousness. The divorce became "final" thirteen months ago. But divorces never become final, he thinks. They just become real.

He needs to call Randi. Will she wonder why she wasn't invited to the White House meeting with him? Will she think something about this request seems odd, as he does? Or will she just be thrilled by the chance to move up to a new level, which this certainly would be? His father, if he were still alive, would be bursting. "The president, Pietro. The president asked for you!"

In the kitchen he mixes a martini, two parts Grey Goose vodka and one part Dolin vermouth. The first sip should come quickly, as cold as possible, while the glass is still frosted. He feels the thick, icy chill rise up his skull.

He takes the drink back to the Morris chair. Two walls of the den are lined to the ceiling with books— biographies, some political theory, a few mysteries, but mostly history. "The argument without end," Dutch historian Pieter Geyl called it. Most Americans barely know the arguments, Rena thinks.

Rena has always been a digger, and at times, he fears, a grinder, someone who gets by more on sweat than talent. He also is engaged in an accidental profession, one he came to late. So he always assumes how little he knows and always arrives—when he was young to soccer matches and classes, now to assignments or meetings—the most prepared person in the room.

As he has tried to learn Washington, he has come to think too many of the political debates that grip the country are histrionic and self-defeating: small arguments over policy orthodoxy portrayed as major differences in core principles. The melodrama may be good for lobbying and campaigning and raising money, but it doesn't solve much. Rena trained to be a soldier, and soldiers have to be pragmatists. Too much faith in orthodoxy loses you wars. Or gets you killed.

"**We can** say no," Brooks says when he calls her.

He knows she doesn't mean it.

"Not without consequences."

"There are always consequences," she says with a laugh. "Especially when the person asking is the president."

"Why do you think he invited me and not you?"

"Oh, that's easy, Peter. You're the Republican. You haven't done a lot of these. When it leaks out they came to you, the optics are different than if they came to an old Democratic hand who had vetted a dozen nominations."

"Maybe."

"What's eating you?"

"I don't like nominations. They've become ugly and ritualistic. Everyone comes away bloodied."

"It's a lifetime appointment," Brooks says. "That's a long time to lick your wounds."

He marvels that the darker side of the city only seems to make her want to fight more. He doesn't raise his deeper fear: that they are being set up somehow. That Nash might secretly want this different kind of jurist to fail so he can pick someone more liberal afterward. Is that far-fetched? Is he being paranoid? Why does he doubt Nash's sincerity? Why does everyone doubt Nash's sincerity?

"Let's sleep on it," he declares. "No decision should ever be made at the end of the day if it can be avoided."

"See you in the morning."

He puts on Sarah Vaughn singing "More Than You Know." In Italy, before he came to America, most of what his father knew about this country was jazz. When he moved the two of them here, his father surrounded them with it.

The martini is gone. Maybe a second would help him sleep. Or not. He fixes one. Vaughn sings about love found after years of searching. He feels vodka in his temples. He closes his eyes.

His cell phone wakes him around 11:00. Caller ID from Virginia. He doesn't know the number. Something tells him to answer anyway.

"Peter!"

It is James Nash's voice.

"Mr. President?"

"I want you to feel you have a direct line to me. Anything you think I should know, just call. Use this number. I won't answer. But I will always get back to you."

Rena hasn't said yes yet. It doesn't seem to matter to Nash.

"I mean it. If there is anything that you need to ask, that you don't want through channels."

"Thank you, sir."

"Excellent. Good night, Peter."

"Good night, sir."

Rena hangs up.

What does James Nash want?

Seven

8:03 P.M.

San Francisco

He sits at a kitchen table and thinks about the unthinkable.

After all this time, it has really begun. After all the dreaming, plotting, thinking, planning. He thought he might be scared. He isn't. He feels incredible.

He watches Mama carry the casserole to the table with that little shuffle in her walk that comes from wearing her slippers.

She slides into her seat without saying a word, gives him a look, just for a second, and then quietly says grace to herself as if he weren't there.

"Eat your supper, Sweetness," she says wearily. Sweetness was her nickname for him from when he was little.

When he got older, and into trouble, he came to think of the name as a mocking thing. He would over-hear her tell people, with a shake of her head, "He has the face of an angel, so sweet, but there is a devil in his heart." That hurt him back then. He wanted to please her. The way Peanut pleased her. And he feared the devil.

But eventually, when he was a teenager and angry most of the time, he fed off that hurt. He thought the "devil's heart" meant he scared her a little. And he liked to think he scared people, maybe especially her.

All that was in the past now, almost twenty years ago, before he was sent away. Before he learned every-thing. Before all this started.

"You wash your hands?"

"Yes," he says.

Mama's head is tilted down toward her plate, her eyes looking up at him. It is the way cons eat inside, he thinks, as if suspicious someone might steal their food. He has been back more than a year, almost eighteen months. But he and Mama don't talk, not really. She thinks he's a boy still. They don't have the years in be-tween.

"I'm older now and I'm changed," he said to her once, about a year ago, as if he wanted to explain to her how he felt differently now about so many things and wanted to make a lot up to her. But she looked at him as if he were throwing prison in her face, like he resented her for it or something, which wasn't what he meant. After that, he never seemed to find a way to explain.

"What you been doin' with yourself?" she asks.

"You know," he says, not expecting the question.

"I don't know. How would I know?"

"Mama, I . . ."

"You're not hanging out with hoodlums I hope."

Hoodlums? He starts to get that old feeling, angry, like a rod of steel has shot up his back and in a second he will explode from it. But he doesn't. He feels the sensation rise and he just waits it out, and then he feels it go down again, and he thinks this is the new him. He has learned.

"No, Mama. I don't see them anymore."

He spends his time alone now. Planning.

"You going to that job?"

Clarke got him the handyman job. He'd always been handy.

"Sure."

She looks at him. "You gotta keep that job now."

"I will. I am."

The job is a joke. An insult. A thing for ex-cons. Something for people who can't get anything better. But he can't say that to her. He can't complain about the few things that people have done to try to help him.

"I hope so," she says.

"Don't worry about it. I've been going to the job." She looks at him, her eyes sunken, and takes a bite of her casserole. She is different, too. Not just older. Hollowed out.

If only he could tell her. How careful he is. How he has worked out all the details.

In that way they are alike, he has come to think. She is the kind of person who lives in the details of things. She and her friends always tell each other everything that happened each day—they went here and what this person said, and this is how they felt about it. It used to drive him nuts, but lately . . . He has discovered he is good at details, too. Now that he has a purpose.

The casserole has a smell from when he was a boy. He takes a bite. The smell is better.

Then he thinks of the day. It almost doesn't seem real. Holding the bag over her head, feeling the life go out of her.

When will he do the next one? Soon. It has to feel right. He has to feel right. He needs to think about it.

For a few more hours at least. Trust his instincts. He is good at this. He can feel it.

He looks over at his mother. She has had so much pain in her life, and he knows he's been one of the causes. That tears at him.

I'm doing all this for you, he thinks. I am sweetness.

PART TWO
The Scrub

April 14 to April 30

Eight

Tuesday, April 14, 11:00 A.M.
Arlington, Virginia

The cars are lined for a quarter mile.

They snake up the road toward the Tomb of the Unknown Soldier, past the sloping green fields and the groves of oak and dogwood and the fallen of seven wars. The land that became Arlington National Cemetery once belonged to Robert E. Lee. His mansion still looks down on the grounds. By the summer of 1864, the Civil War had filled up all the cemeteries of Washington. So the Union confiscated the rebel general's home and began to bury the boys he had killed in Mrs. Lee's rose garden.

Rena watches people in dark colors and good shoes try to negotiate the steep lawn to the interment site. Secret Service has erected a security perimeter with electronic checkpoints, bunching the crowd into three lines. Inside the perimeter, the number of mourners already exceeds five hundred. It will double in the next twenty minutes.

They have come to bury Supreme Court justice Julius Hoffman.

"The old judge would have loved this."

Rena's friend, the journalist Matt Alabama, is standing beside him. A correspondent for ABN News, one of the three old broadcast television networks, Alabama is taller than Rena and about twenty years his senior, with thick salt-and-pepper hair and a dashing but weary handsomeness. He is also older and more accomplished than network correspondents are usually allowed to become these days—he had spent a decade writing for the *New York Times* and had written four novels. Networks like CBS and ABN once had a penchant for hiring people like that, Rhodes scholars and literary intellectuals, back when television was new and trying to prove itself. Today, their audiences halved, network news divisions operate largely as break-even legacies, and Alabama is kept mainly for assignments like this, funerals and inaugurations—historic moments and signature rituals still deemed to require institutional memory.

"The Hoff liked an occasion," Alabama says. "The pomp and circumstance of the town."

"Why here?" Rena asks.

Most memorials for the high and mighty are held at the National Cathedral, across the river in Washington. Large public events at Arlington are rare.

"Hoffman wanted it that way," Alabama says.

"And you know this how?" Rena asks.

"It's an obvious question . . . the journalist's greatest friend." Rena raises an eyebrow. "I asked the son," Alabama deadpans.

Alabama scans the growing assemblage of mourners. "And now I gotta go ask a lot of obvious questions of obvious people," he says. He offers Rena a crooked salute and drifts away.

In the rows of white folding chairs, all of establishment Washington is on display. Such occasions are rare enough. Joint sessions of Congress assemble the elected, but only funerals seem to gather everyone, the elected and unelected, the powerful and truly powerful, and the seemingly ever-growing list of influence seekers.

Rena's partner, Randi Brooks, arrives and offers him one of her big, marvelous smiles. At full wattage it involves her whole face, especially her eyes. She is tall, only an inch shorter than Rena, and heavy, but her soft features and prematurely graying chestnut hair accentuate her natural warmth for people—and hide her lawyer's cunning.

"They could either save the damn country or destroy it if they dropped a dirty bomb right here, and I'm not sure which it would be," Brooks says.

"That's not funny," Rena says.

"I'm only kidding," she says. "It's just that the only person in Washington who's missing is the vice president."

"He's probably at a secret location, to protect the line of succession," Rena says.

"He's balling his mistress at a condo in Bethesda," Brooks says.

"That *is* funny."

"Now I'm not kidding."

She probably isn't. Brooks knows these sorts of things.

A short, broad-shouldered man moves in their direction. Brooks moves aside. The Speaker of the U.S. House of Representatives sticks out his right hand and places his left on Rena's shoulder.

Brooks calls this move "the shug." Half handshake and half hug, it is a staple of Washington. The shug is a way of suggesting something more intimate than acquaintance, though enemies could shug as easily as allies. The shug allows someone to lean in and whisper in another's ear and not be overhead.

The Speaker makes use of this feature now.

"Peter, I want to thank you for this Cartwright thing." His voice is low, signaling his seriousness. "How is Belinda?"

"Still processing," Rena says.

Square-faced, balding, and doughy, the Speaker has a tendency toward dishevelment and a habit of sometimes using not-quite-the-right word, qualities that lead people to dismiss him. But he always looks you in the eye, and no one in Washington could remember him lying.

He ascended to the speakership because he was the only candidate with whom all of the factions in his party were still on speaking terms. None of those increasingly ideological factions fully trusted him. Each thought it could manipulate him. He, in turn, imagined he had outmaneuvered his puppeteers because he had more alliances than they did. "If you have many bosses you don't really have any," Rena had heard him joke. But his power is tenuous.

"Belinda understands the situation?" the Speaker asks.

Rena nods.

"I'm afraid her problem is that she's a fool, but that isn't usually a fire-able offense," the Speaker tells him with a grim smile.

Rena thinks ambition, not foolishness, has been Cartwright's ruin. But politicians are not inclined to see that quality as a vice.

Someone touches the Speaker's shoulder; he nods a parting acknowledgment and disappears into a tide of aides.

Across the expanse of gathering people Rena sees William Stevens of Rhode Island, the second-longest-serving member of the Senate and the last lion of old-style liberals, but one who would also still make deals with Republicans. Stevens is talking to Rena's old boss, Llewellyn Burke, the heir to an auto family fortune from Michigan who seems to move seamlessly among nearly everyone in both parties.

A round man approaches Rena with a smile. "A bad day for the country," he announces.

"Senator," Rena answers. The senator is Fred Blaylish, a Vermont Democrat with a thick New York accent, and a member of the Judiciary Committee, which would review Nash's Court appointment.

"A bad day for everyone," Blaylish adds, "including Justice Goldstein, though he's too arrogant to know it."

Justice Goldstein and Justice Hoffman, both Jews, represented the two polar extremes of the Court.

"How's that?" Rena asks.

"Hoffman made Goldstein's arguments better. And the other way around. Great arguments require great antagonists."

It's the kind of point not many politicians would make.

Blaylish is the most liberal person in the Senate. He's also openly gay, the only one in either legislative body, and considered by many the smartest person in Congress. Certainly Fred Blaylish thinks so.

"What do you think the president will do, Peter?"

Blaylish would be plugged in, Rena thinks. He might even know about the meeting at the White House last night. Rena doesn't answer.

"You know there are seventy million Americans who consider themselves progressives in this country. They need a champion on the Court, too, Peter."

Rena again says nothing, and Blaylish smiles.

The senator had befriended Rena, unpredictably, four years ago when his lover was implicated in a drug scandal. The Democratic Party hired Rena to find out if the scandal might implicate the senator, too. It wouldn't, Rena concluded, but Blaylish had appreciated rather than resented Rena's thoroughness. They also discovered they had friends in common, including Matt Alabama, and a shared enthusiasm for reading history. They had dinner occasionally.

"Peter," he says, "if I can't get information from you, at least I can do a little lobbying while I'm here."

Rena pretends to be confused.

"The question now," Blaylish says, "is how much Nash wants to tangle with the opposition. Especially with Chairman Morgan." Furman Morgan is the chairman of the Senate Judiciary Committee. An ancient southerner, he must be close to eighty-five. He would run the hearings evaluating the nomination of Hoffman's successor.

Whoever Nash nominates will not only need about half a dozen Republican votes to be confirmed, he or she will also need Morgan's assent—however tacit it may be—if not his actual vote.

"And what does Chairman Morgan want?" Rena asks.

"Ah, well. Furman likes to create mystery. Or maybe at his age everything is a mystery," Blaylish says with a lift of his substantial eyebrows.

"Freddieeee." Blaylish turns and Rena sees Deborah Cutter, the head of the liberal interest group Fair Chance for America. Cutter is one of the most powerful and respected women in Washington. She transformed Fair Chance from the second tier to the preeminent liberal interest group by moving further left at a time when many other progressive groups had withered or tried to become more moderate.

A considerable part of Cutter's success was her skill on television. Unlike many liberals, Cutter believed that social values played into the hands of progressives, and she relished denouncing social conservatives as intolerant hypocrites whose insistence on religious faith dictating government policy was anti-American in a way the Founders would have considered repellent.

It helps that she is more beautiful than most movie stars—a youthful forty-three with flowing red hair and a hypnotizing smile—and more ruthless than even the most jaded political consultants. On camera that combination tended to intimidate opponents regardless of creed, color, or gender.

"The president has got to be strong," Cutter says to Blaylish. "He's got to. And frankly, he could use a good fight, Freddie. Really, he has more to gain from picking someone as strong as Hoffman, and losing, than he does from picking someone weak and winning."

Blaylish tries to answer.

"I hope someone tells him that, Freddie. Someone he respects."

"Hello, Deborah," Blaylish says slowly.

"Have you talked to him?"

"Deborah, Justice Hoffman is not yet even in the ground," Blaylish says.

"Freddie!"

Cutter notices Rena. "Hello," she offers, along with a power smile, and pulls Blaylish away.

After a moment, Randi Brooks reappears and takes Rena's arm.

Apparently she has been watching him.

"Making trouble?"

"Trying not to."

"She doesn't like you."

"Who?"

"Cutter. You're unreliable. Too bipartisan."

"What about you?"

"We're old friends. So she absolutely abhors me now. I'm a traitor for working with you."

Rena looks at her. She is only half-kidding, he realizes. Maybe less than half.

Together they scan the gathering crowd. Many of the seats have been reserved for elected officials, senators, House members, the Justices, the cabinet. Behind that section are seats filled with lobbyists, lawyers, and interest group leaders. The press is here, too, or what remains of it. Their fall in influence in a decade is breathtaking. Rena does not try to engage the reporters he sees, but a few catch his eye. Matt Alabama is talking to Gary Gold of the *Washington Tribune,* a relentless character with several friends on Rena's staff. Rena nods.

Alabama wanders over. The assembled crowd has swelled to full size. The day is glorious, clear and mild, a rarity for Washington in spring. April tends to alternate from cold and wet to notoriously hot every other day.

"The armies eye each other from across the field," Alabama says. "There gather the defenders of the helpless." He nods in the direction of Deborah Cutter, who is huddled with about a dozen other progressive interest group leaders and a couple of less judicious members of Congress.

"And there the enemy," says Brooks, moving her eyes to another knot of people. In the center of the group, barely visible, Rena can see Josh Albin, a man who has managed somehow to remain at the epicenter of conservative activism for more than two decades, from the Reagan Revolution to the Bush neocons to the Common Sense rebellion. A neat trick of agility.

"The hard Right gathers under the oaks," Brooks says. "And the hard Left there under the elms. The flesh eaters and the bleeding hearts. A feast."

"No, Randi, they are soldiers in the great battle for the future. It is waged each night on cable," Alabama says.

"I remember when real leaders stayed off television," says Brooks.

"Ahh," says Alabama, "the days of the closed door and the compromise deal. Today victory is found in the public eye, where you can raise money for a campaign PAC," says Alabama.

Justice Hoffman's son Elliott comes to the microphone and asks people to take their seats. The memorial service is quick. Justice Goldstein speaks about their time on the Court as rivals who had grown old together. Justice Miriam Drier, the next most liberal judge, tells personal stories. So does Anthony Shackelford, a former Hoffman law clerk who went on to become commissioner of the National Football League, and then Cory Hundstrom, the president of Harvard, another former clerk. They talk about Hoffman's intellect, his ferocity, his guts. Yo Yo Ma plays a Bach cello sonata. Paul Simon sings the judge's favorite song, "Sounds of Silence." The poet laureate reads verse. Washington knows how to do memorials.

The last speaker is President James Nash. His seven minutes are pitch perfect, funny, eloquent, and moving, about the law, Court relations, and Hoffman's indomitable personality. He offers no clue about what he will look for in a replacement.

As Elliott Hoffman is closing, Rena feels a touch on his elbow. Someone near enough to whisper. "Mr. Rena, if you have a minute." A young man—with solemn aide-to-an-important-person's body language—holds out an arm and sweeps it in the direction of a large black car parked under an overhanging oak tree about forty yards away. "Spencer Carr wants to know if you might be willing to share a word with him," the young aide says.

Outside the security perimeter, the rear passenger door to the town car opens and Rena slides in.

Carr offers a chilly nod and hands Rena a plain piece of white paper, not White House stationery. The paper bears five names without titles, apparently typed on an IBM Selectric typewriter rather than a computer. That means it did not exist on a server. No record.

"Five names, Peter. You're vetting the last one." Carr's tone is irritable. He wants to make one more show of his disapproval of using Rena for this.

Rena takes the list. They never had a choice. He and Brooks knew it this morning without saying a word.

Carr adds a stare and then some helpful advice: "Don't fuck this up."

Nine

The first hours in any investigation are the richest. Your mind is more open and your vision clearer. You haven't formed opinions and, with them, blind spots. Rena calls them "the magic hours."

He and Brooks believe in making the most of them. They assemble everyone, break into teams, and give people just a few hours to produce a "flash report." That initial burst of effort—perhaps five hours—usually gathers three-quarters of what an investigation will learn. It also surfaces the gaps.

If they want to use the magic hours today, they

have to move fast. What remains of the afternoon after Hoffman's funeral is jammed. In twenty-five minutes Rena has a call with Wally Lescher, the general counsel of the NFL team in Philadelphia, who wants him to look into charges that a star tight end was involved in a killing at a New Orleans strip club. Then there is a meeting with food conglomerate Daniels Ford Mifflin, which wants to do background checks on possible new CEOs for a high-end natural foods grocery chain it just bought. And Belinda Cartwright is waiting for Rena to return her call.

They stand at Brooks's desk looking at the list from Carr.

"Why five names? If we're only vetting one?" Brooks asks.

"A game," Rena guesses. "Carr says they have given lists to other vetting teams, each with five names. But every list is different."

"If any names leak, they'll know who to blame," says Brooks.

Rena nods.

"You really think there *are* other vetting teams?"

"Who knows?" Rena answers.

Brooks scans the list. There are the usual names speculated about in the media:

Laura Joiner, U.S. Court of Appeals for the Eighth Circuit in St. Louis, very liberal, African American, from Tennessee.

Patterson Doherty, Eighth Circuit as well, a Nash law school classmate, fellow Nebraskan, appointed by Nash's Republican predecessor, pretty conservative.

Tyson Moore, U.S. Court of Appeals for the First Circuit, Boston, in her forties, perhaps too young.

Amanda Cross, Second Circuit, New York, on lists for years, and maybe now at sixty-three too old.

Three of the four had been Hoffman's clerks.

Then she looks at the last name.

"Edmund Roland Madison, Ninth Circuit Court of Appeals, San Francisco," she says. "Shit, Pete."

"What is it?"

"Nothing but trouble."

The conference room of Rena, Brooks & Toppin is the fourth-floor attic of a mid-nineteenth-century row house. Rena and Brooks had leased the townhouse, at 1820 Jefferson Place, more for history than convenience. Theodore Roosevelt and his family had lived here during the Harrison administration, when Roosevelt was working for the Civil Service Commission. The charm of that connection may have meant less to their employees, who are spilled over the narrow house's four floors. But Washington, D.C., was a city of anonymous thirteen-story office buildings adorned in a brass and marble style that suggested high Soviet Union or maybe low Donald Trump. At least "1820," as everyone called it, was different.

Rena and Brooks had met seven years earlier when they were Senate investigators, after he had to leave the army and Senator Burke, a friend of Katie's family, offered him a job. He was prepping Burke for a hearing on drugs in Olympic sports, a kind of one-day sham hearing designed for nothing other than cable airtime. Rena decided to give it seventy-two hours to find something new, maybe force the hearings into something substantive. Everywhere he turned he came across the trail of the lawyer for the Democrats, who was usually a step ahead of him.

When he tracked her down, Rena found a brassy ultraliberal who cursed like a sailor and tended to think most Republicans were shitheads. He also found an unlikely kindred spirit, a natural, obsessive digger. Skill and craft bound them despite ideology.

They began to make a habit of collaborating, at first without telling their bosses. When Burke suggested four years ago that if Rena created a consulting firm—and was paid a market rate rather than a federal salary—it might calm some of Katie's family's concerns about him, Brooks was the first person Rena asked to join him.

They partnered with Raymond Toppin and his firm Toppin & Associates. "Top," a lawyer and former presidential aide, was mostly a one-man advisor for hire, a broker who knew how to get antagonists to shake hands. Rena and Brooks brought in new people, expanded the business into investigations, crisis management, and communications strategy as well as strategic advice. Sometimes they even did security or surveillance work, subcontracting with Rena's ex-military friends. You just had to be careful about whom you worked for. Top had retired a year later.

The business had thrived. Their gang of lawyers, ex-cops, ex-FBI, and database hunters were good at getting at things quickly, including details that people wanted to hide. Clients tended to come to them when their situations were especially serious—or had gotten especially bad. They were known for their candor. They were used to working fast.

They assemble the team for ten minutes. "Here's the name we're vetting," Brooks says after she and Rena outline the assignment. "All I can tell you is this: Edmund Roland Madison is an iconoclast. He's got conservative impulses on some issues, a libertarian streak, and liberal, even far-left ideas, on others."

Iconoclast was code, everyone in the room knew, for the idea that he would have no natural constituency. People would support him to help Nash. But if there were the slightest problem, those same people would be quick to bail.

They break into three teams—one to look at Madison's writings, his legal opinions and scholarship; a second to look at anything Madison may have written outside the law; a third to look at his personal life. "We will reconvene at five," Brooks says.

Three and a half hours later they are back in the attic conference room.

The people around the table are mostly friends Rena and Brooks collected from their years in Washington. There is Walt Smolonsky, a bearlike former police detective and Senate investigator, a few years older than Rena. And Hallie Jobe, a former FBI agent whom Rena had known in army intelligence, who had acquired a law degree at night along the way, quiet, conservative, the daughter of a black minister in Alabama, one of the most disciplined and driven people Rena had ever met—including the driven crazies from Special Forces.

Jonathon Robinson, their media specialist, is a former Senate press aide and attorney. Maureen Conner is a lawyer, quick, scholarly, sharp-tongued, a tiny wisp of a woman in her fifties with short hair and a hook nose.

Next to her is Ellen Wiley, their chief computer sleuth, a matronly woman with owlish glasses on a chain and a quietly shrewd manner. To Rena, the former librarian of the *New York Times*' Washington bureau is as much the soul of the operation as anyone, the most creative hunter of facts using databases he has ever met. In the office, a computer search is called "a Wiley."

Next to her is Arvid Lupsa, Wiley's protégé and odd-couple workmate. He is thin and has a goatee, a Romanian accent, and a genius for writing code. From what Rena can glean, Lupsa's social life proves that geeks are not just cool now but sexy.

"Tell me, who is Roland Madison?" Brooks asks.

Wiley, who worked Madison's personal background with Smolonsky, begins the resume:

Edmund Roland Madison, known as Rollie, born 1952, raised in San Francisco; graduated University of California at Berkeley, class of 1972, at age twenty.

"Skipped grades," Smolonsky adds. "Back when they did that."

Harvard Law School, 1975. Supreme Court clerk for Justice Fulton. Then two years at the solicitor general's office in the Justice Department.

Madison had spent most of his career as an academic, ten years at Harvard, fourteen at Stanford, the last six as dean. He has been a federal judge for five years.

"The Senate already confirmed him once, five and a half years ago, for the federal bench. What can we learn from that?" Brooks asks.

"Won't help him much," Wiley says. "Committee hearings lasted an hour. He testified for like fifteen minutes. He and four others at the table. Utterly non-controversial."

Madison had been appointed to the federal bench by Nash's Republican predecessor when Nash was president-elect.

"A package deal," Conner recalls. "President Lee got to pick a couple of judges whose appointments were stalled in exchange for appointing a couple of names Nash wanted."

"I remember that," Brooks says. "New spirit of co-operation."

"Yeah, that worked," says Smolonsky.

"So we start from scratch and assume nothing," says Brooks.

Conner spots "a wrinkle" in Madison's resume. Between Stanford and the federal bench, he served briefly as a Superior Court judge in California. That is a conspicuously modest judgeship for a former Stanford Law dean on his way to the federal appellate bench.

"Was he forced out as dean at Stanford and needed a spot to land?" Hallie Jobe asks.

"And he wasn't on Superior Court long before going to federal appeals," Conner notes. "Just eighteen months."

"We'll find out why he left Stanford for a not-so-fancy gig," Wiley promises.

Lupsa describes Madison's nonlegal writings. "Guy has a remarkably wide-ranging mind and he's an amazingly prolific writer," Lupsa says with a thick accent but precise diction, the blend of a childhood in communist Romania and a college education in math and computer science at Princeton.

"He's written for all kinds of magazines—everything from *Runner's World,* to *Outside* to *Science,* and some blog called PCH," Lupsa says.

"That a drug, PCH?" someone asks.

"It's a highway," Jobe answers. "Pacific Coast. The blog is about an open state of mind."

"Oh, great. Sounds like a marijuana blog," says Smolonsky.

A Stanford Law alumni magazine profile after Madison was named to federal appeals described him as "a man of such breadth of interests and depth of knowledge—from history to the constellations—that he seemed as close to a Renaissance intellect as you could find in the twenty-first century—inventive, connected to the past, quiet, moral, and abstract."

"How would they know that he was moral?" Jobe says. The ex–FBI agent speaks in a clipped monotone that people sometime mistake as humorless.

"Journalists can look into your eyes and tell," Robinson says.

"He's written thirteen books," Lupsa continues. "On everything from sailing to legal history to hiking the California coastline to astrophysics."

"What the hell is astrophysics?" asks Smolonsky.

"Astronomy."

"When did they change the name?"

"He even wrote a book on being a single father," Lupsa says.

"He's a widower," Wiley explains. "Wife died twenty years ago. One child. A daughter. Grown. Also a lawyer."

"He is a true public intellectual," Lupsa says admiringly.

"Swell," Brooks moans.

A public intellectual means a long paper trail, or a lot of provocative ideas that can be used to attack him.

A paper trail is what did in Robert Bork, the conservative law professor whose hearings helped politicize the nominating process in the first place in the 1980s. Since the Bork hearings, ironically, presidents had tended to pick people who wrote less, who tailored their resumes toward advancement rather than scholarship and intellectual curiosity. It was part of the politicization Nash had talked about.

"Legal philosophy?" Brooks asks.

Conner, a lawyer, takes over the narrative, with help from Jobe and Robinson, summarizing not only Madison's legal writings but that of other legal scholars about him.

"What you see," Conner says finally, "is a guy searching for a less ideological approach to the law. He talks about stripping away contemporary politics and scholarship, and looking for what he calls 'a more essential American truth.'"

"A what?" Smolonsky asks.

"It may be a bit nuanced for you nonlawyers."

"Explain it to us anyway," Rena says.

"Madison is arguing that the Constitution was the ultimate consensus document and not nearly as ideological as people make it out today," Conner says. "The colonies were about as different from each other as countries would be today. And they were frightened about almost everything after splitting with England. The only way they would approve the Constitution is if it stuck to the handful of things on which everyone agreed."

"Can you say it even plainer than that?" Smolonsky says. "So I can understand it." This was one of Smolonsky's ways of playing dumb and exposing the holes in what other people were saying.

"So what Madison sees in the Constitution is a set of essential American ideas that stand out for their lack of political ideology," Jobe translates. "He argues that the Constitution points mostly to protecting and expanding liberty and opportunity, and that the clearest way to apply the law today is to shed ourselves of current political ideas about original intent. Others writing about him say he is pointing to a new paradigm of legal interpretation that they call 'essentialism.' It's kind of a third way, beyond current politics, beyond loaded terms like *original intent* or *strict constructionism* or *judicial activism*."

"So he's a compromiser?" Smolonsky says.

"No. In fact, he writes about some of the biggest mistakes in legal history occurring when people tried to forge compromises on controversial issues of the day.

The Dred Scott decision that defined blacks as property, he argues, was an attempt at finding a compromise between pro- and anti-slavery positions," Conner says.

"What's the difference between a compromise and a third way?" Smolonsky demands. Jobe regards Smolo with irritation. There is occasional tension between Rena's two top street investigators, Smolonsky the sloppy but charming ex-cop and Jobe the efficient and driven former FBI agent who had made it not only being African American but also a woman.

"Any of these controversial decisions look like trouble?" Rena asks.

"Well, that's the thing. In finding his new way, he has staked out positions that annoy both sides," Conner says. "He is distinctly conservative on guns, for instance, and things like protecting religion rather than keeping religion out of public events. But he seems liberal on free speech, race, and discrimination."

The room has gone silent.

"His iconoclasm is a key point to press on tomorrow in your research," Brooks says. "Where could it make trouble?"

"Ellen, do you have those lists I asked for?" Rena asks Wiley.

Ellen Wiley hands him copies of three long lists, which Rena passes out. "These are the class lists of people in Madison's year at Berkeley and Harvard and the faculty lists from Harvard and Stanford law schools. I want everyone to go through these carefully and tell me if you have any friends on them, anyone you know.

Some called this "cohort asset assessment."

It's the technique of finding people in an investigation with whom, by luck, you have a past connection.

"If there is anyone you know here, call them and talk to them confidentially. What we're looking for is personal behavior that could get him in trouble. But you need to get them to promise confidentiality," Rena warns.

"Will they stick to that?" asks Robinson, the former Senate aide who was a new hire. Rena thinks he may use him to help with Belinda Cartwright.

"If you're scary enough," Jobe answers.

The White House wants an initial status report by Friday night, two days from now. They will meet again at the end of the day tomorrow, then begin drafting memos.

Rena looks at Robinson and Maureen Conner.

"Jon and Maureen, I want you to develop an attack memo, all the reasons Madison would be bad for the country. Hit it hard. Nasty, but serious. All the bad stuff in the worst possible light. Let's see what it looks like."

"On the opposition research," asks Eleanor O'Brien, Rena's new assistant, "do you flag only anything you think the Right will use against him? Or do you flag anything the Left might use, too?"

Not a bad question, Rena thinks. Smart kid.

"Forget the Left," Brooks says, who is about as far to the political left as anyone in the room. "They won't stab Nash in the back in public. Only in private. Whatever they have, they will bring to the White House."

"Let's hope you're right," says Robinson.

"We need to hear back from Hallie," says Rena.

"Hallie?" Smolonsky asks.

"I'm heading to Stanford to talk to faculty about what Madison is like. I'm leaving for the airport in thirty minutes."

"Faculty will talk and talk. Catty knife-in-the-back talk," Conner says.

"I'm telling them I'm from the MacArthur Foundation. Investigating giving Madison the Genius Prize."

Jobe is such a striking figure, a young black woman, military upright, impeccably polite, it seems impossible to people that she would ever be putting them on. It's one thing that has made her such a good investigator.

"Little old for a MacArthur, isn't he?" Wiley observes.

"We're making a statement," Jobe says. "About aging and creative thinking."

She's already in character.

"Listen," Brooks commands. "We operate as if Roland is the nominee and this is the final check. That means scrub within an inch of his life."

"Twenty-four hours, gang," Brooks adds.

"One more thing," Rena says. "Don't pretend to know more than you do. Look for holes. We're not just trying to tell the White House all we know. Knowing what we don't know may be the most important thing we identify."

When the meeting is over and Rena makes it down the stairs to the first floor, Stephanie Hampton, the receptionist, holds up a phone message for him. Hampton has stayed late, waiting until they broke up. Rena and Brooks find having a human being answering the phone a good thing for a sensitive business.

Belinda Cartwright, Hampton says, is holding for him on line two.

"How long has she been doing that?"

"About ten minutes."

A sign of panic.

Rena takes the call in his office.

"Congresswoman."

"Thank goodness, Mr. Rena, I thought no one in town would talk to me."

She is being shut down.

"Busy day. Hoffman's funeral," he says. Trying to make her feel better without lying to her.

"I want to take you up on your offer to help me with a press conference. I'm ready, Mr. Rena, to give up the seat."

"Yes, ma'am."

"You said I should tell the truth."

"Yes."

"I want you to help me find the words to do that."

"Good."

"I want to say that even if I have to resign, that I didn't create this situation. That I am a victim. That I am doing this reluctantly."

Rena sighs. "No, Congresswoman. I won't help you do that."

"I beg your pardon?"

"The next thing you say publicly can have only one message—that you understand that what you did was wrong."

"You said tell the truth. I want people to know how I really feel."

"How you feel is not the truth. They're just your feelings."

"What does that mean?"

"The truth is that you engaged in a cover-up. Unless you acknowledge that, you will be regarded as either a fool or a liar."

"You can be a very impudent man, Mr. Rena."

"I'm told it's my best quality."

It's the first time he's heard her laugh.

"This is hard," he goes on, "because it's so different from the rest of your life. This doesn't feel like you."

He has seen this before—in other successful people who made terrible choices.

"But at a certain point you were not the victim any-more. You were an accomplice."

"How does it help me to say that?"

"If you show people when you resign that you un-derstand you were wrong, they will want to forgive you."

"What did I do wrong?"

Merda, Rena thinks in Italian.

"Congresswoman, here is what I want you to do. Imagine how the people who are disappointed in you see this. Don't try to persuade them. See it their way. Spend a half hour doing this. Then write down how they see it. Five sentences. Then sleep on it overnight and look at it again. When you are ready, call me back."

"This is going to help me?"

"Leaders understand how their people think, Congresswoman. This is an exercise in leadership."

He stays to read through the Madison files Wiley has ready so far, which are saved in a security-encrypted server.

Just before 9 P.M., he realizes he's worked through dinner. Now he's too tired to eat. Tomorrow will be long, too.

At home he mixes a vodka martini rather than make dinner. He slices some Gouda and takes the cheese and the martini to the den. His cell phone rings. Matt Alabama is calling to ask about Rena's day; it's a ritual to which his friend is faithful.

Though two decades apart in age, they had become friends when Rena was a Senate aide and Alabama covered Congress. "You're a rare breed in this town," Alabama had said in a bar one night, back when Alabama was still drinking. "A pragmatic idealist. We're almost extinct. When members of the species meet, they need to help each other survive."

Mentors and self-appointed tutors had played a large role in Rena's life, a soccer coach in high school, a history professor at West Point, many people in the army, Llewellyn Burke in the Senate. Alabama had become a tutor of a different sort. Of what? Getting older? Losing wives?

"You see my piece?" Alabama asks.

He must feel insecure about his story on Hoffman's funeral, Rena thinks. For all his accomplishments, Alabama still agonizes over every story. He feels a sense of responsibility, a desire to do justice to what he covers. It was one reason he hadn't been jettisoned as network news shrank, became sillier, and then as all of journalism imploded. Rena makes a point of recording and watching his friend's stories.

"Just got home. I'll take a look."

There is a long comfortable silence, the kind almost reassuring among close friends.

"You okay, Matt?"

"Too many funerals. They're starting to take their toll."

Maybe his old friend is becoming more idealist than pragmatist, Rena thinks. He was a passionately empathetic man, poetic and emotional, which made him particularly good on television, but he felt too much.

"Hoffman was a towering figure," Alabama continues. "Wonder if someone that big could get through now."

"Maybe these guys are just towering in retrospect."

Rena hears a soft, short chuckle over the phone.

"Maybe," Alabama says. "But I don't know if Nash has it in him to aim high."

Rena cannot reveal being hired by the White House. Washington lives are compartmentalized.

Rena looks at his martini and worries that Alabama might drink tonight.

"You feel like a walk? I could drive over."

"No, if you just got home, you're working on something. How you doin'?"

"In the middle, as always. Fixing other people's problems. Being pulled on both sides."

"Be careful to keep your arms in their sockets."

Rena laughs.

"Night, brother," Alabama says.

"Night, Matt."

His phone is ringing again. His partner.

"Wiley just emailed me," she says. "A transcript of a speech at a small law school in Arizona. Madison's asked about legalizing drugs, and he leaves the door open."

Rena and Brooks spend two more hours looking through the record, scanning for statements to mitigate the remark about legalizing drugs, material to make that one look like a random instance of thinking out loud. "Jesus, Peter," Brooks says over the phone, "you know this is just the first day?"

Rena thinks about that and tries to imagine the days to come.

Ten

10:45 P.M.
Washington, D.C.

Before he leaves the office, Gary Gold scans the stories about the funeral of Justice Julius Hoffman already posted online. Other papers have more up than the *Tribune* does. Jesus Christ, why can't the damn paper do even the most basic digital things right?

Now the judicial spectacle will start again, he thinks, the jostling among the groups over who should be picked, the breathless idealization of the president's selection from the president's media machine, the cartoon criticism from the other side depicting the person as a dangerous freak. The press will be complicit in all of it. The whole nomination game can get empty and cynical fast.

Maybe he could make a difference—or the *Washington Tribune* could. He's the best investigative reporter the *Tribune* has, isn't he? Well, along with Jill Bishop on national security. The paper might be diminished, but it is still the most important media outlet in the world's most important city. Yes, he'd like a piece of this story. When the thing starts to move, he'd like to take a whack at digging into the nominee. Make the man or woman into a real person. And find out if there is anything to find out. Find out what becoming a great judge is all about. Assuming they pick a great judge.

He will need to select the right moment. Good way to stay on page one in between deep dives.

Yeah, he thinks. He will talk to Fiske, investigative editor. No. Hamilton, Fiske's boss.

Eleven

Wednesday, April 15, 6:33 A.M.
San Francisco

He parks and looks around. There is a spot here where the rocks jut out into the bay and the fishing is supposed to be good. Truth is, the fishing hadn't been good here for a long time. People who fish are nostalgic. That makes them predictable. That makes them susceptible and weak.

"You gonna do a guy, it's better in a wide-open space," Bird used to tell him. "Where a guy feels safe."

He can still hear Bird's voice in his head.

There's hardly anything to do in a cell but talk about how to commit more crimes when you get out.

Rumor was Bird had killed for money in the real world. He was big enough that you could believe it and he had dead gray eyes.

Whatever he did outside, he sure knew a hell of a lot about how to kill people.

"No matter what, you gotta know guns are stupid. Traceable. Guys think they're safer 'cause you can be further away. But guns just get you caught. Leave powder. Every gun leaves a signature inside the barrel."

Yeah, Bird.

They talked about it for years.

How it was easier to kill people close up. "People think you must know the guy."

And use whatever is around. A rock. A lamp. Things you pick up at the scene aren't traceable.

How finding the right place, the right scene, was critical. Some place they go a lot. And where you can see who can see you.

See the patterns. Learn their habits. Find the spot. Case the spot. Know everything about it. Then pick your time.

He could recite it in his sleep now.

And "hygiene." So you leave no traces. The cleanliness of killing.

"You keep your head shaved. Scrub your scalp that day, so no flaking, and you oil it up, so no dryness. And then you wear a hat on top of that. . . . And you always wear gloves."

They talked about vengeance, too. Bird used to say, "With enough time, a man dreams of revenge." He liked that. Yeah, a man dreams.

Had Bird ever done it? Or just dreamed it?

Well, *he* is doing it. He gets out of his car and surveys the terrain, a long stretch of bay front, north of the airport, south of the city. It's so early he has the place to himself. He gets out and sees a spot where he can throw a line into the water and also see a fair amount of the shoreline without being conspicuous. He could fish there for as long as he needs and no one would think about it. Or notice him. Just a guy. He walks over to where he would stand and fish to know exactly what he would see from there. Yes, he could wait right here.

Only he won't be waiting for fish.

Twelve

The conference room of Citizens for Freedom is already crowded.

The room is famous both for the meetings held here and the cheapness of the furnishings. The conference table is four rectangular folding tables pushed together surrounded by plastic stackable chairs.

Josh Albin, the founder of Citizens for Freedom, has a theory about office furniture. Albin has theories about a lot of things. When he arrived in Washington in the 1980s to challenge the Republican establishment, Albin decided cheap furniture wasn't a sign of being poor. It was a sign of conservative virtue. It showed that he and his group weren't just Republicans. They were insurgents driven by a cause—cutting taxes and shrinking government. Most Republican conference rooms were plush, with ten-thousand-dollar polished burled wood tables and padded leather chairs; they spoke of money and power. Albin wanted his offices to speak of commitment and revolution, and if people gave money, he wanted to them to know it would be spent on the work, not on the décor.

And thinking it has made it so. Albin has turned shabby folding tables, cinder-block bookshelves, and metal chairs into a badge of honor. A quarter century since coming to Washington, he could afford almost anything. But when people see the conference room, they remark on its modesty, and the story of Albin's views on opulence and commitment is retold.

The legend of Josh Albin grows. Movements are more than ideas. They also require leaders.

Albin has a theory about that, too. At Harvard in the early 1980s, he'd come to hate entrenched establishments. Harvard was so marinated in liberalism, he thought, it seeped into everything, like a stale odor in an old house the residents stop noticing. People at Harvard mistook their liberalism for intelligence and conservatism for ignorance. That, Albin is famous for telling people, is the only thing of value he learned in Cambridge.

The line always generates laughter and applause—though, of course, it isn't true. Albin uses it when he is telling people how they must fortify themselves against haughty self-satisfaction. Never bask in your accomplishments. Always question. Keep your ideas something living, changing. Never let them stultify into dogma.

As new insurgents have come to the party over the last twenty years—the Common Sense crowd is just the latest—Albin has managed to remain among the rebels. One reason was the Pledge. Any Republican elected to Congress must sign it, promising to do nothing to grow the size of government. Nothing. No new taxes. No earmarks. Absolutism. Even the Common Sense crowd loves his most famous aphorism: "I want to shrink the government so small that it can fit in a toilet. Then I want to flush it."

The conscience of the political Right, the enemy of compromise is dressed as he always is, the signature look forever mentioned in media profiles: a daily white carnation in his lapel, black cowboy boots. He is not tall, five feet six, but with his silvery blue eyes and blond beard, he cuts a striking figure people remember.

"Okay, everybody, we've got a major operation to plan here, and a country to change, so let's settle down," Albin says. He lifts his eyebrows momentarily to signal that he is kidding.

Albin is renowned for delivering grand pronouncements self-mockingly, a habit that allows him to articulate the unlikely scope of his ambitions but always in half jest. Doubters will think he's kidding. Believers will marvel at his cunning.

"Today we are going to war-game the battle for the next Supreme Court justice. I want everything figured out by tomorrow so it's ready for the Monday meeting."

The Monday meeting is a reference to Albin's famed Monday breakfast gatherings, held in a room across the hall. Dozens of conservative movement groups meet each week to coordinate tactics and talking points. More than one hundred people show up, lawmakers, lobbyists, pressure groups, and citizen action groups like Albin's. The meetings are another part of the Albin magic. If people imagine that the Liberal Establishment has ruled the country for seventy-five years—with the power elite all gathering at places like the Trilateral Commission to build a web of power—Albin has decided to counter that by creating a ruling conspiracy of his own, consciously and deliberately. Every Monday morning. And he has.

A blond woman raises a hand.

"Any intelligence, sir, from the Network?" she asks.

"Not yet," Albin answers.

The Network refers to a mysterious group of "friends" Albin supposedly developed over the years, and, according to legend, in some cases even helped placed in key power centers around Washington—agencies, rival groups. It began, so the story goes, with Albin identifying the political orientation of all the civil service people in the White House and contacting them.

Sometimes called "the Listeners" or "the Watchers," they represent a secret network of spies that purportedly reports to Albin directly. No one even knows for sure if the Network is real. But Albin nurtures the idea with vague allusions to "our sources" in the "Code Blue Bulletins" he sends to other conservative groups when things are breaking.

"So, how do we want to think about this nomination?" Albin asks.

"We have flexibility, it seems to me," answers Keith Flanders, Albin's new head of research.

"Our focus is on cutting taxes and limiting the size of the government. As you say, Josh, to make it so small we could flush it down the drain. Well, how do we advance that goal here? By predictably opposing whomever the president nominates? Or is it possible that we could gain more leverage by keeping an open mind on the nominee? If we approve the president's pick, or at least remain silent, could we earn a credit from the White House that we can use later, on something closer to our core mission?"

Albin regards Flanders a moment and then answers: "Right definition of focus, Keith, but wrong strategic analysis. But I'm glad it came up, for those of you who are new."

Sarcasm in his voice.

"Breaking away from our colleagues on the right is rarely a useful option. It's the nuclear option, and it has mostly negative consequences. The strength of the center-Right movement in America is its unity. Never make an ally into an enemy."

Albin sees leadership as a teaching role, and repeating aphorisms like this is one of his pedagogic tactics.

"Remember, unity is a key competitive advantage we have over the weakened and dying vestiges of the Left," Albin reminds them. "The leftist groups always fight among themselves because they are scrambling for federal money, and there is a limited amount to be had."

Albin pauses, waiting for nods of assent. Then he continues.

"On the right, we are fighting for ideas, and they are something to be shared and spread. In our unity we gain allies, we gain strength, and we gain power for the next fight."

"But isn't there a risk, then, that in practice this means we just go along?" Flanders presses. "Doesn't that mean we end up opposing whomever the president nominates regardless of who they are?"

"No," Albin answers quickly. "It means this: Now that Hoffman is in the ground we can send a message to the president and the country that we expect the next justice joining the Court to reflect and represent the values of most Americans. So now, in today's news cycle, our first tactic is to frame the debate and set the terms by which we want the president to play. That is leadership. Not followship."

Albin pauses for effect and asks, "And have we got that message ready, Sally?"

Sally Holden is the communications director.

"We're working on talking points for your approval."

"Excellent. Can you have it on my desk by end of day? Basically an hour? What are the core values the next Court justice should represent that reflect the center of thought of the American people, the mainstream American values?"

"You'll have it," Holden answers.

"Here's what I want to have happen. Once I've gone

over this, I want to blast-email the talking points around as a courtesy to the members of the Monday Club by seven P.M. tonight, and I want to let them know that we invite any input they have and we will be emailing to the press at one P.M. tomorrow afternoon. That shares the talking points and gets buy-in and feedback from our allies. And if we have missed anything, it gives us three hours to fix it."

"And helps everyone else shape their message," Holden says.

"Exactly," says Albin. "Unity. Any questions?"

Silence.

Al Thomas, deputy director of Citizens for Freedom, whispers something to Albin.

"We have a new person starting today," Thomas then says to the room. "I'd like to introduce everyone to Jeremy Stone. Welcome, Jeremy."

A chorus of welcomes are directed to a tall, blond-haired young man sitting against one wall.

"Jeremy graduated from Dartmouth last year. He was in the Federalist Society. Worked on the *Dartmouth Review*. Comes very highly recommended."

"Very nice," Albin says.

"I'm excited to be here, sir," the young man says.

"Well, we make our interns really work," Albin says. "There'll be plenty of Xeroxing. Running errands. Taking notes." People laugh. Then Albin leans in toward him with a sudden serious stare. "But we're shaping the future of this country. Right, everyone?"

Smiles around the room at the ritual.

"All hands, then. Good luck," Albin says.

In an instant everyone rises and the room begins to empty.

"That was quick," the new intern who had been singled out says to his neighbor.

"One standing rule of an Albin staff meeting," the staffer tells him: "Any gathering about tactics or administration that takes more than fifteen minutes is too long. Anything longer creates mischief and wastes time."

"He is right on time," the boy says, looking at his watch.

"Welcome to Josh World."

The intern thinks he will need to sit down tonight and write for his minders his first memo on Josh World.

Thirteen

7:00 P.M.
Washington, D.C.

"Good evening, Ms. Cutter, and welcome back to Restaurant Donna. The rest of your party is already here."

"Thank you, Annie."

The hostess is a young Eurasian woman with the cheekbones of a queen and dark, hypnotic eyes. That kind of beauty is a gift, and it can take you much further than you might otherwise go, Deborah Cutter knows. If you have the brains and drive to use it.

Cutter follows the girl to the best table in the dining room's famous back corner. Restaurant Donna, named for owner Donna Fleming, had been the preferred

dining spot for progressives in Washington for a quarter century. During her first five struggling years in
Washington, Cutter had eaten here exactly once—with
her parents. Now she was a regular, and most Wednes-
days they hold this table in case she comes in.

The senior staff of Fair Chance for America—Sylvia
Blechman, Nan Bullock, and Todd Paulson—is already
seated.

"Chardonnay, please," Cutter tells the hostess, who
gives her a flustered "I don't wait on tables" look, but
there is something about Deborah Cutter that defies
rules. The wine arrives a moment later, brought by
the hostess herself. Too bad, Cutter thinks. The girl
wouldn't hold her ground. Her looks might be a waste.

"We're debating two questions," says Sylvia Blechman, Cutter's deputy, a heavyset woman in her late fifties with rimless glasses.

"Don't tell me," Cutter says. "Whether to strike
fast and frame the public debate or wait and coordinate
with other progressives."

"Right," Blechman says, smiling.

They are always the same questions, Cutter thinks,
with a sudden feeling of disappointment.

"We have the prestige to lead on this, to demand
the president pick a liberal," says Todd Paulson, Fair
Chance's new communications guru.

Cutter has just hired Paulson to modernize their outreach. He knows social media and technology and he has a killer instinct, which she likes.

"But we'll have more leverage if we coordinate and speak as a unified progressive community," says Nan Bullock, the most senior of Cutter's team. "This president won't listen unless we're unified."

Bullock, who has been fighting the culture wars for forty-five years, always leans toward unity. But in the digital age, when you are closer than ever to your base, worrying about what gets things done in Washington isn't always as important.

"If we wait for the progressive community to agree, the president will have named a nominee, the Senate voted, and the Court will be in session," Paulson says, only half-jokingly.

Cutter is tired of this debate. Dog tired of it. It's the same one the loose community of progressive groups has on every issue.

"We can have it both ways," she declares, trying to end this. "We prepare a statement pressuring the White House about the importance of picking a liberal, and we give other groups twenty-four hours to join us. No blindsiding."

Her deputy Blechman nods, which ends the discussion. "And what do you think the Right will do?"

Blechman adds so that the conversation moves on. Good ol' Blechman.

"It's possible, if we listen well, we might be able to get a read on that," Paulson says enigmatically.

Paulson should keep his mouth shut, thinks Cutter. Shortly after she hired him six months ago, he had come to her privately and asked her how she would feel if he had people inside other organizations who from time to time reported back to him. She had looked at him a long time, nodded slightly, and said simply, "Don't tell me." He had smiled. But now he can't help himself. He keeps dropping little hints that maybe he has people actually doing it. Like that braggart Josh Albin supposedly does with his moles, or listening people, or whatever they're called. She doubted he had any such people. She isn't opposed to Paulson trying something like that. But he needs to zip it.

Paulson suddenly pulls out his cell. He answers in a low whisper. Everyone is watching him, waiting. Then he closes the phone and says importantly, "I have news. From the West Wing."

"He's picked someone already?" Blechman guesses.

"No. But he's picked who's going to run the nomination," says Paulson. "Peter Rena."

"Peter Rena and Randi Brooks?" asks Blechman.

"Yes," Paulson answers.

"Isn't Rena a Republican?" Cutter asks rhetorically.

"But Randi Brooks is a Democrat," Bullock adds.

Cutter makes a huffing sound and waves her hand in the air. "Randi Brooks is a genuine progressive," Bullock says.

"Or she used to be," Paulson says.

Cutter takes a last gulp of her wine and shakes her head. "I don't care what she used to be. You trust those fighting with you. Anyone else you don't know what you can share." Everyone nods, Cutter notices, except Bullock.

"You stay and eat," Cutter tells them. "I need to make some phone calls. If the White House has already hired someone to handle the nomination, we don't have time to waste." As she slides out of her chair, she sees the dark-haired hostess watching her.

Fourteen

Thursday, April 16, 9:15 A.M.
Washington, D.C.

Belinda Cartwright's email came in at 3:07 in the morning.

Five sentences: how she has betrayed the public trust.

Rena spends the first half hour at the office turning her words into a workable statement she could read in a press conference—as early as next week if she agrees. Most of the words are Cartwright's.

I want, first, to apologize.

To the people I represent. This House. My country. My friends.

I have let you down. I have let my family down. I have let myself down. I am truly so sorry.

In the beginning, my mistake was an innocent one. I allowed myself to be tricked by a man who said he loved me.

Yet if that were my only mistake I wouldn't be standing in front of you here today.

When I found out that my husband was a thief, a man who was stealing my money and my family's money, I made my bigger mistake. I let my vanity and my shame get in the way of my judgment. I didn't trust that the people of Utah would understand. I worried about keeping my high position. I crossed a line. To cover my growing debt, I put my husband on my personal staff though I gave him no real responsibility.

I also began to mislead my staff, my colleagues, and the people I represented, hoping vainly that if I could just manufacture more time, I could somehow untangle everything and put it right.

At that point I went from being a victim to being part of the deceit. The legal system will determine what formal redress is required, if any. I know by my own moral compass that it was wrong. And I must pay the price for that.

I did not make this situation. But I did make it worse.

Now I owe it to this institution and our system of government to allow the people of Utah to choose different representation in Congress that won't be handicapped by what I now have to go through. And I need to turn my own personal attention to correcting what has happened to my family, and to helping any legal authorities find the money that was stolen from me and others by the person who wormed his way into my family's life and began this nightmare.

To do that, I am announcing today that I am resigning my seat in the House of Representatives. I need to begin to get on with the rest of my life by being part of the solution to this matter, not the problem.

She should take questions. She will need legal counsel first to know what she can and cannot say. Courtney Palmer would be a good choice, even if Cartwright already has someone else.

Hallie Jobe is calling from Palo Alto, up early—still on East Coast time. She's reporting in on her day and a half spent talking to faculty about Madison, the kind of personal summary no FBI background check would get. Rena asks O'Brien to get Wiley, Brooks, and Smolonsky to come in for the call. More minds on a problem will find more problems—and that is what is needed.

"In the end, I'd say affable but not warm. Outdoorsy but in a cerebral way. A little crunchy granola—the birding, the astronomy, the sailing—but that kind of thing is normal out here."

Rena smiles to himself. Jobe, who had loved the discipline of the military, is as straight as they come. Crunchy granola is not her thing.

"How political is he?" Rena asks.

"Well, the guy went to Berkeley from 1968 to 1972," Jobe says.

Rena glances at Brooks and asks, "What does that mean, Hallie?"

"I can find people who say he took drugs in college."

"Berkeley in the sixties and all you got is pot?" Smolonsky asks.

"Actually," Wiley says, "he wrote a fascinating article on how the 1960s affected the current generation of jurists. He says that it did lead to a greater judicial activism, but that the activism is in both parties, and he cites lots of cases to prove it."

She doesn't mention the ambiguous speech transcript about legalizing drugs that Brooks called about last night.

"Anything else, Hallie?" asks Rena.

"No, that's all," Jobe says in her clipped, efficient way. "Shall I come home?"

"No. Write it up in the next hour and email it in drop box. And tell no one."

Rena looks at Wiley when the call ends. "Anything more on why Madison took that detour to the Superior Court after being dean at Stanford? Any inkling he was forced out?

"Apparently, the opposite; it was Madison's idea. He argued Superior is where most law is practiced, and he thought he should experience it. My guess is he knew the appeals court job was coming soon enough."

"You buy that it was Madison's idea?" Brooks presses.

"According to the public record at least," Wiley answers. "The university was getting a new president, and he wanted Madison to stay. Madison had been the law school dean for six years and told the incoming president that was enough, and that his successor shouldn't have him skulking around. There was even a quote from Madison. Where is it? 'You probably do your best work as a dean in the first four years.'"

"Humble," says Smolonsky.

"Not the word most people would use to describe him," Wiley says.

Rena's assistant O'Brien tries to suppress a laugh.

"We get much from the class lists from Stanford and Harvard?" Rena asks. "Anyone know people on those?"

Rena knew two people and had called them the day before, a journalist who had gone to college with Madison whom Rena knew from Pentagon days and a law school classmate of Madison's whom Rena had done work for as an investigator. He hasn't heard back.

"Details. Nothing significant," Brooks says.

These calls are delicate. Calling people about a nomination that isn't public risks tipping a hand. That is why many federal background checks actually occur after someone is hired and working provisionally in a federal job. And why Rena and Brooks rely so heavily on database research. Databases don't tattle.

They are getting close. They'll have to send something to the White House later today. For better or worse, they are in it.

Fifteen

3:30 P.M.
Washington, D.C.

The three memos about Roland Madison are drafted. Randi Brooks, sitting on the couch in Rena's office, reads them on her laptop. Rena reads the printouts at his desk.

The personal background profile, written by Lupsa, has woven in Jobe's notes from Stanford. The legal profile—Rena can see Brooks's fingerprints on it—is even better, erudite and insightful, signaling potential flash points in Madison's legal philosophy and offering initial defenses.

The attack memo by Jon Robinson and Maureen Conner, though, is the most interesting. "Professor

Madison's judicial philosophy is a mix of sixties Berkeley campus radicalism masked in New Age California rhetoric," it reads, reminding people in one sentence that the guy went to Berkeley, is a professor, and is from California—code words for elitist, academic, lefty, and out there.

"For all his discussion about a third way," the attack memo says, "Madison is no real friend to conservatives." And the proof is his criticism of the core conservative legal concept of strict constructionism—the idea that judges should go no further than reading the text of the constitution and applying the facts of a case to that original intent. Madison dismisses the theory as "a political argument, not a serious legal one." His attitude about this vital legal doctrine "is both arrogant and dangerous," the memo says.

When you add it all together, it concludes, Madison's thinking "is based on the misguided, discredited, and repudiated legal detour" the Court took during the latter half of the twentieth century.

"Legal detour." Nice phrase.

"Madison's ideas call for an activist, overreaching judiciary."

Attack memos are a way of imagining how your worst enemies will come at you. They're fun to write, like a pan of a terrible movie. They're also the most important documents you produce.

Rena and Brooks insist they be done well.

What was it that Lily Tomlin once said about Washington? "No matter how cynical you become, it's never enough to keep up."

Rena looks up from the attack memo at Brooks. His own cynicism is nagging at him. He'd better tell her soon what has been bothering him. Most investigations go wrong because people lose sight of something they thought about at the beginning and then let go in the sweep of other details. The neglected early suspect. The doubt that you never got around to checking. It's what you forget that will bite you.

"Randi, there is one thing to talk about. You brought it up yourself when you first saw Madison's name. You said he was 'nothing but trouble' because he has no natural constituency."

"Okay." She makes a point of closing her laptop, then leans back on the sofa to listen.

"Something like that has worried me from the start," he says, "before we even saw Madison's name. When Nash invited *me* to the White House and not you and told me how he wanted to change the country with an unusual choice."

"What are you worried about?" She crosses her arms and gives him a serious look.

"If the president actually picks Madison, you think it's possible he might want the nomination to implode? The Right gets a win. Then Nash can pick someone more liberal. That we're being set up?"

"That's pretty paranoid, Peter," she says, uncrossing her arms and leaning forward. "Why do you think that?"

"There are so many long shots in one plan. The extraordinary jurist idea. That he would ask people outside the White House to run it—especially *us* since we don't belong to either party. It's like he wants to keep his distance. Then Madison himself, not just someone unusual, but a guy with such a long paper trail there are a lot of things grab on to if you want pull him down."

Brooks has a habit, when she concentrates on something, of pursing her lips and tilting her head up slightly and focusing her eyes just ahead, as if the idea were floating physically in the room in front of her.

"Maybe this town is so screwed up," Rena adds, "the only way Nash thinks he can get a liberal on the Court is to give the other party a pound of flesh."

"Madison's the pound of flesh? And us?" she asks.

"Yeah. We're part of the sacrificial stew."

"You make Washington sound like cannibal town. And Nash pretty cynical."

"Henry Kissinger said just because you're paranoid doesn't mean someone's not after you."

"Is that who we're aspiring to be now, Peter? Kissinger Associates?" After leaving government, the controversial secretary of state assembled many of his advisors into a consulting firm that made millions advising foreign governments.

"No, I'm just saying we should think through the paranoid scenario. On that score, Kissinger isn't wrong."

"Is Nash that devious?" she says. "I don't know. I need to ponder that."

At 5:00 P.M. the memos are copyedited and ready for the White House. Rena calls Spencer Carr. "Hand-deliver them, someone from your staff. Sealed envelope," the chief of staff says. "Have them call my office before they come. I will get them clearance. They come directly to me."

Should he have his assistant O'Brien do it? Too new, he thinks. He asks Stephanie Hampton, the longtime receptionist, whom they had used for confidential matters before and he knew would get it done.

At 6:00 Rena slips out of the office and walks the mile down M Street to his apartment in the West End. A few years ago, that walk would have taken him from a bustling commercial district to a quiet neighborhood. Now the bustling doesn't end.

Rena needs to clear his head. The sleeplessness of the last few nights is catching up to him. He could use a run.

On the stoop outside he stretches his calves and starts out toward the river. At the Kennedy Center, he gets on the path that runs along Potomac and heads in the direction of the Lincoln Memorial. He crosses the over the Memorial Bridge and runs toward Arlington and the cemetery.

He began running in the army, after he decided he'd had enough soccer. He looks forward to it, but he doesn't crave it. He likes that it keeps him fit. But more than that, he enjoys that he disconnects—no cell phone, no email. Just his body and mind until the ritual—from first stiff steps, to the shower afterward—is complete.

An hour later, he is home. He drinks water thirstily, takes a long shower—cool, then cold—and shaves again, dresses, and picks up his cell phone. There is a text message. It says "WH: Jordan Lyman" and contains a phone number. He doesn't recognize the name.

"May I help you?" a male voice says at the end of the line.

"Jordan Lyman, please. Peter Rena calling."

"Thank you. We will call you back." The tone is polite and officious at the same time. Rena guesses ex-military.

Twenty minutes pass before his cell rings back.

"Peter," the voice says at the other end of the line.

"Mr. President."

"I read your memos."

Why, Rena wonders, is the president of the United States calling him back personally about a preliminary background memo?

"A brilliant man, then, your vetting suggests, if an unusual one."

"Apparently, sir."

"You called your review preliminary. How long till it's not preliminary?"

It's a man's life, Rena thinks. The *Los Angeles Times* sent two people to live in Little Rock for eighteen months in 1991 to scrub Bill Clinton. Took them a year to unearth his draft notice, the one Clinton said he never got.

"Another week would tell us more."

"Can we assume," the president asks, "that anything that took you longer to dig up will be harder for others to find, too?"

"It doesn't work that way, sir." There is a randomness to investigating. "Someone might stumble across something the first day that we might not find for weeks."

"The power of chance?"

"The older I get the more I believe in it."

"You say if I'm serious you need to question Madison face-to-face to see how he reacts?"

Rena calls this the Watching. It is something on which he always insists.

"Yes."

"Then I think you need to get yourself to California."

Sixteen

Friday, April 17, Slightly before dawn
San Francisco

D amn truck drives like a washing machine.
Thumping and bumping.

He pulls the beat-up blue Chevy pickup off the 101 northbound onto a small dirt access road that moves out past where Candlestick Park once stood. The predawn light peeks over the Bay to the east, streaking the horizon with slashes of apricot and scarlet. The left headlight is askew, its beam crossing into the path of the right. A cross-eyed Chevy with a shit engine.

He navigates the pickup toward the fishing spot along the bay where the rocks stick out.

He stole the truck thirty minutes earlier on a side street near the Cow Palace, the old arena where the Warriors once played basketball after they came west from Philadelphia. Before they moved to freakin' Oakland. Now the old arena is a place for pet shows, coin conventions, and an annual tattoo expo. The high-class stuff long ago moved downtown. South San Francisco is just a place people drive by.

Good place to die, he thinks.

He wasn't positive the guy would be here, but for about half the Friday mornings in the last two months at daybreak he had been, with his fold-up canvas chair, his radio, cooler, and gear. Guy couldn't sleep no more, probably. Too old. Too many memories.

A stupid man becoming more stupid as he gets older. Wasting time at dry fishing holes, catching nothing, listening to the traffic whoosh by on the Bayshore Freeway.

You should be in church, old man, paying for your sins. You can pay me instead. And someday you and me can discuss it in hell.

He pulls up to the far end of the dirt road a little past where most people usually park. So when the guy sees the truck, he won't think someone's fishing near his favorite spot.

He sets up, pole in the water, and waits awhile. Seems like hours. What if he actually caught a fish? That'd be pretty damn funny.

He doesn't smoke. He doesn't do anything. No DNA.

Sometime soon he hears a car drive up and the engine turn off, a door open and close, a trunk slam.

He waits a few minutes more and wanders up toward the parking area to look and sees the old Buick LeSabre.

Navy blue. Cop blue. Guy has no imagination.

He takes a deep breath in and lets it out.

It's gonna be today, he thinks. With the sun rising.

"Shit," he hears himself say under his breath.

He picks up his rod and returns to the spot where he can see the guy's old Buick.

He waits a few more minutes. Then he heads down the rocks to the water and starts to make his way along the shore, stepping carefully so as not to slip, toward the figure now settled in at a small point jutting out into the bay.

Calvin P. Smith.

SFPD detective, second class. Retired.

Smith is wearing one of those padded olive green coats with the furry hood. The hood is down, not over his head, fortunately. Not that it should matter that much. But it might.

The other good news is he is sitting. He's in one of those folding canvas chairs you get at Target for less than ten bucks. It's low and, at Smith's age, getting out of it would be hard. Probably need both hands to push on the arms to get up.

Smith has two poles into the water, both propped up on little stands you can buy to hold them in place. He has a cooler set out, and he's sipping a can of Coors.

Breakfast of champions.

Smith glances at him from a distance of about thirty yards, then back out at the water.

It is cold here, even in summer. That's good. Means the gloves don't look out of place.

He is close now, fifteen yards. Then ten.

"Mornin'."

Smith doesn't look up. Takes another pull on his Coors.

"I think this hole is played out. Ain't got nothing here for a couple seasons. I think I ain't gonna come no more."

Smith still doesn't look at him.

Mean cuss. The worst kind. The kind you can't talk to. Who thinks if you didn't do this crime, you did another.

"You catch anything?"

As he says it, he puts his rod down and leans over a

little more and puts his hand around a rock he figures is large enough. Smith still isn't looking. He straightens up, standing sideways, so the rock is behind his body now.

"Hey, you remember a kid nicknamed Peanut?"

Smith turns just a little, as if the name registers only vaguely.

The rock comes down on the older man's left temple before Smith utters a word.

He can feel a crush of bone and hear a sloshing sound.

There is no blood, not at first, but Smith's mouth has opened as if he were going to say something.

"Well, this is for Peanut, man."

The guy is leaning slightly now, tilting away from him. That makes the temple a little harder to reach squarely. So he brings the second blow down on the top of the man's head, just slightly toward the front.

Blood is flowing now from Smith's ear below the left temple. Mouth slack.

One more blow to the temple. There is no crush sound, and it feels softer this time.

Smith falls out of the folding chair, and it topples over with him. Smith is lying sideways, the bloody temple facing up, and one of Smith's legs is caught in the chair.

He feels something on his shoe. Smith has grabbed his shoelaces with his left hand and clenched.

He has dropped the rock.

Where the hell is it? Damn it.

He sees the rock, with a little bit of blood and hair on it, and picks it back up. He thinks of crushing Smith's fingers, but then he remembers that will mean hitting himself in the shoe.

He brings the rock down on Smith's elbow. Smith's body rolls.

"Fuck you," Smith's bloody mass of a head manages to say, the "you" coming out garbled, sounding more like "uh."

He only vaguely sees the gun.

Somehow, this piece of puke with his head caved in has managed to pull it out of his coat or somewhere and get it into his right hand. But he can't seem to aim it properly.

Smith's eyes aren't even fixed on him. It's as if Smith is reacting from memory.

He smashes the rock on Smith's right wrist holding the gun.

Then without thinking about it he sees himself hitting Smith on the head again. Then again.

The old cop's head has opened now, revealing a mixed red, clear, and white mass inside. It looks like bloody cottage cheese.

The gun is still in Smith's hand, but the arm has stopped moving.

"No, fuck you," he says to the body.

He realizes he is crying.

Shit. SHIT!

Did it drip down, the tears?

Will there be DNA?

Smith's beer has toppled over, but it's still half-full. He takes the can and pours it all around where he's been standing. Then he opens the cooler. There are two more Coors inside. He takes one, opens it, and pours that all around, too.

His heart is pounding. He hasn't noticed it before. He drops the beer can, standing there, panting.

Time to move. If you're seen standing here, someone will wonder what you are looking at. He begins to head back toward the truck. Slowly. As calmly as he can. Make anyone who might see him now think nothing out of the ordinary is going on.

For an instant he wonders about the fishing lines. Why would he do that? Why would he care if a fish had struck?

When he gets back to the dirt road, he drags his feet to make sure he doesn't leave footprints that give away his shoe size.

Truck fires right up.

He turns around and drives back up the dirt road to the access road toward the freeway. He looks out toward the office buildings near where Candlestick used to be. Any lights on? They couldn't see the rocks, but they might be able to see a pickup. Not that it would matter.

In ten minutes he will ditch his fishing rod that he had touched the night before without gloves in the first dumpster he can find. Five minutes after that he will ditch the truck, put the overalls in the grocery bag he brought, get on the bus, and later burn the clothes in the furnace at the building where his aunt lives.

What about his shoes? Smith grabbed them.

He sees the old shithead hanging on to them. What was in the old guy's mind? Did anything register? Or was he fighting like some animal by just instinct? He sees that hand on his shoe, and the gun. And the skull open, with the brains pouring out.

Then he realizes he has driven too far. He has gone an extra exit, past the place where he had meant to ditch the pickup, the one without surveillance cameras and near a dumpster. Should he go back?

No, get rid of the truck. The cameras on the freeway will spot you if you go back and forth.

He pulls off at Cesar Chavez Street and turns right toward the bay. He parks the truck on the street near nothing in particular. He grabs the fishing rod out of the back and walks away.

He looks for an alley, or somewhere where there might be a dumpster and where there won't be surveillance cameras.

He finds one eight blocks away. He writhes out of the overalls with the blood on them and stuffs them into the grocery bag.

He imagines Smith's dead eyes following him, the way a picture's eyes follow you around the room.

Stop thinking.

He picks up the grocery bag and the fishing rod and looks for a dumpster. He wants to lose the fishing rod. In a few more blocks he finds one. Maybe he should have thrown it into the bay?

Once he has dumped the rod, he picks up the grocery bag full of the bloody overalls and looks for a bus stop. No, he should walk farther. Give himself more distance.

Walk all the way back if you have to.

He decides in the end to do that. It wouldn't be safe to get on a bus with a grocery bag full of brains, with blood and beer spilled all over them. They would probably smell.

He hadn't thought of that.

In an hour, he is at his aunt's building. The basement is open. The furnace is going. He takes the bag and pushes it in, with the overalls, through the square door that he holds with one of the gloves. For a while the bag just sits there, as if impervious to fire, as if it has become magical, something that will never disappear. He imagines that the furnace will go out and they would come down to see what was wrong and find the bloody clothes, or maybe they would burn up and then reappear again, like a curse in a horror movie.

He needs to stop thinking.

Then all at once the bag explodes into flames.

It burns white. His forehead is searing. He watches the bag become engulfed. The heat of the furnace is so intense the clothes are gone in a minute.

"Bye, bye, Calvin," he whispers so softly he can barely hear himself.

Seventeen

Saturday, April 18, 9:51 A.M.
Woodside, California

"This guy the Unabomber?"

Brooks looks out the passenger window of their rented Buick and scowls at the redwood trees rushing past. The country makes her uneasy.

Roland Madison must love it. He lives in a town south of San Francisco on the top of a mountain. To get there, Brooks and Rena have to navigate a steep, curving two-lane country road.

Brooks feels carsick.

"These hills remind me of Tuscany," Rena says, grinning. Her partner knows the drive is making her nuts and he's rubbing it in. "But the forests here are thicker."

Rena was born in Tuscany and spent summers there with his grandmother.

Brooks takes another pull of her double venti Americano for support and frowns.

"Give me buildings. And concrete. And streetlights imposing order on the traffic," she says. "We build cities for a reason. They're civilized."

They enjoy teasing each other about how different they are, maybe because so many people can't believe they are partners. Nearly everything about them seems mismatched. Their politics is just one of the more obvious items. She is loud and opinionated and works out her ideas through arguing. He is cool and quiet and puzzles things out by listening. He still looks like he could play midfielder for West Point's soccer team. Her? Jesus, she thinks, what could she say? She is only four years older than her partner but has already begun to thicken into middle age. Somewhere around forty, it's like she started shapeshifting.

She sees their differences as complementary, their secret weapon, the combination that makes them so good. She is linear and lawyerly. She can build a documentary record of someone's life and make out patterns even the subjects of the investigation don't recognize about themselves. Rena adds something she cannot. He can read people. He can interview them, sense things that were never in the record, things that have to do with character and motivation, and somehow get the person to reveal them. If she is the documentarian, she often thinks, he is the ethnographer.

But in one respect she thinks they are utterly alike. They are both retrievers. They can't help it. Once given something to probe, they share an almost pathological need to know the whole of it.

She also senses in her partner a lingering doubt. He never meant to have a career like this, part politics, part rich companies, fixing problems for powerful people, some of whom would be better punished than rescued. Her partner, the soldier, she knows, would prefer his lines of demarcation to be bolder and thicker—country and enemies, duty and patriotism. He isn't sure he belongs doing this. But *she* is sure he belongs. He wouldn't be so freakishly, instinctively good at it, she thinks—especially the political stuff—if he didn't.

"I'm telling you, Peter, if this guy is some kind of mountain loon . . ." she grouses. "It's bad enough he's from California." She's just feeling irritable. "Why can't Nash pick a southerner? At least that might be worth a couple of votes." Maybe Rena's doubt about

Madison being a pound of flesh for the right wing isn't entirely far-fetched. Well, she needs to meet the man.

At the top of the mountain, they come to a crossroads with a gas station, a restaurant called Alice's, a general store, and a realty office. The place is crowded with an odd mix of luxury cars, pickup trucks, Harleys, and expensive road bicycles.

Brooks and Rena look out of place, like easterners who made a wrong turn, she in a suit, he in gray slacks, tie, and blazer. Rena is apparently thinking the same thing, she notices. He is pulling off his tie.

A left turn and five minutes later they are in front of a nondescript sign hanging on a wooden fence: Portola Heights. But there's a locked wooden gate. For all the funky, rustic woodsiness, she thinks, the place is a gated community. Rena punches in a code on a security system that opens the gate and they head down a gravel road, the passing houses hidden behind redwoods and unpaved private drives, until they come to Madison's, signified by a wooden address sign nailed to a tree. Two hundred feet down a gravel driveway they come upon the house, Frank Lloyd Wright–inspired, all glass and redwood and horizontal lines, jutting out over the mountain's edge.

It all irritates her, the woods, the queasy drive, the dirt, the hidden affluence. There is no doorbell.

She bangs on the door like a bounty hunter.

"Really, Randi?" says Rena.

"They can't afford a ringer?"

A woman dressed in tan hiking shorts and a Princeton T-shirt opens the door.

It's Roland Madison's daughter, Victoria. A lawyer, age thirty-six, they knew from the file, who lives in nearby Palo Alto. She is more striking than her photos, slender and athletic, dirty-blond hair streaked from the sun cut short in a bob, with eyes the color of smoke flecked with yellow at the irises. She looks like a girl in a Beach Boys song grown up and gotten more poised.

Rena is staring. Do men have any idea how obvious they are? Brooks thinks. She gives her partner a stare to prevent him from embarrassing himself but then thinks it's already too late.

"Morning," the woman says as if they were already friends. Confident, strong voice.

"I'm Randi Brooks, and this is Peter Rena. We're from Washington. You must be Victoria."

"It's Vic." She smiles. Rena smiles back in a way that Brooks thinks stupid.

The signs of outdoor life are everywhere. By the door sits a basket filled with trail-running shoes and hiking boots. On the wall, hooks with field glasses, walking sticks, and various hats.

The house inside, Brooks has to admit, is dramatic—a large open space with dark wood, varied elevations, and large windows surrounded by a huge deck. Everywhere you look you see the outdoors. The forest in one direction. Green and gold hills dropping toward the sea in another. In the distance hangs a thick layer of fog over the Pacific.

"Well, no doubt you want to meet Rollie," Vic says, and she leads them to a small den on the other side of the open living room.

"Dad?"

They hear a chair squeak, then footsteps, and a lean, angular man appears in the doorway. He is tall, perhaps six four, and long legs make him appear even taller. He has the same sandy hair as his daughter, a thin patrician face, a high forehead, strong cheekbones, and a long chin—the face of an English vicar. He is wearing a cardigan sweater, blue jeans, and hiking sandals with padded hiking socks.

Too goddamn crunchy granola, Brooks thinks. They will have to get rid of the sandals and socks.

"Dad, this is Randi Brooks and Peter Rena from Washington."

"Welcome, welcome, come in," Edmund Roland Madison says, extending a bony, enormous hand. The voice is disappointing, thin and brittle—not good for television.

The room is Roland's personal study. Brooks notices Rena scanning it, drinking in details. Rena believes you learn the most from a room used primarily by one person, and he is much better at learning from such spaces than she.

A few things stand out to her. The range of topics of the three walls of books for one—logic, theories of math, physics, music composition, biography, sailing, running, birds, parenting. No ego wall with photos of famous people, plaques, or awards is another. The only photos—and they are on a desk pointed so he can see them rather than at visitors—are photos of Vic at different ages on trips in various places in the world. The room's also packed with stuff. And tidy. She'd like to ask Rena what he has seen, what's she's missing.

She and Rena have a routine for interviews they conduct jointly. She begins. He watches. He might say nothing. He might add a few questions. He might become aggressive and take over. It depends on what he thinks will loosen whatever the subject is holding back.

"Your honor, we talked on the phone," Brooks begins.

"Yup, yup," he says. "Please sit."

With a glance that suggests his patience for even this amount of small talk is nearing exhaustion, he adds, "So, what do you need?"

"We'd like to ask you some questions about your record, your judicial philosophy, and your background," Brooks begins.

"What is it you can't get from my judicial record and my academic writings?"

It's a bad start, Brooks thinks. If Madison has to make rounds of Senate offices and charm people who disagree with him, lack of patience for empty talk with people he considers dull will not do.

"We need to get to know you a little better," she says.

"Why?"

She glances at Rena, whose expression tells her they're wondering the same thing: Is Madison ill at ease or trying to provoke them?

"Well," Brooks says, "we need to know, sir, how you'll answers questions you might be asked if nominated. We want to go a little deeper on some matters in your background. And, frankly, we need to observe you over a number of hours."

"Ah, to see how I will withstand the withering glare of the national media and penetrating scrutiny of Senate questioning," Madison says to Brooks.

"Dad, play nice," Vic says from her chair on the other side of the room. Madison holds up his hands in mock surrender.

"Yes, Judge, we need to size you up."

"You are the direct one," Madison says to Brooks.

"Actually he's the direct one," Brooks says, looking at Rena. "I'm the nice one."

Madison can't suppress a small laugh.

Eighteen

About a quarter mile away, on the opposite ridge, a man raises large field glasses to his face and focuses at a house in the distance. He can see into it easily through the big picture windows.

He'd discovered months ago that this was the house, found it on Google satellite maps. That's the key—advance planning—right, Bird? Plan it all ahead of time, down to the last thing. Then, when you start, they all go in rapid succession, different people, different places, different ways. And you're gone before anyone realizes any connection.

He hasn't been here in weeks. But after doing Calvin yesterday, no rest for the righteous. Or is it the wicked. Or just the weary?

He needs to be careful. The judge is hard. No freaking way you can do crap at a courthouse. Up here in the freaking woods seems great, at first. It's so remote. But it's also hard to get out here. You can get into the woods from public land, but you have to hike on private property to get this close. He has done it a dozen times, a day here, a day there, over the months of planning, but it's been a while. Who knows, maybe he'll just do it today.

Rapid succession. Before anyone knows there's a connection. That's the plan, right?

He puts the field glasses back to his eyes.

Nineteen

"**Y**ou know that the hearing process is a sham, don't you?" Madison says. "The senators ask questions to curry favor with interest groups. The nominees score points by not actually answering them. No one learns anything. It's become a disappointing, meaningless ritual. Surviving it says nothing about whether someone would be a thoughtful constitutional jurist."

Not exactly a revelation, Brooks thinks, but not what you expect a job applicant to say to butter you up.

"Does that mean you would turn down the nomination if the president offered it to you?" Rena asks, jumping in for the first time.

Madison gives Rena the kind of flinty look a professor might give a student who has asked an impudent but intriguing question.

"If you want to size me up, shouldn't you know how I feel about the process? Or should I lie to you to be polite?"

"If you lied to us, we would learn what kind of liar you are," Rena says.

"Is that useful to know?"

"If you are going to lie," Rena says.

A full smile this time from Madison and then it's gone.

"What do you mean by the process is meaningless?" Brooks asks, trying to take the testosterone level down a notch.

"It's theater, not inquiry. You know this idea that everyone should testify didn't even begin until 1955, which, of course, coincides with the birth of TV. Southern senators were worried John Harlan would spread integration in the South."

"So it's all for show?"

"Before John Harlan, only two nominees had ever testified in a hundred and seventy years," Madison says. "Harlan Stone in the 1920s and Felix Frankfurter in the 1930s, in both cases, to answer doubts by southern senators about desegregation."

"Isn't testifying still a way to settle doubts?" Brooks asks. "And if you cannot do it competently, you don't pass muster."

"If there are real doubts about a nominee they don't ever get to hearings. The last nominee to be done in by them was Robert Bork in the 1980s. And his mistake was he answered the questions honestly."

"In that case, Judge, we need to know if you will insult the senators by telling them how you feel about their process," Rena says.

"Why don't you ask some more questions, and you can tell me how I do?"

"Why don't you stop sparring with us," Rena says. "Are you so afraid of this that you want to scuttle it? Do you really think it is too much for you to handle?"

Vic begins to chuckle. She is looking at her father, trying to suppress breaking into laughter.

"Dad isn't sparring," she says. "He's being dense. But I have to say I enjoy watching him being challenged by you."

Madison turns and stares at his daughter.

"Am I?"

"Well, I doubt that there is anything Randi or Peter can do about the nomination process, Dad. They're here to assess how well you will survive it. Arguing with them isn't going to help."

"Yes, of course," Madison says. "I apologize."

Rena smiles, but Brooks thinks it's a hunter's smile, the one that means Madison's not off the hook yet.

"Judge, now that you've revealed you can be evasive, we need to know whether you can be charming or you know only how to be offensive while you do it," Rena says.

Madison's eyes dance with interest. "Ah," he says, "then we can begin."

After questions about Madison's resume for fifteen minutes or so, Brooks asks, "Do you believe the Constitution guarantees a right of privacy?"

"Certainly there is a right to privacy in the Constitution. But—though I wouldn't bring this up in a hearing—I wouldn't say guarantee."

"Why not?"

"The word *guarantee* is political babble."

"Yeah, don't bring that up," Brooks says. "If you think there is a right to privacy, why did the Founders not include it among the Bill of Rights?"

"Because it went without saying. Privacy was simply a fact of life in the eighteenth century—beyond anything we can imagine now. Time moved slowly and people spent a good part of it in private thought, and in nature. In many ways the whole purpose of the Bill of Rights was to protect privacy. Privacy was integrally linked to the terms happiness, liberty, and opportunity in a way we don't think of today, that didn't require separate enumeration."

"So do you see a right to abortion?"

"Ah, so here we are now."

"Yes, here we are," Brooks says.

"I thought the White House didn't ask nominees whether they believed in a right to abortion or supported *Roe v. Wade* anymore," Madison says. "That's how they finesse that it isn't a litmus test. Don't ask, don't tell."

"We're not the White House," Brooks says.

"A semantic difference, don't you think?"

"She asked you an honest question," Rena interrupts. "If you care so much about candor, why are you afraid to answer it?"

A flinch in the eyes. Madison's voice slows, a sign of irritation under control.

"Legally the Constitution offers a right to privacy *and* to life, both. The question is how do you balance them? And that is the problem. Our modern political discourse doesn't accommodate balance."

Madison uncrosses his legs.

"One party is attached to life, the other to choice, as if there is nothing in between. But real life exists in the middle. Modern politics does not."

"How about modern jurisprudence," Brooks asks. "Where does it live?"

Madison nods at the distinction between politics and law.

"That is one of the fallacies of the conservative idea that judges simply read the Constitution, understand its intent, and then see if the facts fit that intent. The Constitution articulates sometimes conflicting values. A critical part of being an appellate judge is balancing those conflicts."

"Would you say that in a hearing?" Rena asks.

"What you mean, Peter, is would I offer the same evasion as everyone else who testifies," Madison answers. "Would I say I don't think it is wise to engage in hypotheticals and I believe in precedent? Or would I try to turn my hearing into a national teaching moment on the law?"

"And?"

"As a professor, I lived in the world of ideas. As a judge, I now live in the real world."

"What does that mean?"

"It means, Mr. Rena, I am no fool."

Twenty

"Peter, this is Henry Weingarten. I'm sorry I'm late returning your call."

Rena's cell had vibrated and he excused himself from the interview with Madison and wandered outside to the back deck for the call. Though it is spring, it is cold, a cloak of silver fog moving swiftly down the mountain toward the ocean.

Rena called Weingarten two days ago, part of the process of calling people he knew who might know the judge. Weingarten had gone to Berkeley in the late 1960s and early 1970s, the same years as Madison. He'd also gone to law school—Berkeley not Harvard—and then became a journalist. He'd covered legal matters and labor for the *Los Angeles Times* for twenty years and now taught law and journalism at the University of California, Irvine. Rena had met him years earlier. Weingarten was the only reporter who had come close to getting the real story of the incident involving the general that had ended Rena's military career.

Their acquaintance is enough for only a few pleasantries before Rena says, "Henry, I want to ask you something from your life before you were a reporter. I want to ask you about something off the record."

Silence. Then: "Why would I agree to that?"

"Because I want to ask you something you learned about in college, under circumstances that were personal. The basis of your knowledge about this has nothing to do with your being a journalist, and your responsibilities are personal, not journalistic."

More silence. "You have thought this through pretty carefully, haven't you, Peter?"

"I hope so."

"From college?"

"Do you agree to my conditions, Henry? Off the record. Not for you to use? I am interviewing you, Henry. The shoe on the other foot and all that."

Another pause.

"Ask."

"Do you know Roland Madison?"

"Why?"

"No, Henry. Off the record, about something you learned before you were a journalist."

Weingarten laughs. "Okay, Peter, you have me cornered. I am too curious to say no."

He and Madison *had* been friends in college, close friends, Weingarten says. They were both serious kids, both interested in law. They were the same year, though Madison was two years younger. "Rollie really was a prodigy, an extraordinary mind. Immature, obviously, on top of the awkwardness that usually comes from being serious and bookish."

"Is there anything in his past I should know about, Henry?"

There is a silence on the other end.

"Henry, you do him a favor by telling me. And you do him harm by withholding it. You know that. No one should know that better than a reporter."

"I can't believe you have talked me into this, Peter."

"I haven't talked you into anything, Henry. I've leveled with you."

Weingarten laughs again.

"What is it you want to tell me, Henry?"

"Nothing . . . no, it's . . . Well . . . There may be one thing. Something we've never told anyone, never needed to. But if this background check is for what I think it is, maybe you should know."

Rena lets the silence do its work.

"One year, Rollie and I and two friends created an antiwar group that engaged in activity that was illegal."

"What do you mean by illegal?"

"We called ourselves the New Walden Project—you know, Thoreau, civil disobedience—and we talked about the limits of civil disobedience to protest an unjust war."

"What was illegal, Henry?"

"Well, we talked ourselves into some things. Rollie was seventeen years old. A very young college sophomore. The rest of us turned, what is it, nineteen during that year."

"What things?"

"Well, expressions of civil disobedience that we wanted to explore—something different from mass protests. Something with a more defined message, we thought. But it seems absurd and naïve in retrospect. There was vandalism of an army recruiting office. We wrote a manifesto and spray-painted some words on the front window of the storefront where it was located. And another message on the hood of a recruiter's car. We also made contact with groups advising people on how to evade the draft. Contact with groups shepherding people to Canada. We let a few people stay in our dorm. We didn't really know who they were. But we thought we were part of the new underground railroad. It lasted a year. Then we moved on. We fancied ourselves the heirs of Thoreau."

"Is that it?"

"Well, and this is why I think you might need to know, we were detained briefly, by a military guard. Caught doing the car."

"Detained? You mean arrested?"

"No. He let us go. We cleaned the glass and the car. We explained the whole Thoreau business. I think he thought we were idiots more than threats. Look, people had just been killed at Kent State. It was late May 1970. School was almost over for the year. The army was in no mood to overreact. And this was Berkeley. He knew what he was dealing with."

"That it?"

Weingarten hesitates.

"Henry, it's worse if some detail we missed comes out later. Much, much worse."

"There was a woman," Weingarten says, "who stayed a night on her way to Canada, or someplace. There was a rumor she might have been on the run, a member of the Weather Underground or something.

We were never sure. Never knew her real name. But that made it seem a little too real. It was the beginning of the end of it."

Damn, Rena thinks.

"This was forty years ago. How come it's never come up before?"

"Of the four guys, three now work in government, all now pretty high up. Two of them started there pretty young. And those two guys didn't divulge when they started out because they were afraid."

Weingarten pauses.

"Since it had never come out, they just kept it buried, assuming it was lost to history. I am assuming, Peter, off the record, we are talking about something different from that now."

Rena doesn't answer but says, "I need the details, Henry."

There aren't many more. The messages painted on the army property are lost to memory. There were self-important echoes to Thoreau and puffery about the significance of citizens to articulate their objections to laws considered unjust or immoral. Harboring a fugitive from the Weather Underground would have been a serious crime, but even that, if it was more than just a rumor, was lost to the mists.

Weingarten is worried now, as people usually are

after they are persuaded to be candid in a situation they do not fully understand.

"Peter?"

"Yes."

"I'm trusting you. This is no trick."

"No trick. I'm working *for* Madison. Not to hurt him."

"If you're screwing with me, I won't forget. And I won't forgive."

Weingarten's career stretched back to a time when a newspaper like the *Los Angeles Times* could really hurt you if you crossed it. And Weingarten, one of the smartest and shrewdest journalists Rena had ever met, would know how to do it. That shrewdness is probably why he had trusted Rena. Weingarten had always operated as much as a social activist as a reporter and thrived most when the two jobs coincided.

That was why Weingarten hadn't published what he'd learned about the incident involving Rena years ago. He'd decided the harm to some innocent people would outweigh the good.

Today's transaction, however, bound them in a way they had never been bound before. Or at least put Weingarten at Rena's mercy.

"I'm trusting you, Peter."

"You can."

Could he?

Rena can imagine the portrayal. A domestic terrorist. Aiding and abetting the enemy. Perhaps a harborer of a murderer on the FBI's Most Wanted list. He needs to find Brooks.

"Jesus, Peter, you called a reporter?" she says after he has retrieved her from the den and brought her out to the deck.

"He won't publish it, Randi."

"The hell he won't."

"He learned it in a context in which he wasn't a reporter."

Brooks grimaces.

"Learned what exactly?"

He relates what Weingarten told him.

"And why the hell did he tell you?

"Because he became convinced it was better that we know than if it is discovered some other way."

"He became convinced?"

"He listened to reason."

Brooks looks doubtful.

After a few more questions about details and why it has been kept buried, Brooks announces: "Twenty-Five Year Rule."

The 25-Year Rule is Brooks's time guideline for bad things in politics: Anything someone did twenty-five years ago or longer is considered a "youthful indiscretion" and could not hurt you. Politicians could smoke pot in college, or even worse, and no one cared.

Rena isn't so sure how far any rules fully apply. As far as he can tell, politics is more like sandlot baseball than geometry. You make new rules whenever the ball ends up somewhere it has never landed before.

"Anyway, it's bullshit," Brooks says. "It was the height of the antiwar movement. The government was shooting people. The only people who weren't engaging in antigovernment activity were asleep, drugged out, or too dumb to know better."

Rena can think of a lot of people who don't fit that description. He looks at his partner, a woman he trusts implicitly and admires. She is as smart and good as anyone he has ever met. But they come from different worlds. He says nothing.

Twenty-one

The restaurant they had passed at the junction is called Alice's. That's where the Madisons take them when they return from the deck and suggest a lunch break. The combination restaurant, gas, and propane-filling station reflects the mixed culture of the mountain neighborhood where Madison lives, a remote rural enclave in the hills above Stanford University and Silicon Valley. Alice's menu features "Harley" burgers, grilled salmon and tofu sauté. They choose a table on a back deck where they can't be overheard.

As the plates clear, Rena asks Madison to "describe your life to us as if it were a story."

Madison regards Rena a moment and then tells a spare tale of growing up in San Francisco in the 1960s, attending Berkeley, then Harvard Law, clerking on the

Supreme Court, and then working briefly in the solicitor general's office in the Carter administration before entering academia.

The man is astonishingly articulate. The fruit of a thoroughly examined life, Rena wonders? Or something rehearsed and practiced?

"What was Berkeley like in the early 1970s?" Rena asks.

"Boiling over."

"With radicalism?"

"Depends on your definition of radicalism."

"I'd say talking about overthrowing the government. Being anticapitalist. Defying the law. Left-wing extremism."

The cool, vaguely detached smile on Madison's face is back. It may just be the way his face breaks, Rena thinks. But the guy often looks like he's smirking. That would bother the shit out of senators. They like to be the ones doing the smirking.

"The whole country was left-wing back then by today's standards, Peter," Madison says. "Kent State happened in Ohio."

"Not the whole country."

Madison nods.

"Were you into criminal civil disobedience?" Rena probes.

A hesitation. Just a hint.

Then Madison says, "These conversations always lack a sense of time."

"Sense of time?"

"Context."

"Try adding some."

Rena looks at Brooks. She usually enjoys when her partner is about to interrogate someone, but something in her expression suggests says she doesn't like the vibe that is developing between him and Madison.

"Martin Luther King was assassinated my senior year in high school," Madison says. "A few weeks later, Robert Kennedy. Then the Democratic Party nominated Hubert Humphrey for president, who didn't win a single primary and said he'd continue LBJ's war policies. Johnson lied to us about the war. Then Nixon escalated it and lied some more. My generation felt trapped and betrayed. The whole system seemed to be splitting apart. What did Joan Didion write about the era? 'The center was not holding.'"

"And Harvard?" says Rena. "What was that like?"

"The country was exhausted. We had gone from killing kids at Kent State and a secret war in Cambodia to proof that the president was a criminal with Watergate. It is hard to imagine now. I think we wanted it all over."

"Tell me about the radical group you formed at Berkeley with three friends your sophomore year: the New Walden Project."

Madison's face registers a millisecond of surprise and then changes to pained and a little sad.

"You're not serious."

"Your opponents will be," Rena says. He fixes his melancholy eyes on the judge, his interrogator's stare.

"What a farce," Madison says.

"How so?"

"If you were worried about this, why didn't you ask me two hours ago?"

"I'm asking now, Judge."

"We were sophomores," Madison says with a sigh. "Idiots. We were opposed to the war, and we imagined that we were the first people to ever think of the things we thought."

"You helped people evade the draft."

"Virtually everyone who could tried to evade the draft. Certainly the majority of men in college, including most of the Republicans my age in Congress."

"You helped people flee to Canada."

"We let people stay in our dorm. We talked about driving them to Canada. We talked about a lot of things."

"One of them, a woman, might have been a killer,

might have been a member of the Weather Underground."

"Or she might have been someone's cousin," Madison says with lawyerly precision. "I always thought that
particular speculation was an urban myth."

Rena holds Madison's gaze a moment, examining the
tall face of the judge before asking his next question.

"You also vandalized an ROTC office, and an army
recruiter's car. And wrote a manifesto defending the
right of people to resist the government and break laws
you considered unjust."

Madison is a reader of faces, too. He and Rena are
studying each other's.

"This is garbage," Madison says finally. "This didn't
mean any of the things you're suggesting."

"Then why hide it? All four of you. All these years.
It's called conspiracy."

Madison sighs again. "No, it's called life."

Rena can feel Vic Madison's eyes on him. He wants
to know if they are disapproving, but he doesn't break
his gaze from her father's.

"You're going to have to explain it in Washington,
later, if you're lucky. So you should explain it to us now."

Rena glances at Brooks. She is looking at Madison.
But she won't interrupt this, he knows, and won't try to
defuse it with humor or by playing the good cop. When

they do interviews together, they always let the other have their runs, like musicians who've played together a long time and don't get in each other's way.

Madison nods and says, "All kinds of things that would be explained and dismissed today seemed more significant then. We lied on job applications about taking drugs and protesting in illegal demonstrations. Something you don't hide now. But these things weren't forgotten and forgiven back then."

Maybe they are forgotten and forgiven by most of the people Madison knows, by the young, and most people in this restaurant, Rena thinks. But they aren't by everyone. Not by the motorcycle guys he saw on the front deck of the restaurant with the Vietnam vet badges on their leather vests. The guys who felt betrayed by rich college kids like Madison.

"We better go back," Brooks says. "I have more questions."

Twenty-two

Rena and Vic are standing in Madison's kitchen, exiled there by Brooks so she can have some time with the judge alone. "I get you're trying to break his defenses, Peter," Brooks had whispered to him as they returned to the house, "but that was getting to sound personal." She asked for some time with the judge. Vic suggested she and Rena make tea.

"Is this what you do, Peter?" Vic asks. "Check out nominees for the government?"

"Not really. Most of our work is private. Background and security. Law firms on criminal cases. Companies looking for CEOs."

"So you're modern private investigators, Washington-style?"

"It's not as romantic or dramatic as you make that

sound," he says. "It's hardly Philip Marlowe in a trench coat or the TV show *Scandal*."

"More like NSA spying?"

"More like trolling people's lives on Facebook and then asking the ones tagged in the photographs exactly what happened before the picture was taken."

She laughs.

"But Randi's a lawyer. You do legal work, too?"

"Randi and a few others in the firm, but no, we don't. It's just good to know the law."

"And you?"

"Not a lawyer. Army. West Point."

"A soldier," she says, as if she doesn't know many.

"A past life."

Vic smiles, apparently at the idea of past lives.

"Have you investigated a Supreme Court nominee before?"

She is good at this, he thinks. Asking questions.

"They don't come along very often."

As she prepares the tea, he notices how delicate but strong her hands are. He feels something he hasn't in a long time. It's not just a physical attraction, though he feels it, to her athleticism, to her fit body, and to her intelligence. There is something warm and disarming about her, an informality, an empathy, as if she inherited her father's perceptiveness but not his remoteness.

Rena hasn't been interested in dating much since he and Katie split two years ago. He suddenly wishes he and Brooks were spending more time in California. Then he wishes Vic lived in Washington, and that she were somebody else's beautiful daughter rather than Roland Madison's.

"And how's my father doing?"

Rena smiles and shakes his head sympathetically.

"Sorry, Vic, my opinion can only be offered to the president. That confidentiality also protects your father. But I'd like to know how *you* think he's doing."

She stops, her hands suspended over a tray on which she is arranging mugs. "I think he will be fine. He is always fine."

She smiles at him, more thoughtfully this time, not in jest but in recollection. It's a great smile. The smoke-colored eyes shine even more.

"You know, earlier, when he was being difficult, well, that was just Rollie trying to be honest. He dislikes falsity. He takes pride in that. And he didn't want to be false with you. So he tries to disarm people by being candid, even provoking, to get them to be honest with him. You have to remember he's been in a position of absolute authority—a professor and then a judge—for a long time."

It's clear Vic believes this. Rena wonders if he will

come to agree. And then he wonders if can get the judge to knock it off if he comes to D.C. to be confirmed.

"Are you married, Peter?" she says suddenly. She has some of her father's directness, too. "I'm sorry," she adds. "It's none of my business. I don't know why I asked."

"I used to be," he answers.

She blushes and says, "There is no better way to say that, is there? How long ago did it end?"

"Two years. Divorced just over a year. What about you?" She's divorced, too, he knows from the file but he asks anyway.

"My own story isn't so raw," she says, drying her hands on a dish towel. "Not anymore. We were law students together. We weren't well matched, but we were the kind of people who didn't fail at things. So we worked hard not to fail at this."

She pours tea into four mugs and then opens a cupboard, pulls out cookies, and begins to arrange them on a plate.

"It must have been a different kind of childhood," Rena says, hearing himself changing the subject, "growing up in this house. So far in the woods."

"Just Dad and me. Yes. You have a take a car everywhere. But it's not as remote as it looks. And you?"

Rena thinks she is asking about his parents.

"Also just my dad and me. We came from Italy when I was almost two. My father was a stone artisan. Churches."

Then he realizes she was probably asking where he grew up, not how.

"He carved the National Cathedral in Washington. The gargoyles, the balustrades."

"Makes you close, when it's just two of you," she says. "No room for rebellion."

Rena thinks of his dad, and feels the familiar sense of loss, which makes him think about Katie.

Vic picks up the tray of tea and cookies and says, "Follow me, soldier."

"Dad, it's almost four p.m.," Vic announces a half hour later after observing more questions by Brooks.

Madison glances at his watch.

"I like to run on weekends, around now if I can," he explains. "A trail run, not far from the house."

"My father is a creature of habit."

"A believer in routine," Madison corrects her. "It's amazing what routine can do for productivity. I write in the mornings before work. Exercise late afternoon. Read at night."

"Yes, routine is the way to master time rather than squander it," Vic teases, repeating what is apparently a favorite paternal aphorism.

"Perhaps I should stay and we keep going," Madison says.

Rena wants him to leave. He'd like to comb through the house to help get a better fix on the elusive judge.

"Go ahead, Judge," Rena tells him. "Randi and I could use the time."

On a distant ridge, a man watches the judge and the daughter on the trail and notes the time.

Twenty-three

James Nash is not good at waiting.

It is more than a week since Julius Hoffman died. Nash has given the ex-army investigator Peter Rena and the veteran judicial reviewer Randi Brooks two days with Roland Madison in California. But he has asked that they come straight from the airport to the White House on their return. He likes to hear things immediately, and unrehearsed.

"They're here, Mr. President," Sally Swanson buzzes at last.

"Send them in."

Brooks enters the Oval Office in a rumpled gray pantsuit looking exhausted. Rena looks as if he's just showered. A steward brings lemonade and ice tea.

Nash asks them about the flight and their hotel—small talk that keeps him in touch with details of regular life—then leans back on the sofa, draping a leg over the couch's arm.

"Do you know the biggest mistake most presidents make?" Nash says.

Brooks shakes her head.

"They become too isolated. They get too much information filtered through a handful of senior aides, and let one or two of their staff know as much as they do. This cuts off the person with the best instincts for decision making from fully understanding problems and creates alternative power centers in the White House."

Lincoln, he tells them, monitored battlefield news directly at the telegraph office. Reagan divided the chief of staff's role into three jobs—in his first term anyway. Franklin Roosevelt enlisted special envoys who reported directly to him.

"That's why I asked you to take this on and why I've asked you to report back to me immediately before you've had a chance to speak to anyone else."

"Of course, sir," Brooks says.

Nash slides his leg off the arm of the couch, leans forward, and takes a sip of his iced tea.

"So what did you think of him?" he asks Brooks. "Should I put Roland Madison on the Supreme Court?" Nash knows her history, a dogged and astute attorney who has vetted a lot of judicial nominees for a past president and in the Senate. Now in her forties, she would be at the peak of her skills.

"Mr. President?" she says, caught off guard.

"That doesn't sound very positive."

"I, it's just a question with a lot of dimensions."

"Should we go one dimension at a time?"

She laughs. "It would be less intimidating."

Good. She's relaxing. One of the most frustrating things about being president is getting people to calm down enough to be honest with you.

A knock on a side door. "Come," the president says. Spencer Carr steps halfway into the room. "May I?"

Nash had wanted this meeting without Carr. Spencer has been fighting him on this whole thing. But William Barlow Nash's son is also not going show up his chief of staff in front of outsiders.

"Of course, Spence," the president answers. "I was just about to ask Randi how would it change the Court if I replaced Julius Hoffman with Roland Madison? Randi?"

"It might confuse everything," she says after a breath.

"How?"

"Judge Madison strives very hard to be an iconoclast, in the best sense of the word. Someone free of cant and orthodoxy. He tries to push back against the liberal 'critical legal theorists' who argue there is no such thing as objective law—that it's just all ideology. But he pushes equally hard against conservative orthodoxy that sees the Constitution in what he considers too rigid a way."

"So he'd be an unpredictable choice . . . politically unreliable."

"He might relish it."

"How would the other justices react?"

"Some will be annoyed. But it might inspire other justices to be more freethinking. History suggests that is hard to predict."

Nash looks pleased.

"What's his most unorthodox position?"

"His theory of 'essentialism.' That's the idea that the Constitution was a document of political consensus that articulates sometimes conflicting ideas. As he puts it, the Constitution is brilliant, but human, not divine."

She was a good choice for this, Nash thinks.

"How does he come across personally?"

"You mean how will he do in hearings?" she asks. "To be honest, he can be challenging. He's brilliant, but he doesn't have much patience for what you might call social niceties."

The president doesn't react.

"Have you met him, Mr. President?" Brooks asks.

Nash smiles and glances at Carr. "Oh, yes." He and Carr have met a lot of possible Supreme Court nominees privately over the course of the last year, often out of Washington, spread out in a way that the meetings would go unnoticed.

Nash turns to Rena. The man has a lethal stillness about him, Nash thinks.

"You agree, Peter?"

"I'll defer to Randi on the law, sir."

"Then tell me about the politics."

The ex-soldier is an unusual Washington fixer, the president thinks. He came to it not entirely by choice, and he is a little too independent. All of which, according to reputation, has made him an unusually cold-eyed and objective political tactician.

"The Right will be caught off guard but the hard Right will conclude Madison is even more of a threat because he is unorthodox," Rena begins. "And the cultural cues will grate on some people—Berkeley, the sixties, articles about everything from birding to single parenting."

"What about my own party?"

"They'll be conflicted between supporting you and being disappointed you didn't pick a stronger liberal. And that ambivalence will embolden your enemies to fight you more."

"And the press?" Nash asks.

"They despise the current state of politics so they'll be impressed by an iconoclastic choice. But they're fixated on winners and losers, so they'll note the lack of enthusiasm in your own party. Ultimately, they'll say it's another enigmatic move," Rena says.

The president has a taut expression and then his face softens. The soldier does live up to his reputation for frankness.

"No credit for trying to change the dynamics of the Court?"

"That's too subtle a narrative for a hundred and forty characters."

The president looks at Brooks and then to Carr for rebuttal, but they are looking at Rena. Nash creates a pause by taking another drink of iced tea, then moves on.

"You find anything that could damage us? Any dirty laundry that can't be cleaned? I don't mean some random phrase taken out of context from a law review article. If we can't handle that, we don't deserve the White House."

"We found one thing," Brooks says quickly, and Nash wonders if she has jumped in before Rena can answer.

"And that is?"

"Vietnam antiwar protests."

Bemused, Nash says, "Why is that a problem?"

"Because Madison and his friends have hidden it all these years."

"Why have they done that?" Nash asks.

Brooks tells the story and she puts it as nicely as it can be put, Rena thinks. But she includes everything they know—the vandalism of the ROTC office and car, detention by an army MP, contacts with other groups, including those shepherding people to Canada. She uses the phrase "civil disobedience group" and says "Madison was seventeen."

Nash shifts around uncomfortably on his sofa, as if a spring were suddenly poking out of it.

"They actually ferry anyone to Canada?"

"Not that we can find. They put people up. They didn't know where they went after."

"One of them may have been part of the Weather Underground. That would be a felony," Rena adds. "That is serious."

"But there is no evidence of that," Brooks says. "It was a rumor. And they were never charged with a crime of any sort, and laws at the time mean the statutes of limitation have run out."

Nash looks at Carr, then back at Rena and Brooks.

"If it's been hidden, how did you find it?" Nash asks.

"Isn't that's why you hired us?" Rena answers.

Rena is trying to read him; the president can sense it. Nash's grandfather, a great card player, used to call that "listening with your eyes."

"Why the hell did they try to hide it?" Carr says from the other side of the room.

"It seemed more controversial at the time than it does now," Brooks says.

Nash rises from the sofa and begins to pace, marking a path back and forth. "Would Madison volunteer it?"

"Yes," Brooks says. "The problem is two of the others, who've insisted from the start. They work in government and they think they would be damaged now. A judge and a high-ranking government official."

Nash stops pacing and scans the faces of the three people in his office.

"Mr. President, in my view, this is innocent," Brooks says. "And it was forty years ago."

"Peter? Something bothering you?"

"It may be a youthful indiscretion. But to some people this will sound like acts of treason. And the fact that they have hidden it makes it worse."

"Treason, that's ridiculous," Carr says. "By that standard millions of Americans—"

Nash raises a calming hand. He is standing next to the sofa so the four of them form a circle, the three aides sitting, the president standing over them.

"Your recommendation, Peter?"

"I think you have three choices," Rena answers, as he might a commanding officer in the army, where you lay out options rather than tell the boss what to do.

"You could choose to volunteer this information. You might even make it a condition of a Madison nomination.

"You could choose not to reveal it and hope it remains hidden. But if it leaks, he's probably done and your presidency would be hurt. You have picked a radical and hidden it.

"Or you could decide that his silence over this, if not the protests themselves, disqualifies him from being nominated."

Nash looks at Carr again, but with a slight shake of his head the chief of staff indicates he has nothing to add.

"Mr. President, may I ask you a question that isn't my job to ask?" says Rena.

Nash, still standing but looking restless again, says, "Fire away."

"Why don't you pick Laura Joiner from Tennessee? She's more liberal. She's African American. She's younger. She's probably more confirmable."

Rena wants to read Nash responding to a direct question about this. He wants more clues about what the president really wants. And whether Madison and they are being set up.

"Because Joiner rebalances the Court, but that's not what I want to do. I don't want to rebalance it. I want disruption.

"Now it's my turn for a question," Nash says. "If you found this hidden Vietnam stuff why won't others?"

"We can't guarantee they won't," Rena says.

The president stares at him. Then a mischievous grin crosses Nash's handsome face, and it makes him look younger.

"Makes life interesting, doesn't it? A politically unreliable iconoclast who might just move the Court in an important new direction, but who may never get confirmed. And there's a secret that could blow up in our face."

The president is enjoying the moment, the stakes, the decision making.

"Time for bottom lines," Nash says. "Randi, yes or no?"

"I doubt, sir, there are a dozen people with his kind of legal mind in the country, and that includes the eight sitting on the Court already," Brooks answers.

"Peter?"

Rena can feel something welling up. He isn't sure what he is about to say. In his soccer days he learned to prepare by actively emptying his conscious mind, a form of trusting yourself so your fears didn't overwhelm you. The technique had helped him cut it in Special Forces, a place where you dedicate yourself to going beyond the limits of what you thought you could handle.

He sees Madison's face at lunch, the dismissiveness in his eyes, as he described the thinking that went into the war protests when he was seventeen.

"My father used to say, 'There are a lot of people who are smart. Not so many who are wise.'"

"You don't think Roland Madison is wise?"

"What the hell was that?" Brooks says after they get into the car waiting for them outside the White House. "You don't think Madison is wise enough to be on the Court?"

She is somewhere between furious and amused, but she hasn't made the whole journey between them yet. "Jesus, Peter, we're sitting with the president of the United States in the goddamn Oval Office. You're not at some D.C. dinner party throwing out bullshit."

Brooks is falling for Madison, Rena thinks, or falling for the idea of picking a different kind of person for the Court.

"You afraid we might lose?" she demands.

Rena looks at his partner across the backseat.

"Because he spray-painted an ROTC window when he was seventeen and let strangers stay in his dorm room?"

The limousine taking them home stops at the security gate behind the White House on Seventeenth Street.

Rena suddenly realizes what he is feeling. It isn't the prospect of losing that bothers him. It's the idea of helping Madison win.

He was mentored by men who had fought in Vietnam. Those men, his friends and teachers, bore a triple scar. They had been damaged by the war in the way soldiers always are. Then they had come home and were despised for their patriotism, and that was a national disgrace—as much as persisting in fighting a war that couldn't be won.

But the third scar was the worst. The soldiers were also despised for losing the war.

People don't admit that last one. It makes everything more complicated. But a good many antiwar protesters were simply afraid of going. They didn't know if the war could stop communism in Asia or not. How could they? All these kids knew was that the war seemed hopeless.

Had it been winnable, everything would have been different. Or if Johnson had pulled out in 1964 when he was first told he couldn't win, or even in 1966 or '67. But that's not what happened. And a lot of the country condemned the soldiers who went anyway as if they were to blame.

To Rena that made the sacrifices of these soldiers more tragic and valiant, not more shameful.

It didn't make Vietnam right. But it dishonored the protestors. And it had cleaved the nation in two, a split that still hasn't healed, even if half the country is too young to remember or have been alive.

Roland Madison, like most people his age, seems to consider his protests of the war a badge of honor, or something humorously young and hardly worth reflecting on. Maybe that isn't so unusual. But Madison is supposed to be extraordinary.

As the car heads up Seventeenth Street Rena sees a collection of protestors gathered near the White House.

There are always some, a constant but changing and motley troop, carrying hand-painted signs.

"The Army Tested LSD on My Father." "Save Our Country: End Foreign Aid." "Please Find My Daughter." "Will Anyone Help Me?"

Twenty-four

Saturday, April 25, 4:04 P.M.
Woodside, California

The position is perfect.

From here he can see the house and also sections of the trail coming down from the house and he can still be hidden as someone on the trail gets close.

There is a rock outcropping, and when he slips behind it he can remain hidden from almost every angle. Yet with two steps forward he easily has room to swing a club and kill anyone coming down the trail.

Whoever is coming down that path is defenseless. And the faster they run, the more lethal the blow. A good spot. A killing spot.

The weapon was a challenge. He needs something found here, in these woods. Like Bird said, anything you bring from somewhere else reveals more about you. And it had to be a hardwood, thick and long enough to be struck across a man's head with enough force that it could crack the skull. That meant it couldn't break. It needed to be strong. A killing stick.

The blow is simple. It's a backhand swing, like a righty batting left-handed. And the force would be even harder 'cause the runner would be coming at him down the hill. Sure thing.

A man would go down easy. And once he is down, well, he has another plan for that. At one end, the stick he's found will also work like a spear. He can drive it down into the judge's chest, crushing the rib cage. Like a knight with a lance. Righteous. A goddamn avenger.

The only problem is if someone is coming up the path from below at the same time. The path curves there, and so he wouldn't see someone coming up. He could hear but he couldn't see. So he will need to listen in both directions.

And there's one other risk. The biggest one. It came to him like a flash, as the whole plan had formed in his mind over the last month. This hiding place, this killing place, changed something. When they come out with their tape, and their chemicals and their bullshit, the police will figure someone had waited, had stalked. Unlike the other two, they would know this wasn't random, and they will try to imagine all the people who might want to kill the judge. They would ask everyone and make lists, and in time, they might begin to connect the other two, and begin to figure it out.

But by then he would have vanished.

That is the plan. That is the trick of the whole thing, the plan of doing them so close together.

Always plan, right, Bird?

He has looked at it both ways, pro and con. Cost and benefit.

The cost of doing them all at once is he wouldn't learn as much from the first kill, from the woman. He took months, worked them all out, and he couldn't do the first one until the last one was all figured, down to the last thing.

But now he feels rushed.

Maybe it's all the better. Like a raging fucking hail storm coming down. Before anyone figures out anything. That is a benefit.

The other cost, he figures, might be his own panic. What if he gets excited? Or hurt? He will have no time to calm down. No time to regroup.

But he is good at this. He can feel it. He sensed it right away, even before the woman. So much of it, little things, things many people wouldn't think of, seem to come into his mind right away. Like it's natural.

He looks up the ridge, trying to pick up the early parts of the trail.

About time.

The judge usually runs alone. Weekends at 4:00 when he's home. Like clockwork.

You gotta love it. Routine makes a man vulnerable.

He puts the binoculars to his face again and scans the ridge, trying to find the trail.

He sees him . . . distant. In the trees and shadows.

Time to slide into the spot, the little crevice, where he could hear the footsteps on the trail. He waits. It seems forever. And then he hears. Yes.

Wait.

Not yet.

He feels the stick in his hands. Lighten the grip. Be cool. Be loose. Listen.

The footfalls are getting closer.

Fifty feet.

Easy.

Now forty.

He can hear himself breathe.

Thirty.

Can he move? Can he slip out? Yes, he is loose. Don't make a sound.

Twenty.

Deep breaths. Relax. Relax, man.

Time the footfalls. He feels that syrupy feeling again, the one he felt the first time with the bitch in Berkeley. Yeah.

Ten.

Now.

Wait. Just as he begins to move, he slides back, into the crevice.

And he sees the runner pass.

Shit. Goddamn it. His heart feels like it is going to blow out of his chest. Breathe.

He looks, through the tiny space, and watches the runner move down the trail, leaning back just slightly as the trail steepens.

But it's a woman. Not the judge.

She reaches the curve of the switchback and is gone.

He cannot calm his breathing. His heart.

But he feels pride, too.

That he sensed something wrong.

He isn't here for the daughter.

Twenty-five

Monday, April 27, 2:40 P.M.
Washington, D.C.

The president walks to the microphone alone.

The Rose Garden had been the president's idea. "An august occasion, a Supreme Court nomination," he'd said whimsically. "And it's springtime. Get the wretches out of the press room."

Rena and Brooks sit in the first row of white folding chairs set up on the grass, beside senior White House staff, plus the attorney general and solicitor general and their chief aides. The press is seated in the rows behind. A Rose Garden press conference vaguely resembles a small wedding.

The president carries no note cards with him. He looks down at the portable lectern to center his thoughts and then up at the "pool" camera at the back.

"History shows us that among the lasting impressions of a presidency, a so-called presidential legacy, perhaps no element is more significant in its implications on the lives of ordinary Americans than the jurists you place on the country's highest court. Today I make my first nomination to that court."

Brooks is leaning over her cell. "Still no name," she whispers to Rena, meaning it hasn't leaked. The reporters must be livid.

The president's remarks touch on the significance of the Court, the importance of consensus, the desire of Earl Warren that as many decisions as possible be unanimous. It's a veiled slight at the decisions rendered by the Court under current chief justice Stephen Forner.

He invokes, as he had the first night with Rena, what the Federalist Papers said about what a president should seek. "Nothing but judgment," Nash repeats. "Wisdom, judgment, that is a judge's power. That is the gift we seek, the temperament we need. No jurist in America epitomizes those qualities more than the judge I introduce to you now."

At the word "now" the door that connects the Oval Office to the Rose Garden opens, and Edmund Roland Madison emerges, followed by Victoria Madison.

Reporters whispering. You can hear typing on wireless devices as people scan the Web to ID the man. At least for some, the White House has achieved actual surprise.

They'd worked on Madison's statement last night and most of the morning, ever since Carr called to say Nash had decided on him. Madison had chafed at the vagueness of it. "Dad, just go with it," Vic advised.

"Your only job is to be grateful and humble," Brooks said.

"Should I wear a monkey's cap and be tied to the organ grinder's wrist?"

"If it will help," Rena said. That had prompted Vic to laugh—sending a message to her father: "Stop, Dad."

Madison pulls the statement now from his jacket pocket.

"It is with great humility and gratitude that I stand before you today. I have spent my adult life studying the law, practicing it, teaching it, presiding over it."

The statement offers just enough biography to introduce Madison without any hint of what he thinks or believes. He mentions being a widower and a single

father. He acknowledges Vic. He thanks the president
and his home-state senators.

Press conference by numbers. No questions. "Your
nomination is the news. You don't want to make it any
more with anything you say," Brooks had told him.

It all goes fine until a reporter yells out asking
whether he looks forward to appearing at Senate confirmation hearings. Perhaps the inanity of the question
pushed a button.

"You know that isn't required by the Constitution,"
Madison responds.

"Oh, God," Brooks mutters.

"That protocol, having nominees testify, is really a
creature of television. Before that, it almost never happened."

Madison ad-libbing. He means it as a joke. But it's
not funny.

"But if the Senate Judiciary Committee asks me, of
course, I look forward to it, and to answering whatever
questions they have."

**Senate Cloakroom
2:53 P.M.**

Senator Wendy Upton isn't quite sure if she heard
right.

Did the man whom President Nash nominated to the Supreme Court just take a royal piss on the Senate confirmation process?

Right there on television?

It was subtle, but it was there. His appearance before the Senate isn't required by the Constitution. He would appear "if the Senate asks"? And something about a "creature"?

The talking heads on TV seemed to have missed it. The anchorwoman, a redhead made up to look more like a porn star than a college graduate, is reading some biographical factoids about Madison she probably got from a White House handout. It depresses Senator Upton that cable channels insist on making women look like that. The same information about Madison is repeated in graphics running down the side of the screen and again in text crawling across the bottom.

Upton looks around the cloakroom to see if any other senators noticed. A half dozen are on their cell phones texting or on Twitter, probably trying to assess reaction. A few senators don't even have smartphones yet, but some of her colleagues reveal more on Facebook than they tell spouses or staff.

A maverick on the Judiciary Committee who rose to prominence as a crusading attorney for the Judge Advocate General's Corps in the U.S. Army, Upton had caught the eye of the GOP in her home state of Arizona after being profiled by *60 Minutes*. She had a reputation on Judiciary as the house intellectual, a freethinker, an instant star because of her obvious legal intellect and as a woman. Well, what should *she* should think about Nash's choice for the Court? She has questions. Certainly she has questions.

She sees Senator June Blanchard, a new member on Judiciary, and catches her eye.

"June, you see the press conference?"

"Yes, I will need to know more, but he seems like an interesting choice," she says with a practiced senatorial vagueness.

Upton can't decide whether the honorable Senator Blanchard is careful or vapid, a distinction sometimes difficult to make with politicians.

"This will be my first Supreme Court nomination as a member of Judiciary," Blanchard says.

"Yes, they are always interesting," Upton offers. She had worked on a Supreme Court nomination during her brief stint as a staffer for Judiciary chairman Furman Morgan after leaving the army. Her time as a Senate staffer was followed by four years in the House, then a successful run for the Senate.

Blanchard's cell phone vibrates, and she is instantly absorbed by it. Upton excuses herself and wanders over to eavesdrop on four other senators, three of them liberal members from the Northeast, standing near another television talking. She hears the words "moderate," and "California," but the tone is hard to discern.

"John, Marty, Sandy, Fred," Upton says in greeting.

"Wendy."

"You see the president's announcement?"

"No, but we were just talking about his pick. Seems like Nash is trying to avoid trouble," says John Rasmussen of Connecticut. "Madison is a moderate."

"Smart," says Marty Rogers of Massachusetts.

"Or gutless," says Fred Blaylish of Vermont.

"I don't know. Berkeley. Harvard. He's not exactly getting to the heartland, is he?" says Upton.

It's obvious that none of them knows any more about Roland Madison than they had just heard on TV.

"You going to play the culture war here, Wendy?" Blaylish shoots back.

The culture wars? Fuck you, Fred.

Blaylish seems to think that what he calls the "culture wars," the social values politics of the 1980s and '90s, were cynical rather than sincere. They weren't. And they are a lot simpler than the pressures from constituents Upton faces now to keep her seat. Today she has to have the right position on abortion and guns, and then also worry about where the Common Sense vote is on taxes, and health care, debt, climate change, evolution—and who knows what will be next.

She will find out when she "dials for dollars" tomorrow. That's how she spends most of her time now, it feels like—on the phone raising money. It is up to four to six hours a day, depending on the time of year. When she started it was maybe one or two—and many days none. And most of these hours are spent talking to your most angry supporters, extremists so aggrieved they will give you money only if they're sure you're as zealous as they are. Or the transactional jerks, people who want something hard and expensive for their contribution and are willing to pay for it. You need these angry and demanding people's money to serve. But they want assurance you are as angry as they are, or that they will get a return on their investment. Once you say yes, you owe. You owe and owe. The money game is so out of control and people don't seem to realize these aren't supposed to be bribes. Well, it's the age of accountability, baby.

The Common Sense phenomenon awed her most of all. It is less a movement than an emotion—anger directed at almost everything, the economy, race, multiculturalism, modernism, taxes, the Chinese, the Koreans, aging, change, about the whole goddamn state of things.

One of her closest friends, Randall Stone, saw his bid to retain his seat in the House in South Carolina fail in a primary loss by 3,200 votes to a Common Sense candidate, and Stone was probably the most conservative person she knew. Randy taught Sunday school and took a hard line on almost every social issue there was. His sin was that he believed that climate change was real, and he had voted to raise the debt ceiling. "You either get with the program or get run over, Wendy," Stone had told him. "Even if you think they are crazy you have to agree. Either that or get out."

She looks over and sees her mentor, Senator Furman Morgan, the senior senator from South Carolina and chairman of the Senate Judiciary Committee. Morgan will chair the Madison hearings. She walks over to him.

He is asleep, slumped in a red mahogany leather armchair in the Senate Cloakroom with his eyes closed.

Of course, she thinks.

Morgan hides in one of the cloakroom's plush armchairs with his eyes closed many afternoons around 2:30—at least on those days when the Senate is in session. Out for about twenty minutes, give or take.

Morgan even bragged about preferring to nap in the cloakroom, the sprawling offices just off the Senate chamber, rather than his office across the street in the Dirksen Senate Office Building. Only senators and

aides are allowed in the cloakroom, and what occurs in
the cloakroom is strictly private. It may be one of the
few places in Washington where nothing leaks. Every
senator spends time here. Which means everyone is
vulnerable. So everyone is safe.

Upton owes the old man a good deal. She had met
Morgan when she was a young JAG lawyer, at a time
when women were far and few between in key military
positions. Morgan, who had a reputation for staffing
his office with beautiful women and marrying a succession of younger wives, had surprised her by encouraging her, then grooming her to run for a House seat
and eventually the Senate.

But it is not clear anymore whether Morgan is conservative enough, passionate enough, energetic enough,
for what is to come. The old man has sat on Judiciary
for forty-three years. He was the committee's staunch-
est conservative in the culture wars of the 1980s, was
enraged by the Bork hearings, had done more than
anyone to carry the conservative cause during the Clar-
ence Thomas–Anita Hill hearings in the 1990s. But
Morgan came to the Senate in another time, an age when
senators fought in public but socialized in private—and
measured a large part of their senatorial value in the
deals they made. Two years from now Morgan will
face a primary challenge from any number of Common

Sense advocates. A lot of folks doubt the old man will survive, if he is stubborn enough to try.

You never know. The man is a sphinx. But more and more Upton worries.

Upton heads toward the door of the cloakroom when she hears Senator Morgan's voice.

"Wendy," the old man says in an impish whisper.

"Senator?"

She looks down at Morgan. The old man, usually so natty, so vital, appears shrunken in the big chair, his suit bunched up at the back of his neck. Morgan still has his eyes closed.

"Looks like we are goin' to have to a little fun with Judge Madison," Morgan says, drawling his vowels and dropping consonants for effect.

"Sir?"

"If, uh, we, 'insist' on his testifyin'? Well, I am afraid perhaps we shall."

"Yes, sir," Upton says.

"We won't insist, of course. We shall humbly request. We would never imagine insistin'."

"No, sir."

"This isn't a great sin on his part, Wendy. But I believe we may conclude that we may have to instruct this young judge from the western state of California in the value of humility and polity. Washington is, after all, a southern city. Manners still matter."

"Yes, sir."

"So you noticed his impudence, Wendy."

"I did, sir, yes."

"I'm pleased to hear that."

"Thank you, sir. I thought you were sleeping."

"Oh, just listenin'. Not sleepin'. But, Wendy, there is little that will happen in this town that has not happened before. And after forty-five years I have even seen some of these things that have happened before for myself."

"Yes, sir."

"So you learn, Wendy, when you need to listen, and when you need to watch."

"Yes, sir."

"Sometimes, listenin' is better."

"Yes, sir."

The old man still had his eyes closed.

Twenty-six

9:30 P.M.
Washington, D.C.

Before she starts, Brooks calls Rena. She is sitting at her kitchen table with her laptop, tablet, and phone, ready to pore over the first cut of press coverage and social media building in response to Madison's nomination. She is feeling exultant.

She knows her partner still harbors doubts—personal ones about Madison and Machiavellian fears about Nash.

"Here we go, partner," she says to him over the phone.

It's a line they share when they have passed the point of no return on a project.

"Here we go," he answers back with a soft laugh.

Brooks can hear jazz playing in the background through the phone. He is probably sitting in his den, she thinks, reading some tome about the planning of an obscure Revolutionary War battle. But he sounds more relaxed than he has in days.

"You remember when you told me that in the back of your mind you still couldn't shake the idea that we're being set up, that Nash *wants* Madison to implode?"

"I remember," he says wryly.

"How did you put it—give the other party a pound of flesh and then Nash can pick someone more liberal. It was your Washington as lawless frontier, dystopian theory."

"I still think the paranoid scenario is worth considering," he says.

Now she laughs, an outsize wholehearted laugh, a release of tension of the past week.

"Well, I've been thinking about that," she says, "and I don't think it's that simple. Jim Nash is too clever for that."

"Okay, I will call Dr. Kissinger and tell him I want to stop my therapy sessions," Rena says.

"Oh, Madison could implode all right," Brooks adds. "But I don't think Nash wants him to. The brilliance of picking him is that Nash wins either way. That's what became clear to me today, Peter, as we were sitting at the ceremony. If the judge makes it, the president has done something big. If he goes down, Nash still gets credit for trying, *and* gets another pick. Men like Nash always play with more than one option. That's how you get to *be* president."

In his den, Rena closes the book he is reading and lays it in his lap. It's a fair theory, he thinks.

"So we're not being set up to fail, Peter. We're being set up to succeed. If we're up to it."

Meaning get with the program, partner. Madison's the guy and it's up to us now to get him confirmed.

"You feel me, kemo sabe?" she asks.

Now Rena laughs.

"I feel you, Lone Ranger." He pauses and says, "You're the white guy, right? I'm the Indian? 'Cause that's how I'd cast it."

"See you tomorrow, Peter."

Nash had decided on Madison the day after they returned from California. Despite the judge's lack of respect for the process. Despite his oddness. Despite the fact that Madison refused to disclose the antiwar activity—and Lord knows they had tried. Madison insisted he wouldn't betray "a promise to my friends."

Nash went ahead anyway.

Brooks never had any doubt he would. She had walked out of the Oval Office six days ago convinced Nash was genuine about wanting to change the Court.

She sensed that he was ready to flout his own party and the opposition and be unconventional. She believed him when he said Madison is just the kind of judge the Founders had in mind.

In a way, she had told Rena, Nash is picking himself for the Court. Someone who aspires to be original, free of cant, and wants to inspire others to try to be.

Rena is more skeptical, but then he hadn't voted for Nash—twice—as Brooks had. And he's right: There is still plenty to go ass over heels.

Republicans controlling the Senate, Madison's criticisms of conservative ideas *and* liberal ones, his California eccentricities, his refusal to talk about the Vietnam protest group, and his resistance to being handled. Culminating in today's ad lib.

So now they will have to balance her enthusiasm and his doubts. If they're going to succeed, Brooks thinks, that's how they'll do it.

She pulls out her iPad. Time to see how Roland Madison's nomination is playing. She taps the icon for the *New York Times*.

For all the changes in the world, the most important scorecard in Washington is still the *Times*' front page.

Only now you read it the night before—via Twitter feeds.

Along with the White House, Rena and Brooks are dealing with Madison's greatest vulnerability—his criticism of the cherished conservative idea of strict constructionism—by running at it headlong. They've uncovered all of his criticisms and put them out there for all to see, along with a simple narrative. In many ways, Madison is the ultimate advocate of original intent. He just realizes it's more complicated than some of the slogans, and requires more of judges. And his arguments are beginning to change the view of legal intellectuals about the whole concept of intent.

It's a plain enough strategy: Exhaust the subject before any critic could get a hold of it.

She pores through close to forty pieces from a couple dozen sources.

The longest story is a biographical profile in the *New York Times*.

"Roland Madison: Pegged Early as a Prodigy, 'a Mozart of Law' and Renaissance Intellectual."

The piece is a tour de force of White House message control, and the sheer weight of assembled detail will make it effectively the basic public biography. If opponents want to attack Madison now they will have to alter this narrative. The story quotes almost two dozen people from Madison's life—nearly all of them sources she, Rena, and the White House had lined up.

The other side's criticisms, for the moment, are vague and ritualistic. "Madison is a liberal activist of the first order who poses as a moderate and puts his own philosophy above the Constitution," says Wally Short of a group called Judicial Confirmation Alliance. The same quote appears in several stories—it was emailed.

So they have achieved one goal: surprise.

She feels a rush that goes with knowing you have momentum. She loves this.

They could fix Madison's faux pas in a day when they made initial rounds of courtesy visits in the Senate. A bad joke. No harm, no foul. But it was a sign that they had to watch him. One faux pas they could handle. More than one could become its own problem—a sign of insensitivity or arrogance.

Her phone chimes. An email from Ellen Wiley—with a link to a list of 150,250 social media posts. Wiley has hired a firm whose algorithm files and categorizes the posts into Pro, Con, and Neutral. She can scroll through quickly to scan them. They are grouped by Facebook, Blogs, and Tweets.

A third firm is tracking the "network" relationships among the tweets, to find out who the most influential

tweeters are on the subject, based on how many follow-
ers each has and how often their tweets are retweeted.
This identifies influential voices in social media they
might have to target and either feed with positive messages or discredit by feeding bits of misinformation.
The Web is the Wild West. You can pull absurd stunts,
and if you get caught no one seems to mind all that
much.

She should stop. She's exhausted. But she's riveted.
She goes another hour.

Twenty-seven

Tuesday, April 28, 11:19 A.M.
Washington, D.C.

G ary Gold has chewed the plastic stick from his coffee into a twisted mess.

"Max, you should be in jail," he says into the phone. "You know you should. I should have put you there." He is grinning like a thirteen-year-old boy playing a prank that is just a little deliciously dangerous.

It is one of Gold's more curious habits. He loves to needle his sources, especially his shadier ones. He has one foot on his desk, and the other on the floor, and he is leaning back in his chair so that one of its wheels is off the floor. His cubicle is located almost precisely in the middle of the *Washington Tribune* newsroom; anyone sitting within twenty feet of Gold can hear his conversation. At fifty-seven, Gold has never fully mastered what his mother still irritatingly refers to in his presence as an "inside voice."

"Oh, shit, Max," Gold says, interrupting the man on the other end. "Please. Who do you think you're talking to? You're not in jail because I love you. And you always help the ones you love. Even if they don't help you. Even if they hurt you, Max. Because that is what love is." The grin broadens.

Gold is rolling the coffee stirrer between his thumb and forefinger. Now it is flipped back into his mouth. Suddenly it is out again.

"Bullshit. I never would write a story that way. I always throw straight down the middle. Hard slider. Like Mariano Rivera, baby."

Gold pulls his foot off the desk, and has both feet on the ground, so he can concentrate. The foot that was up is now vibrating, the toes on the floor, the heel bobbing up and down at high speed.

"If Cameron told you that, he's lying. He's testing you. And I'm ashamed of you for falling for it."

Gold listens for longer this time.

"If that were true I would have put it in the paper."

Another line lights up on Gold's phone. Then the light goes out and the message light comes up. Then the second line lights up again.

"So you gonna help me? And then I can help you?"

He is laughing in a way that suggests Max is laughing, too.

"Yeah, the Tune," he says, referring to the Tune Inn, a bar and restaurant on Capitol Hill. "Around one thirty . . . Sure, he can come, too."

The phone is down and the pulpy stick is back in his mouth. He ignores the message light.

He grabs the plastic stick and flips it toward the trash basket under his desk. It hits the side of the basket and bounces onto the floor near a dozen others.

Now Gold is up and walking toward a glass office in the front of the room facing out to the street. Inside Jack Hamilton, the assistant managing editor for national news, is talking to his deputy, Marjorie Watson. Hamilton sees Gold and shakes his head signaling that he is too busy for him. Gold heads right in.

"Jack, you're gonna have to give me a Sunday slot for a Slavin story. Page One. I'm gonna nail that guy. He's dirty, and I'm this close. This close. I was just on the phone with my source, and he's absolutely ready to confirm. Maybe this afternoon."

"Gary, not now."

"But before I finish that, I have a better idea. Let me in on Madison. You've done the basic quickie bio thing today. Good grief, Jack. Did they pay us? Huh? Huh?"

"Stop it, Gary."

"Let's not do what everyone else is going to on the next one—the *Times* and the *LA Times* will do, and the *Journal*—breaking off different sides of the guy. One piece that tracks a few quirky decisions. Another that traces his intellectual influences. Another one that explains his independent streak. Talk to his professors, his colleagues, his spunky ma, blah, blah. I can write it for you now. 'Undeniably brilliant. Iconoclastic decisions that could make trouble. Extraordinary guy people always thought might be on the Court.'

"Let's do this thing differently for once. Just once, for God's sake. Let's scrub the shit out of the guy. Do it investigative. Not soft. Not human interest. Really dig, Jack. We have a responsibility to, ya know. Money. Connections. How did he get to the top? What were the compromises? Do it right. Cold-eyed. Do it cold-eyed, with some courage.

"Mad Dog," Hamilton says to stop him.

Mad Dog is the nickname Gold earned thirty years earlier. Not that many people in the newsroom actually know it. But Hamilton does, and he uses it now to get Gold's attention. During a virtual monsoon one summer in Washington the elaborate stone entrance to Gold's apartment building was flooded, trapping the tenants inside. They had a party for the day, everyone's doors open, the apartment turning into a dormitory. Except for Gold. He jumped out of a window and swam across the parking lot in his underwear, then dressed on the street and went to work. When he arrived, soaked, and bragged about how he had made it in, his boss, the editor of a struggling Capitol Hill wire service was appalled rather than impressed. "Gary, you are like a mad dog. The only way to stop you is to shoot you," said the boss, a now-forgotten Washington editor. Gold knew instantly the nickname should spread so that his sources would hear it. And maybe they would fear him for it, just a little. When a decade later he made it to the *Tribune*, after winning a Pulitzer in Chattanooga and being a finalist twice more, he tried to shed some of his more legendary eccentricities. The nickname, now no longer necessary, was one of them. But it lingered, now embarrassing rather than impressive, mostly forgotten but not entirely.

"Jack, don't be a pussy. Oh, sorry, Marjorie. Jack, don't be a wuss. Don't do what everyone else does. The usual, the safe—the boring. The thing that just makes you want to kill yourself because the same friends and neighbors and relatives are quoted in every story to the point that it sounds like it was written by the Madison nomination team. Jack, you know I'm right."

"Did you read what was in the *Times* today?" Gold is holding it in his hand and begins to read. "'. . . described as a surpassing legal scholar and a remarkably wide-ranging public intellectual . . .' Barf bag, Jack."

Gold flips inside the paper. "And the bio profile is even worse. Two full pages that sound like they were written by the president's press secretary. 'Roland Madison: Pegged Early as a Prodigy, 'a Mozart of Law' and Renaissance Intellectual.'"

Thirty seconds ago Hamilton had had every intention of telling Gold he was too busy to talk to him, that he and Watson were trying to put out a fire and that he would have to wait. Now that had been superseded by this other challenge. Gold was insulting. But not wrong.

"What if, just supposing, Gary, there is nothing about Madison that merits a prosecutorial expose? You don't want to hang the man for nothing, to make something sound sinister only because you were looking for it."

"You won't know if you only send out feature writers," Gold says. "Send feature writers and you get features."

Hamilton looks at Watson to see if she would have a faint smile of assent on her face or a stern look telling him not to back down. He cannot tell what she is thinking. He has begun to care too much about what she thinks, and he worries that people may have begun to notice. Especially his wife.

"We have a goddamn responsibility, Jack. We ought to do these things right for a change. Hell, just for once. Just to see what it feels like. Eh?"

Gold looks like a whippet, about five feet six and couldn't weigh more than 140. Paradoxically, the man is both a runner and smoker—the common denominator there being obsessive behavior. And he is the worst-dressed man at the paper, his shirt always untucked on one side and his mud-brown tie he wears several days a week pulled to one side from compulsive tugging.

Yet Gold, somehow, is impossible to dislike. He is infuriating as hell, and he is incapable of not making a pest of himself. Gold knows exactly what he is doing, and everyone else knows it. That is his charm. Gold has perfected it.

"Huh? Jack? Right?"

Hamilton is trying to think.

"And, Jack, I know the folks who are handling the nomination. Rena, Brooks. You know, that former Senate guy and the gal lawyer, they're like super private investigators or something. I know a bunch of the guys who work for 'em. Old, old friends. I can get inside."

More hesitation.

"But you'll nail down this Slavin thing, first, right?" Hamilton says.

"Nail what?"

"Slavin. The bribery story. Congressman Slavin."

"This afternoon. The man is as good as in prison."

"I mean it."

"It's in the bag."

"And Mad Dog, the Madison thing is a team effort, okay. Team, as in cooperate and collaborate."

"Of course, Jack! That's me. No *i* in *team*."

"Okay, Gary," Hamilton says warily.

Gold heads back to his desk.

"But there is one in *win*!" he shouts over his shoulder.

Twenty-eight

Thursday, April 30, 6:30 P.M.
Washington, D.C.

Deborah Cutter looks at her watch. Straight-up 6:30. She has called a meeting for 6:45.

She recalls an old habit and clicks one of the old broadcast network nightly newscasts. There was a time when this was how she ended most of her days in Washington. Everyone did. Twenty years ago, the news cycle ended around now, and everyone watched the network news to see how they did, how they scored, how the day played out. Today the news cycle never ends, and nobody she knows catches the network news anymore. . . . No, that's too strong, but it almost seems that way.

But tonight she is watching. It almost makes her feel nostalgic for simpler days. On the screen, network anchorman Alan Tessier smiles at the camera, the swirling symbol of his network behind him:

> *Tonight, new research on how to avoid cancer . . . A mystery involving wild mustangs in Wyoming . . . And the man who would be the next Supreme Court justice visits Capitol Hill. We begin tonight with the Supreme Court. Matt Alabama has our report.*

Cutter remembers a time when guys like Alabama, dashing and accomplished figures on TV, were considered the coolest people in Washington—hell, in the whole country. Alabama's Marlboro–and–Jack Daniel's baritone booms through the television's speakers. He is narrating pictures: Madison mounting the stairs from the carriage entrance to the Senate . . . Madison walking down a marble stairway . . . Madison shaking hands with old Furman Morgan. In the video's background, Cutter sees various people she knows, Senate staffers, senators, and journalists. In Washington, watching the news, Cutter thinks, is like watching your friends' home movies. Alabama's voice intones:

It is, by Washington standards, an ancient ritual—which is to say one about fifty years old. Each Supreme Court nominee makes the pilgrimage up Capitol Hill, a mountain of some hundred and seventy-five feet, to pay homage to the Senate leaders who will decide his or her fate.

Political people have to be pretty savvy about media, especially television, and about dealing with journalists personally. As she watches, Cutter realizes this is the kind of television writing she doesn't hear much anymore. Alabama's script is subtly ornate, witty, and without the usual painfully obvious puns that mark so much current TV writing. The pacing and syntax are carefully matched to the pictures. Most of what she saw on TV now, on cable, is live, usually interviews, people talking off the top of their heads or reciting stale talking points. She plays that game, too. Live TV gives you more control. But she has to admit, it lacks something.

In public the ritual demands Senate supporters drape the nominee in gossamer praise.

Democratic senator Michael Fuller, standing in a marble Senate hallway, says into the camera, "I cannot imagine a more qualified candidate."

Meanwhile, senators of the rival party, while insisting they will be fair, send signals to their interest groups that they will also be tough.

Republican Wendy Upton says in a sharp, lawyerly tone: "Certainly Judge Madison is qualified intellectually, but academic credentials alone are not enough. On our highest court, we also need wisdom and respect for the Constitution. I hope and trust Judge Madison possesses those."

All of this is in code. To conservatives, any judge who leans left is often labeled a judicial activist, a term that suggests deviation from what the founding fathers intended in the Constitution. A judge who leans right is called a strict constructionist, a term suggesting they are interpreting the Constitution just as it was written.

Republican Ralph Norris of Alabama says: "We need to know that Judge Madison will interpret the Constitution as it was intended, not reinterpret it to suit his own whims."

In private, away from cameras, something else occurs. Senators may not be constitutional scholars, but they tend to see themselves as keen judges of character. They like to size up the nominee as a person, something like a bouncer deciding whether to let one into a select downtown club.

Senator Fred Blaylish of Vermont, the second-most-senior Democrat on Judiciary: "For me, meeting the man one-on-one, eye to eye, away from the stagecraft, tells me a lot."

Alabama narrating over more pictures:

Some nominees have stumbled at these private sessions. Some years ago, White House lawyer Evelyn Miles was so evasive that she struck senators as uninformed, perhaps even ill-equipped. Two decades earlier, Robert Bork seemed too arrogant. Madison has raised concerns that he looks down on the confirmation process. And he can be shy, which may strike some as elitist. Today, he apparently avoided any obvious traps. Listen to the senator considered perhaps the most astute legal mind among Republicans in the Senate.

Wendy Upton of Arizona says, "Madison is an impressive jurist, and I think he did well today."

Then Matt Alabama appears on camera standing outside the Capitol, the dome in the background.

Today's visit is the beginning of a shadow dance. The nominee must avoid saying too much, for fear of creating controversy. But he must also say enough to impress. He must be polite, humble, and erudite—but not so erudite as to show up the senators. It is a bit like meeting the parents of a prom date. You want it to go well, but fundamentally you are here for the date, not the parents. At bottom, Judge Madison is interested in the Court, not the Senate. Alan.

Alan Tessier appears: "So, Matt, is the first hurdle in Madison's confirmation cleared?"

The camera cuts back to Alabama: "Privately, aides tell me yes. No bumps in the road over philosophy or personality, and there has never been doubt about scholarly merit."

Tessier: "Any word from the chairman of the Judiciary Committee, the legendary Furman Morgan, a man who can influence votes?"

Alabama: "As a rule, Senator Morgan and his aides don't talk to reporters before hearings. It keeps their options open and builds more mystery. And today held true to form."

Tessier: "Thanks, Matt."

Cutter's senior staff has begun to collect in her office for their meeting. Cutter clicks off the television.

Crap. When Madison was nominated Monday, she not only discovered he had not been on their list of possible nominees, no one had even put together a background document on him. They've been utterly blindsided. She had to hand it to Jim Nash in the White House. He might not have much political spine, but he knows how to play the inside game in town. Like keeping things under wraps.

"Explain to me how we missed this again," she demands. She knows she is grinding her people; she means to.

"We had seven names," explains Todd Paulson, whose job as communications director includes monitoring the White House and identifying likely candidates. "He wasn't among them."

"I'd heard his name mentioned on TV, for chrissakes," Cutter says.

"No one took it seriously, Deborah," says Nan Bullock. "He's is an oddity, a loose cannon."

They have been having a variation of the same conversation for three days.

The judge came out of that door into the Rose Garden like some prize on a game show.

Were their sources at the White House that bad? Or the West Wing that battened down?

Is the other side as surprised as they are? She wonders, for an embarrassing half second, what Josh Albin knew, that ridiculous man. Does Paulson have an inkling?

She is overcome suddenly with a sense of losing control.

"Listen, everyone. A nomination is a test. A moment when attention is fixed on Washington. If we are not relevant, we become irrelevant. At ten o'clock tomorrow morning, I want everyone back here with suggestions on how we become more relevant."

Josh Albin does not like what he is seeing, either.

In the days since Madison's nomination was announced, the White House has been winning. The groups on the Left, whatever their private ambivalence, are publicly echoing the White House narrative about him: an "extraordinary legal mind . . . what the Founders intended . . . nonideological." It is better message control than the Democrats usually muster.

The messaging on their side, meanwhile, has been slow. The most visible presence has been a guy named Willy Lopes from the Coalition for Justice: "We have concerns," Lopes keeps saying on three different cable channels. And, "There are things that need more study." Concerns and more study? That the best he can muster?

The thought gives him a feeling of hollowness, as if the loss of momentum is something personal, a reflection of his own, Josh Albin's, loss of power.

As he fends off the feeling, Albin's deputy, Al Thomas, pops his head in. "We're ready." In the conference room the staff of Citizens for Freedom is already assembled. He can sense their eyes on him. He finds a seat, eases into it slowly, and begins.

He tells them they've been "caught off guard," that the White House enjoyed "the element of surprise. . . . I salute them."

The staff is listening closely, especially the younger ones. He can sense it. He recognizes the new intern, the Dartmouth boy, sitting against the wall. Good. A time for a lesson in strategic communications analysis.

"We have time. And we have two primary ways to regain momentum. One, counter the narrative before it settles in. But to do that we need unity—all opposition groups telling an identical story. Remember, the White House always has the biggest microphone.

"Alternatively, we can find some fact about Roland Madison that is so disturbing and clear it will change the narrative by itself. The battle can be won late, but only with the right weapon."

Albin pauses to see if his message is getting through. He fixes his gaze for a moment on different faces individually. Make them feel he is speaking to them personally.

"We have to operate on both tracks simultaneously. So, next steps. First, Keith Flanders and staff in research need to dig. No rest. No diversions. All your attention: Here. Now.

"Sally Holden and communications, you need to coordinate with other groups and see where they are."

Another pause, this one for effect.

"Third, we need to have a Monday Group meeting ASAP. Al," he says looking at Thomas, "can you put one together for tomorrow, Friday midday? That means working late tonight."

Hauling everyone's ass this way will send the messages he wants. This matters. He finishes abruptly, the way he prefers.

He makes eye contact again with several people.

"Josh, is there a fourth step?" Holden asks. "Run the Network?"

A hint of surprise flickers across Albin's face. Why does Holden allude to the watchers every time they have a meeting on this? He will have to talk to her about that.

He offers her a tight smile. "Yes, run the Network," he says. Then to the whole room: "I want status reports twice daily on research, Keith, starting close of business tomorrow."

People are unsure if the meeting is over. No one apparently has anything to add.

"Does it matter if we think he is going to be easily confirmed?" one of the younger staffers asks. "I mean he appears to be qualified on experience. So he will be hard to stop on those grounds. And if he really is a moderate . . ."

It's a good question. He's pleased.

"The point to keep in mind is this: Nominations are an opportunity. If you don't seize them for your own gain, you've squandered them. We need to emerge from the battle stronger than when we went in. Even if this nominee is confirmed, we can succeed if we weaken our opponents by what they have to spend to win. That is how losing battles helps you win wars."

There is another pause.

Good. Albin seizes it. "Let's make the most of this battle. Let's win the war."

Twenty-nine

Wednesday, April 29, 10:47 A.M.
Burlingame, California

Nothing like a public library. The security is for shit. You could grab a library card and most people don't notice they've lost theirs for years. He has three different ones.

At the front desk, the woman hands him a slip of paper from a stack next to her with a code on it, written in pencil—numbers and letters, a password to get on the Internet—and points over his shoulder to a bank of old computers against a wall.

He likes this part, the research. It's like a secret he is planning and no one knows. He's figuring how everything will go, and then it does just like he planned. Like he is making up a story. No, better. Like he is direct-ing a movie, only the movie is real. And he is the star. The freaking scary dude, like in the Charles Bronson movies he watched when he was a kid.

Only everything isn't going like he planned. The judge is all over TV.

He had spent months watching the guy, while he also researched the cop and the lawyer. Up on that stupid mountain, taking his hikes, watching birds, going to work, wandering around San Francisco. He would al-ternate days following the others. A week ago he had almost done it. Now what?

Now the guy is moving to Washington? When does that happen? For all he knows, there will be guards and all kinds of shit.

Plus there is Mama. She hasn't said anything, but he could tell this morning she knows about the judge being promoted. She has to. It's all over the news. And she just had a look this morning. Like the Lord had hit her with another blow.

If something happens to the judge now, the whole country will be watching. Headlines. TV news. The heat would be incredible. So he has to change the plan.

It takes him a few minutes to figure out how to type in the code until the words "You may now use the In-ternet" appear on the screen.

He types in the name. "Alan Martell." Martell. The prosecutor.

He has seen his share of prosecuting attorneys. From what he can tell, they all seem pretty much the same. They think you must be a dumb shit. Otherwise, why would you be on the streets, getting arrested? If you aren't a goddamn hump, why didn't you stay in school and have a good job? Like them.

You sit there in court, knowing you're going to lose, with some lawyer you just met, and, of course, you look sad and angry. You know the system is rigged. And they think the expression on your face means you are guilty.

That's when your education about the system begins. It all goes so deep, is so tangled up with so many things, you don't know where to start. If you're poor, you're more likely to live in a shit neighborhood, go to shit schools, live with crime all around you, without any fucking hope. You live in those places, you're more likely to get arrested. If you're poor, you are more likely to have a bad lawyer, or one too busy to do his job. So you are also more likely to get crap sentences. Everything has a reason.

Shit. He's just been sitting here dreaming. This thing with the judge has got him sideways.

Alan Martell. Prosecutor. He had put off the prosecutor before now. He'd looked it up months ago and found the guy had moved away. So he just put him out of his mind. He was going to play the home stand first. If he survived, he would turn to Martell. But now things have changed. Martell moves up in line.

He saw Martell once, after Peanut was gone. Watched him in court one day. Squat guy. Sweaty. Thinning hair, like medical gauze you could see through over his shiny scalp. Even though back then he was probably still in his thirties. But then the guy left town.

He clicks on the name. There are some pictures. Mostly old.

He clicks through more links. There is a lot of crap that isn't connected to the guy. And of what is, most of it is old. Plenty when the guy was a DA. Stories from the local paper about cases.

Not much since he moved away.

He picks up the trail in snippets. And he's not quick about this Web stuff. Never a great reader. But he can't give up now. He is learning how to stick to things. In about an hour he has all he thinks he can get for now.

Then he begins to feel a strange sensation.

Yeah, a new plan forming.

Be like a long-distance mission. Road trip. He'd have to figure out how to get there, where to hang, learn all new places.

Would take all new planning—and whatever charm his Mama thinks he was born with. But let's play a doubleheader.

The judge and Martell. Both in D.C.

PART THREE

Murder Boards

May 18 to June 19

Thirty

O ut of the arch-shaped window in his office Rena
sees a black town car double-park on the street
below. A minute later, Eleanor O'Brien appears in the
doorway. "Roland Madison is here." She mouths the
words in an exaggerated stage whisper.

Madison is back in Washington to begin the confirmation process, three weeks after being nominated.
Rena nods to O'Brien.

Rena finishes the call he is on with the general man-
ager of the Philadelphia NFL team about a player in
trouble.

"Judge Madison and his daughter are in the conference room," O'Brien tells him when he hangs up.

Rena doesn't like what he sees. Madison is sitting in a folding chair in the corner with his briefcase in his lap, the picture of a man uncomfortable in the moment. His blue pinstripe suit, American cut, loose and conservative, is old enough that Rena can see fray spots and hanging threads. The effect is a kind of American Mr. Chips, too effete, distracted, or uninterested to care how he looks. That would only confirm the suspicions most Americans have about professors and intellectuals. It wouldn't sit so well with members of the U.S. Senate, either—a group inclined to hair dye and Botox.

Madison, willful by nature, had wanted to do all of his hearing prep from California. Rina and Brooks had said no. Is he going to pout for the next two months? He's too bright not to recognize the shabby, disrespectful impression he's leaving. He had looked fine for his tour of the Senate a couple of weeks back. They need to get the judge some other things to wear in public. More than that, they need to get the judge to accept a bigger change of terms.

In the center of the room is Victoria Madison. Her father has asked her to come with him to D.C. to help him through the confirmation process, and she has taken a leave from her law firm for the duration.

She looks stunning in a tan skirt and pastel yellow top. She reminds Rena of the women in those ads from that New York designer who uses her friends rather than teenage models to feature her clothes. Adult good-looking women with good taste.

Rena is excited to see her—surprised by how excited he is. Then she offers him a smile that he knows instantly will be the best part of his day.

"I heard you were coming to help," he says.

"I doubt Dad needs it."

"I think we're the ones who need it."

"I doubt that, too," she says with a sly smile.

He had forgotten how smoky her eyes were. Maybe, Rena thinks to himself, the nomination might drag on for months.

"It's good to see you, soldier," she says.

He remembered when she called him that in California. He liked it then, too.

"I'm very glad you're here," he hears himself say.

"I don't know the city well. Maybe you can show me around."

Just then Brooks bursts into the room with an enthusiastic "Hey, you two" and envelops both Madisons in an enormous group hug. When the bubbling and cooing are finished, Brooks releases them and everyone finds a chair around the conference table.

In the three weeks since Madison was nominated, the first wave of press about the nomination has surged and subsided. The first visit to Capitol Hill for meetings with senators three days after the announcement had gone fine after a friendly talk with Brooks to ensure he behaved. Good-cop stuff.

The political scorekeeping so far is fair—better than it might have been. The far Right was digging but hadn't unearthed anything serious. "He's a bit kooky if you want to know the truth. Lives in a log cabin, a Berkeley Birkenstock type" a group called Justice for Justice had emailed widely, quoting from a blogger who called himself "Freedom's Patriot 76." If that was the worst they have, bring it. The Common Sense crowd was also quiet so far.

Two Madison positions seemed to be causing the most trouble with conservatives—his repudiation of the Court's recent decisions on free speech and his criticism of strict constructionism on original intent. But Madison had support from some conservative scholars, and there were signs at least one important political group, the National Rifle Association, might endorse him.

Disappointed liberals have been mildly supportive. That includes the abortion rights groups.

Rena looks at Madison. Does the judge have any notion of how slim a margin he has? He still doesn't have a good read on the man. Their real preparations begin now.

He takes a breath, exhales—old timing techniques from soccer—and begins to outline what will happen next.

The plan has been carefully crafted with the White House and a team of party veterans who have been through this before, with refinements by Rena and Brooks.

"Today is the first day of Phase Two, the process of preparation. You may know all this, and if so, bear with me, but it is best to go over all of it step by step. You already toured the Senate, those courtesy calls we did after you were named. Well, there will be a few more of those, a chance for key senators to meet you privately, one-on-one. It's sizing you up. Like meeting the new neighbor. Are you nice? Are you smart? This time without the TV cameras. You need to be charming with these senators. Be interested. Be humble. Be smart. Answer their questions in the most general way. And don't tell them, please, that you think this process is a sham."

Vic laughs a little.

"Then we start preparing for your testimony."

Brooks takes over this part of the narrative.

"We're going to begin today by showing you tapes of the testimony of past nominees. We also have transcripts of the questions that have been asked of the last four nominees, and some of the answers, but we will spare you most of them. You will take the transcripts home to study them. Look for patterns. And we will talk about them when you're done."

Vic nods. Her father catches her eye, turns to Brooks and Rena, and nods as well.

"And then we will start your murder boards," Brooks says.

"I'm sorry, our what?" Vic asks.

"Murder boards."

"Sounds dangerous," Vic says with a questioning smile.

"They're the practice sessions for your Judiciary Committee testimony. Think moot court. Lawyers who've worked in the Senate or the White House will ask you questions they think the senators will ask. In the last one or two sessions, the lawyers helping with this will actually play the role of the specific Judiciary Committee members, asking the questions we think that particular senator will pose."

"Why are they called murder boards?" Vic asks.

"Because they're supposed to be murder," Brooks says. "The military coined the term, preparing brass for hearings. It's a trumped-up name."

Rena notices Madison shift in his chair. The prospect of rehearsing his ideas probably irritates him. And the notion that answering senators' questions could be murderous or even difficult probably strikes him as absurd.

"Understand, Rollie, this process is not about the senators getting to know you or what you really think. You get that, right?"

"I do, Peter."

No, he doesn't, Rena thinks.

"Let me put it this way. Assume you start with a hundred votes to confirm. All you can do by answering questions is lose votes. . . . You will get the Republicans you need, if you don't give them a reason to vote no. That is what we are trying to do for the next month. Not give people a reason to vote no. That's all."

In other words, don't tell people what you think. Be superficial. That's how you'll get ahead. Be everything you don't believe in.

"There are no second chances to be on the high court," Brooks says. "There is no learning curve. You only get one hearing."

If they push this too hard now, Madison will push back. Rena wants to make this seem more mundane, more mechanical. But he also needs to be clear. "These sessions will be held at the Justice Department, and some at the Old EOB," he says, referring to the Gothic building next to the White House.

"Okay, let's review where you are. With a 53–47 Republican majority, you need four opposition party votes. If we lose any Democrats, we'll need more than that."

"We know the math," Madison says.

"To get there, you will need to win some people over personally in private, to persuade them you're someone they would like to have over for dinner regardless of your legal theories. Okay?"

Madison nods.

"So let's go over the committee," Brooks continues. "You'll have every Democrat. You need two Republicans minimum, and you want to try to get the majority of them."

Another nod.

"Your best chance to start with the Republicans is Wendy Upton of Arizona. She's a former military prosecutor. She's the sharpest lawyer on the panel in either party. Upton also sees value in compromise. But she's struggling to navigate a new harsher political world.

Still, if you can get her, you may get some other Republicans."

Vic is taking notes, but not her father.

"When we did our visits, only one senator seemed rude, Jack Fiddler of Wyoming. He's the most conservative member of the Senate, and one of the twelve who identify themselves as Common Sense members. You aren't likely to get him. But you need not to enrage him.

"Our biggest worry, though, is Aggie Tucker of Texas. He's cagey, and while he is disliked almost universally, he's also feared because he understands the mood of the country almost better than anyone today. He was the first incumbent to recognize the power of the Common Sense movement. He was also a Supreme Court clerk to Justice Goldstein, Hoffman's great antagonist on the Court. Senators don't like Tucker. He can be as mean as a rattlesnake, and selfish. He is a leader of a new breed that puts faction above the Senate, even above the party. But other senators recognize he is smart and fearless and they trust his instincts now because he is in tune with the populism that is sweeping the party. Tucker can change the dynamics. And he's unpredictable."

Tucker was gracious but noncommittal during Madison's visit and has remained that way since.

"Among the Democrats, you have some fence mending to do."

The biggest surprise, and potential problem, is William Stevens, the senior Senate liberal. The old bull had scorched Nash over the nomination in a private meeting at the White House. The president, Stevens said, would unwittingly pull the country to the right, not help the Court be less polarized, by nominating an iconoclastic moderate.

"I know what you're trying to do, but it won't work, Mr. President," Stevens had said. "The way to change the Court is by making sure progressive arguments are made passionately, not trying to find someone with a new way of framing them."

Publicly, Stevens has kept quiet. But he did the president a courtesy in that private warning. If there are problems with this nomination, he had signaled, he will bail.

"Okay, Rollie? Ready to move on?" Brooks asks.

Madison nods.

Rena and Brooks alternate their presentation—a way to keep a subject more alert.

"When the hearings start, here's what you can expect," Rena begins. "About a third of the questions are going to be easy, basically softballs. Only a few will

be serious questions, respectful and genuine. The rest
will be nasty. Some will be aggressive. Others will be
intellectual traps, asking your opinion of some seemingly benign statement by a legal scholar or a judge that
they consider radical and dangerous. Over the course
of several hours, this will amount to dozens of negative,
even accusatory questions."

"The questioning has become more negative over
the years," Brooks adds. "Just to give you an idea, in
1955, Justice Harlan was asked just one negative question. Today, a third of the questions are negative. Some
of them aren't questions at all. They're speeches."

Madison interrupts her, unable to control himself.
"Yes, Ms. Brooks, I have the read the literature, too."

Rena gets up from the table and walks over to the
small window overlooking Jefferson Place. A cold wave
rolls down the back of his neck. He's tired of the judge's
passive-aggressive behavior.

He isn't sure Madison and his friends have been
entirely honest about their Berkeley past. And Rena
doesn't want this to go up in smoke because of lack of
preparation on the part of him and his partner. They
aren't going to be done in by the man who hired him
and the man they were hired to help—not without a
fight. Enough.

"Randi, Vic, may the judge and I have the room?"

A look of surprise flashes in Brooks's eyes and then passes. She nods and stands, and Vic follows her outside.

Rena walks over and closes the door. He returns to the conference table in the center of the room and sits down on the tabletop in front of Madison. For many seconds, he says nothing.

Then, almost in a whisper: "We're not going to play this game anymore, Judge. Today is the last day. You will not treat the people trying to help you as if you are smarter than they are. You most especially will not treat the United States senators you meet that way. It's rude. And you're going to be in their house. They already know you're smart, Judge. You've been nominated for the Supreme Court. Frankly, people with your kind of intelligence don't impress them all that much. Most of the people who work for them are smarter than they are. U.S. senators are people who have spent their lives accomplishing more—acquiring more money, more power, more everything—than people smarter than they are. What they really want to know is if they like you."

"Mr. Rena, I don't believe it is necessary to—"

Before Madison finishes his sentence, Rena slams a fist down on the table. Madison stops.

Rena speaks the next words so softly that Madison has to strain to hear them.

"Judge, you only need to understand one thing today. And when I am done telling you this and you understand it, you can watch some video."

Rena takes a deep breath and speaks with an unconcealed fury, slowly, the way you would talk to a teenager in trouble.

"The power and history of this city deserve your respect. Regardless of what you think of its current inhabitants. You may be the smartest person in the room. You may even be the smartest person you ever met. But you are not the smartest person who ever came to Washington."

Madison attempts to return Rena's stare, but the judge is not as angry as the man standing over him. Rena leans closer. "As far as Washington is concerned, Judge, you are a rookie. Without a hit or even an at bat. And like any rookie, you will be hazed."

"Are you through?" Madison asks.

"Nope. It's a long way to confirmation. When you're done here tonight, I recommend driving around Washington, not just the monuments, but also the lousy parts: You can see some of the worst poverty and deprivation in the world in Anacostia, next to the world's most polluted river. Then the memorials; the Lincoln,

Jefferson, and Roosevelt are the best. Give yourself a couple of hours. They're especially beautiful at night."

Rena slides off the table and opens the door. "Because they don't make those memorials for Supreme Court justices, sir. They're not important enough."

"Show the man some goddamn TV," Rena says as he passes Brooks in the hallway.

"What was that about?" Brooks asks, appearing at his door a few minutes later. She looks more amused than angry.

Rena, who is sitting on his sofa, puts his feet on the coffee table and sighs. "People always accommodate the most difficult person in the room. But there can only be one. And for the next month, it cannot, under any circumstances, be Roland Madison. So I have decided to occupy the space."

"Okay then," she says, and without a word heads back to Madison.

He opens the laptop on his desk. He checks the schedule his assistant O'Brien has set for him for the day. Not too bad. O'Brien has learned not to overbook him. He is looking through the software that tells them where they are on different client projects when his cell phone rings.

"Peter, how are you?"

Senator Llewellyn Burke, his former boss.

"Senator, good morning."

"Been too long, too long."

Burke sounds tired. Rena can hear the eastern prep school influence sneak into his flat Michigan accent.

"You need to come to dinner. I will talk to Evangeline," he says. Evangeline Burke, if possible, has even more social skills than her husband.

"I'd like that very much."

Llewellyn "Lewis" Burke, who was connected by blood to two different Michigan auto dynasties, had made a name for himself on his own in venture capital while still in his twenties, multiplying his family's old millions into roughly a billion in new, mostly in technology. When he moved to politics—Burke's father had been a senator briefly—he had made it clear he had no higher ambition than to serve Michigan in the Senate, and he derived much of his power in the body operating behind the scenes, guiding actions in surprising ways and doing favors in unexpected places. He operated with enormous freedom in part because he had accomplished what seemed today a political magic trick: He was a northern Republican with a secure seat.

"How's it going with this Madison nomination?"

Burke isn't on the Judiciary Committee. Why is he calling?

"Not the easiest job I've had."

A soft chuckle and then: "Those visits up here went well, Peter. Congratulations." He meant the trip to the Senate.

"Thank you, Senator."

"But he needs to come visiting again. Some private chats. With senators in the opposition party, whom you think you might persuade. You understand?"

"Yes."

"Make sure he is as available as possible."

Rena considers the implications of Burke, a Republican who has no role on Judiciary, advising him about this.

"Thank you, sir."

"Good. That's fine. I want to see you at dinner soon."

"Thank you, Senator."

Rena hangs up and imagines invisible hands all around him.

Thirty-one

Monday, June 1, 6:00 A.M.
Bethesda, Maryland

Gotta love a white van.

Throw phone company magnets on the side and you could park the damn thing anywhere. With orange cones you don't even need a parking place.

One morning with Verizon magnets. Another from a gardening company. Magnetic signs. Best invention ever. Steal them and no one cares. Add a white van and you gotta a fleet of cars.

He has been watching Martell now for two weeks.

Learned one thing for sure. Guy's life is a bore. Marriage over, getting fat, up at 6:00 every morning. Walks his big black dog at 7:00. Drives to work by eight. Martell eats lunch at one of three places within two blocks of his office. Goes home at 7:30. Eleven-and-a-half-hour workdays.

He eats frozen dinners. Seen him carrying 'em from the car. Watches TV—thing is always on—then walks the dog, goes to bed.

On Friday afternoons he leaves early and picks up his kids. Has them until Sunday around midday.

Alan Kevin Martell, esquire, age forty-four.

On the Internet they have his life story. In one paragraph.

"Alan Martell is an attorney at the Office of Professional Responsibility at the Department of Justice in Washington, D.C. Prior to moving to Washington, Alan was an Assistant U.S. Attorney for the California Northern District, in San Francisco, where he specialized in criminal trial work, and before that he had worked as an Assistant District Attorney for the City and County of San Francisco. At OPR, Alan makes use of his years as a federal prosecutor to investigate allegations of ethical and professional misconduct by federal agents and the nearly 10,000 attorneys employed by the Department of Justice. He has two children."

He doesn't have to guess much where Martell will be. But there also aren't many choices then about where to do him. Work. Home. Weekends with the kids.

That leaves picking up the paper in front of his house in the morning—too open. Or with the dog. On Sunday afternoons sometimes the guy walks the dog on a path along the Potomac. Too crowded.

Some mornings he drives the black Lab to a place nearer his house. Parks, then walks, in a field near some woods. It's part of the big narrow stretch of land that curls through the city called Rock Creek Park. Strikes him as not really much of a park. More of a road with a creek and bike path and woods. But they call it a park.

That is his best shot. Most people with dogs stay in the field. But not Martell. His Labrador likes to run into the woods, and Martell lets him. All he has to do is get close once. Martell's dog makes that easy. You can always walk up to someone with a dog.

That's the play.

It took an hour of driving one day to find a spot where he could park and enter the woods unseen, a little turnout on a secluded street. In the last week he has walked the woods mornings and evenings.

This whole thing looks simple. Simplest one yet.

It's getting on 6:30, almost light, the time Martell takes the dog out.

If it doesn't happen today, he can wait. Only he can't sit out here every morning. Has to switch it up. Some days he should go to the woods and wait. Tomorrow do that.

Movement. Front door. The big black Labrador, wagging, jumping, pulling the leash, yipping. Martell, at the other end of the leash, a tired smile, holding car keys in his left hand. Getting ready for a morning walk in the woods.

He senses that sweet syrupy feeling he has felt twice before.

He waits for Martell to get in his Honda, then pulls the van out and drives.

About eight minutes later he is parking. From the back of the van he pulls out the stick. Heavy. Thick. Same idea as he had in California, the one he never got to. He spent time finding it in these woods.

He closes the door quietly and heads into the woods, slowly making his way across the hill. Then waits.

Nothing.

Looks at his watch. Ten minutes. Seems like an hour.

Maybe Martell didn't let the dog off the leash into the woods. Or maybe they went somewhere else.

A noise. Animal? Then nothing.

Maybe he should go.

"Ryan?"

The dog's name.

"Ryan!"

Martell is coming across the hill.

"Ryan?"

The freaking dog has disappeared.

He starts to move. Don't want to be just standing there waiting.

"Ryan?"

He begins to make his way up the hill, into Martell's path. The lawyer is scanning the woods, looking for the dog. Martell isn't even looking his way yet. Then the lawyer hears his footsteps and turns.

"Morning. Is Ryan your dog?"

Martell looks at him. "Sorry?"

"Ryan. Is he a dog, a Lab?"

"Yeah," Martell says.

"I think I saw him. Over there. By that stump."

Martell's eyes move in the direction of his pointing finger.

"Thanks," says Martell, and starts to head that way.

He waits until Martell's back is to him. He lifts the stick above his shoulder.

Then he hears the dog. Coming from behind him.

Martell turns to the sound, facing him.

He brings the stick down. Martell lifts his arms. The crack reports something breaking, probably an arm.

"Ohhhh," Martell gasps.

With his good arm, Martell grabs the stick.

Asshole is stronger than he looks.

He pulls it away from Martell, but the leaves on the ground are still wet with dew, and he slips, then staggers down the hill a little. Then the fucking guy surprises him. Martell doesn't try to run. He closes in instead and lunges for the stick.

"Ahhhhh." Martell groans with pain from whatever's broken, but he gets a grip with his good hand, and the momentum and the hill stagger both of them a little farther down the slope.

The end of this won't be in doubt. He is stronger and bigger than the lawyer, and he has both his arms.

But then he hears a growl. A gut sound. Vicious. Pure. And close.

He feels the bite before he sees it. The dog's teeth entering the fatty part of his forearm, hot, sticky, and more a tearing than a bite. The teeth feel like razors, and the real force is coming from the jaws.

Chhhhrriiiiiiist! The pain is searing.

He yanks his arm, but the move just lifts the big Lab without it letting go. He swings his arm back and forth. The move tears his skin.

But it releases the dog.

The Lab is rearing, growling. Sounds like a freaking werewolf.

His arm is on fire.

Where is Martell?

He swings the stick like a baseball bat in both directions to keep the dog back.

A mixture of slobber and blood hangs from the dog's mouth. He can see a piece of his flesh hanging from one of the teeth.

The Lab wants to lunge.

He is gonna have to deal with the goddamn dog before he can do the man.

"Who are you?" Martell hisses. The lawyer is behind him.

"Fuck you."

"Do I know you?"

God damn it. His arm is hurt. It's bleeding everywhere. The dog is growling. Now Martell is talking. Damn it.

"Why are you doing this?"

Keep your eye on the dog.

"What's your name?"

Don't listen. Eye on the damn dog. Wait for the lunge.

"Attack him, Ryan. Get him, boy."

The dog is barking.

The man is yelling.

He swings the stick to keep the dog back.

The lawyer circles so it is hard to keep the dog and the man both in view. Swing at the man and make the dog lunge, he thinks. He swings again and sees a blur, the dog jumping. He hears a strange howl. The dog has got him again; it has set its jaws on his left forearm.

With his free arm, he swings the stick down on the dog's head, but he makes contact with his left arm, too. The pain is incredible, but the dog, stunned, loosens its grip.

Another blow and the dog drops to the ground.

Pain shoots up his left arm like he injected it. He can feel it up in his gums.

But the dog is down. He swings down on the dog's head, two hands on the stick. Hard. He doesn't want to kill the dog, just knock it out. One more blow should do it. In the corner of his blurry eye he sees Martell move sideways. Is he going to lunge?

One more strike to the dog, hard but not lethal.

Then he realizes the mistake. Martell is running.

Straight up the hill, his broken left arm held in his right. With the slope, unable to swing his arms, Martell is stumbling, unstable.

He closes on him fast.

"Help! Help me. Police!"

Shut up, asshole.

One strike is enough. The back right of Martell's head gives way. The lawyer takes another step and a half, diagonal, then a kind of skip. Then falls facedown.

He raises the stick in both hands above his head and plunges it into Martell's back just off the spine, aiming for the heart. It slides into Martell's body easier than he would have guessed. It's harder pulling it out.

He hears a cursing sound in his ears, like he can hear the pain in his arm. It's the sound of his own voice.

He stands a moment trying to catch his breath and slow his heartbeat.

He looks down at Martell's body. "Yeah, you should know me," he gasps.

He is bleeding.

Leaving trace all over the scene. Maybe the dew will wash it away. Or there is so much dog blood, and Martell's, all mixed up. Nothing he can do. Except go. He turns and heads to the van at a fast walk, not a run. One shout for police is probably not enough to bring anyone. No need to hurry.

That freakin' dog. The thought stops him. That dog has his flesh in its mouth.

He should go back and take the dog. That flesh could get him caught.

Does he have time?

Damn it. DAMN IT.

He can't afford not to.

Without thinking, he pulls a hunting knife he bought in Wyoming out of his pocket. He wasn't even sure why he bought it. He walks back to the dog.

What is he going to do?

He looks down at the dog; its eyes are closed but it's breathing.

He drops the stick. It's got the blood of Martell and the dog on it. But his blood is at the scene, too.

Damn it.

He turns and walks away.

The van seems like miles.

Did anyone hear them? See them?

He almost loses his footing on the wet leaves.

Easy. Breathe.

He fumbles for keys. No time to open the back.

Get in. Get out of here.

He opens the door. Slides in. Turns on the engine.

God damn it to hell.

The screaming in his head doesn't stop for a long time.

Thirty-two

Tuesday, June 2, 9:48 A.M.
Washington, D.C.

On a table in his office Peter Rena has dossiers on all the power centers of Washington.

Every interest group and elected official of consequence is represented by a folder, the contents compiled by Wiley and Lupsa, each one describing the group and its leader. Rena is gradually digesting them, trying to understand each major interest group as he might study suspects in an investigation.

There is a folder for every member of the Senate Judiciary Committee, and dozens of so-called public interest groups, People for the American Way on the left, and Citizens for Tax Relief on the right. One for Fair

Chance for America, another for Citizens for Freedom. The Common Sense movement groups, the Family Research Council, the New America Foundation. And more.

"Finally trying to find out who matters in this town?" Brooks teased when he began a few days ago.

"I only care if they matter for Roland Madison's nomination," Rena answered.

"They do."

"I should have boned up on them when we started this in April. Not in June."

"We're doing fine."

"Are we?"

She is sitting in his office again, talking about a meeting this afternoon with Senator William Stevens's staff.

Walt Smolonsky, six feet six inches and 230 pounds of him, appears in Rena's doorway with Hallie Jobe, who at 125 pounds and five nine makes a striking contrast. Smolonsky, who has spent his life trying to avoid intimidating people with his bulk, rarely exercises. Jobe, a woman who feels she constantly has to prove her physical and intellectual abilities, is a gym rat.

Jobe has a grim look on her face and is holding a copy of the *Washington Tribune*.

"You see this?" Jobe says. It isn't clear what "this" means until she points to the paper and hands it to Brooks. It is folded to a small story on page B-4:

Lawyer found dead in Rock Creek.
Police say Justice employee murdered.

There are nearly four murders a week in D.C., but most of them are drug-related crimes that don't make much news. A white lawyer in Northwest D.C.—what people called Upper Caucasia—that makes news.

Brooks and Rena scan the story.

"What are we looking at?" Brooks asks.

"Check the last paragraph," Smolonsky says.

The murdered lawyer was an assistant district attorney years ago in San Francisco, it says.

"I wonder if Madison knew him," Jobe says.

Rena nods.

"This thing is weird," adds Smolonsky. "Bludgeoned and then impaled with a branch. And a dog was attacked, too. The dog was knocked out but survived."

"The dead man's dog?" Rena says with professional curiosity.

"Doesn't say," Smolonsky answers.

"Killer knew the victim?" Rena wonders aloud.

"Or gets harassed by his dog and they get in a fight and the guy loses control," says Jobe.

"You three getting your old cop jones on? How do you know it was a guy?" says Brooks.

Rena looks at her. "The killer was definitely male."

"The Madisons are here," O'Brien announces from the doorway.

They are spending the day prepping for Madison's moot court, plus the late afternoon meeting with Senator Stevens's staff. All of this is Brooks's department. Rena remains in his office studying his dossiers.

The judge starts wonderfully, Brooks thinks, deft and succinct, but he soon loses patience with the dull answers they want him to give.

"Eye on the prize, Dad," Vic chides. "Remember your goal: Do no harm."

"I would vote against me for insipidity."

"I recall something you once said about how to teach new one-L's," Vic says, referring to first-year law students. "You said you imagine talking to highly intelligent fourteen-year-olds—people capable of understanding anything but who know almost nothing."

"You don't have a very high opinion of the Senate Judiciary Committee."

"You miss my meaning, Your Honor," Vic says. "You were trying to get the right outcome with these kids. You were trying to get them to relax, and you weren't trying to impress them."

"Your point, Vic?"

"Think outcome. These senators expect you to say nothing. And the ones who might oppose you are waiting for you to slip up with an authentic answer. Don't accommodate them."

Brooks doesn't know what they would do without Vic. She's learned the process faster than her father and knows how to regulate him better than they do.

"I need a break," Madison says.

The judge is given to short walks to relax. A walker, runner, surfer, sailor, he uses physical activity to free his mind.

When he leaves, Brooks gets and up walks over to a small refrigerator in the corner, pulls out two water bottles, and lifts one to Vic in invitation.

The two women have spent a good deal of time together over the last few weeks. Vic takes the water and says, "Can I ask you something, Randi?"

Something in her tone makes Brooks raise her eyebrows.

"About Peter . . ."

She has been wondering when Vic would get around to this. Whatever is going on between the nominee's daughter and her partner has been obvious since the day they met. He has squired her around town, usually with Madison in tow. They steal looks at each other like teenagers at school. Vic tends to wander into Rena's office during breaks. Brooks has even wondered, once or twice, whether to raise the subject with Rena. But she and her partner generally avoid crossing the line into their personal lives. Work is their terra firma.

"Yes," Vic says with a girlish smile followed by earnest look.

"Go ahead."

"Why did he stop being a soldier?"

"That is a story better coming from Peter," Brooks says uncomfortably. "But let's just say he refused to bury something, a scandal, that the army would have preferred buried. He did the right thing. And it cost him his career."

"And then he went to the Senate? Where you met as investigators working for senators in different parties?"

Vic knows some of this already. She's fishing for Brooks to tell her more.

"Yes. Peter was rescued, you might say, by a member of the Senate Armed Services Committee who admired what he'd done, Senator Burke of Michigan, one of the few Republicans I like. That's where we met."

"Can I ask you something else?"

"You can ask me anything, Vic."

"Why does Peter get . . ." Vic searches for the word ". . . so remote when he feels he doesn't understand something?"

Brooks feels a little guilty she didn't answer Vic's first question. She also wants Vic to trust her and Rena. She likes Vic enormously. And Vic's trust is key to winning her father's.

"Vic, here, look," Brooks tries to begin.

"What, Randi?"

"Okay, I'm going to tell you something about myself that almost no one here knows, no one except Peter."

"Okay."

"When I was in college, my roommate was murdered."

Vic just listens.

"I found the body. The cops assigned to the case struck me as incredibly stupid. And I was a total mess. I took a leave from school. I couldn't focus. You know what saved me?"

Vic shakes her head.

"I set out on my own to solve it. I found one sympathetic detective who let me dig into files. I found a half-dozen similar cases the police had missed. There was even a suspect they had overlooked, someone who showed up in early interviews in multiple cases. I delivered the information to the police on a plate. They convicted the son of a bitch."

"That's incredible."

"But I was never quite the same. I suspect that's why I went to law school. And why I do this. Because in the end you have only yourself to trust. You can take nothing for granted. And in some sense, trust no one's word."

She can see the slow recognition register on Vic's face.

"Peter has some story like this, some secret?"

She has to stop, now. Any more would be a transgression of Rena's privacy he would not forgive.

"Let's just say we are wired in similar ways."

Vic searches Brooks's face trying to decide how far to probe.

"Does Peter think my father is keeping secrets?"

"I think he isn't sure. But he worries that your dad's disdain for what is an admittedly bad process is getting in the way."

Vic makes herself larger in her chair. She is about to make a point she thinks is important.

"Randi, I think you and my dad work well together. But I think Peter is misplaying this. He doesn't get my father."

"Peter is pretty intuitive."

"Dad doesn't like to be handled. Peter should try to put him at ease and earn his trust."

"Is this what your father thinks?"

Vic smiles. "My father probably hasn't thought about it. He takes people as they come. He is, in his way, mostly obtuse when it comes to his own feelings about people. He loves being a judge, a teacher, and he loves being a father. And to him it's that simple. He amuses himself by playing games in conversation mostly because his mind doesn't focus on people, not in the same way most of us do. He lives in the world of facts, of words. And he doesn't like artificiality."

"I think he's lucky to have you around."

Almost on cue Madison returns from his decompressing walk. He sits down in the chair where he was before and says, "Okay, Ms. Brooks, I am ready to accept my training as a witness who does not want to help the prosecution."

"That's it, Pop," Vic says.

They're reviewing questions Judiciary members asked in past confirmation hearings, talking through what questions each member might ask now, trying to make a puzzle of the process to engage Madison. The judge is amazing when he wants to be.

An hour and a half later, Brooks sticks her head into Rena's office. "We're breaking up. You want to pop in?"

Rena thinks Vic looks tired.

"I've got some potentially painful news," he says. He tells them about the murder of the former San Francisco assistant DA, Alan Martell.

"Did you know him? He was there when you were on Superior Court."

Madison rubs his chin with his right hand. "I think I did," the judge says.

"He appeared before you?"

"I think so."

Rena hands Madison the newspaper. There is a picture, from Martell's Justice Department employee tag, a tiny head shot, a balding man who appears to be in his mid-forties.

"He was beaten to death."

"My God," Vic says.

"The killer also attacked what may be Martell's dog."

Roland rubs his fingers over his cheekbone. "Horrible."

"Vic, did you know him?" Rena asks.

"No."

"We've got to get ready for Stevens," Brooks says.

"Before you go, do you have a minute?" Rena asks his partner.

"Sure."

Back in Rena's office, he calls Smolonsky. "I need your brain in here."

Brooks glances at a copy of the *Weekly Review,* the conservative opinion magazine, sitting on the coffee table: "What a Court Pick Tells About the Still-Enigmatic President," the headline reads.

"What's up?" Smolo says when he arrives.

"You still got friends on D.C. Metro homicide?" Rena asks.

"A couple."

"I want to keep tabs on what the police know about that murder in the park, if you can do it discreetly."

"Sure," Smolo says. "Why?"

"Abundance of caution. If anybody else makes the same connection we did about Martell, they are going to ask the White House, and the White House is going to ask us, and we need to know what we want to say."

Smolo's face settles into a deceptively dull expression. "Okay."

"And we should ask Wiley to check Martell's name against Madison's on cases," Rena says.

"What was it?" Brooks asks Rena. "A twitch of Madison's left eyebrow when he said he barely knew the man?"

Rena laughs.

"No. But if it occurs to us that they might know each other, it will occur to somebody else. So we better know if they ever had any cases together or if there is a photo of them at some fund-raiser."

"Hell, it's San Francisco. They could be kissing," Smolonsky says.

"When you see what your friends in homicide have, be subtle. Don't make it seem like we're that interested."

"Peter, we can't ask and not make them curious."

"I'm sure you'll figure something out. What's the Polish word for charm?"

"*Urok.*"

"Oh . . . well, use your *urok.*"

Thirty-three

12:34 P.M.
Neenah, Virginia

His arm feels like someone poured acid on it. He can't look at it, and at the same time he can't get it out of his mind. It looks like meat being dressed after hunting.

This has to be the turn. He slows, and makes the left onto the dirt road. He'd gotten the name of these folks from George, who once lived in Virginia. George said they could help. It has taken hours to get here. The place is out by the Chesapeake Bay, near someplace called Neenah, out in the middle of nowhere. No, not the middle. Way past that.

He turns at a battered rural mailbox on a post and heads down a long dirt drive until he comes to a cluster of buildings. This is not the kind of farm you see in a movie. There are three houses in a clearing, none of them matching, all of which look like they belong in a poor neighborhood in a city, and nearby something that looks more like a garage than a barn.

He parks and walks up slowly to the front door of the first house. He rings the bell three times. Then waits. They said he might have to when he called ahead. "Don't run off," the man had said on the phone. "May take us a minute."

Finally a man in overalls rounds the back of the house. He's young, probably thirty-five, the face dark ebony, weather beaten and tired looking.

"You Scott?" The name he had given them.

"Yes, sir," he says with a smile.

"You called?"

"Yeah, that was me."

The man in the overalls is wiping his hands on a red handkerchief, which he stuffs in his back pocket when he is done. He is squinting in the summer sun. He doesn't hold out his hand to shake.

"Who's your friend again?" Suspicious.

"George Rockford. He used to live out here. And do some sport dogs with you."

The guy's overalls aren't like work clothes from the city. They are full of dust and dried manure. Farm work. The man inside the overalls blinks several times, as if it helps him think.

"Wait here."

He goes back around behind the house and leaves him there by the front door. A few more minutes pass. Finally, from back of the house, a woman who couldn't be more than twenty-two appears and heads toward him. She's wearing shorts and a T-shirt, and has the same weathered face as the man.

She looks him over, tilting her head in a funny way. She steals a quick glance at his arm, which he is holding at an angle so it hurts less.

"Follow me," she says.

He does as he's told. They walk past the first house and toward the smaller one behind it. They enter it into a living room being used as an office. There are two desks and papers piled everywhere.

"So you got tangled, huh?" the girl says. She says it more like an observation than a question.

"Yes, ma'am."

"Okay, then."

She leads him down a hallway into what looks like a bedroom. There's an examination table there made of plywood and two-by-fours, with a pad on it.

"Get on up here," she says. "Lemme see it."

A screen door slams, then footsteps and the man who greeted him enters the room.

"We fine here now, you don't need to be hoverin'," the woman says.

"Don't worry about it," he says. The man stares with fierce eyes. "You say your name was Scott?"

He nods.

"Come on now, lemme see it," the woman says.

He takes off his shirt and shows her the arm.

"My, you tangled all right."

There are three wounds in his forearm. The worst is a series of tears to the flesh. One of the bites is fairly superficial.

"You been like this all night?"

"Yes, ma'am."

"Why didn't you go to the hospital?"

"They'd get nosy. Ask questions. I'd lose my dog. Get my friends in trouble."

"You not from here," the man by the door says.

"No, sir. Arizona. Visiting my sister. Brought my dog with me. Thought I'd get some action in. But we had some trouble separating some dogs. Yesterday, up in Pennsylvania. So I called George Rockford, who I knew had lived 'round here."

The man eyes him.

"George is from out farther west," the man says suspiciously.

"We know each other from fightin' dogs."

"T, the man needs help. He obviously ain't fakin' being hurt."

So the man's nickname is "T," he thinks. He realizes they have not shared their names and he gave them a false one.

"You'll need a rabies shot," the man says.

"I figured."

"And antibiotics, and painkillers, and you need stitches," the girl says. "And then you need to rest. You got to heal this. But if we can stop it from becoming infected, I think you'll be okay. You don't need skin grafts or nothing. But this was a big dog. Not a trained dog. Not a killer. It didn't know what it was doing. That's what saved you."

"You got money?" the man asks. The voice is cold.

"I can pay."

"T, I swear. If you're gonna stay here, you gonna keep your mouth shut."

"You'd fill the house with birds with broken wings if I didn't stop you," says the man.

"And what would be wrong with that?"

She turns her attention back to the wound. "This wasn't your dog, was it?"

"No, of course not."

"Too bad. If you knew it had its shots . . ." she says without finishing the sentence.

She pulls a long, syringelike thing out of a plastic sandwich bag and dips it into a jug labeled "saline."

"I'll give you the first shot and what you'll need for the rest. But you will need to take them on the schedule I tell you."

He nods. He'd heard rabies shots were a series.

"We're going to wet this all up. Irrigate the wound. Then we're going to make sure it's all cleaned out. We're going to be here awhile. Then start to stitch."

"Okay."

"You take anything? For the pain?"

"A lot of ibuprofen."

"How many?"

"Maybe six."

"Well, you shouldn't take so many. Just four. No more. But if you okay with that, then that's good. 'Cause the prescription stuff will make you loopy. Lie down now."

The girl looks back at the man behind her.

"Hell, this man too messed up to do anything to me, T. You might as well go back outside."

"I'm fine here," he says.

"Suit yourself."

He looks at the girl. She has her eyes on the wound. She hasn't made eye contact with him. Then he looks over her shoulder.

T hasn't taken his eyes off him.

Thirty-four

Monday, June 15, 10:46 P.M.
Alexandria, Virginia

Josh Albin isn't sure he has read the first line correctly.

Maybe he only hoped it.

"Urgent News: SCOTUS."

SCOTUS is short for Supreme Court of the United States.

For a moment, his mind passes over the miracle that such an email could come to him at all. The email is from an alias set up for just one group. The Watchers.

He dreamed of the Network all those years ago, contacted people he thought might help, just as the legend suggests, but not much has come of it. The Watchers at first were an aspiration, if not quite a lie. In time, some who had heard the stories were inspired and came to him, first one, then a few. They come and go, and usually, if he is honest about it, they don't offer much he doesn't already know. It's the idea of the Watchers that's important—that has power. The legend became the truth. Perception became reality. *Behold the power of ideas.*

This might be different. The second line of the email reads: "I have information that will end the nomination of Edmund Roland Madison."

He feels a surge of adrenaline. If this were real, it would be the most powerful thing to ever have come from the Watchers. How should he handle it?

The next day, just after 1 P.M., he has an answer.

"What's going on in the flesh-eating zombie world, Josh?"

Gary Gold calls it doing his "rounds." Once a week or so, he spends a few hours making phone call after phone call, checking in with friends, sources, people who have helped him, even victims of past stories. He taunts, jokes, cajoles, threatens, and generally reminds folks he is out there. And then, brazenly, Gold brags about how much people leak to him. "It is amazing how often sources tell you things just because you called."

Gold calls almost every week.

"Why do you try to provoke me, Gary?"

"Because you, Josh, understand the secret of politics, which is also the secret of journalism."

"What is that?"

"That grievance and fear are more powerful than hope. Hope is for church on Sunday. Politics is for fear. And you are a savant of fear."

Gold has elevated obnoxious to an art form.

"Gary, I thought you told me you were digging into Roland Madison's background. I haven't seen much."

Albin could goad people, too. But he needs to play this right.

"Oh, hell, you gotta do better than that. The guy is on a slipstream to coronation. He keeps doing kissy-face on the Hill. He's tall, lean, looks like a wholesome Peter O'Toole, he's courtly. Charmed the moderates even more than the liberals. They should vote now, skip the murder boards and hearings and save the taxpayers five million bucks. You guys have been shooting total blanks."

"Not so fast, Gary. There is a good deal you and the rest of the country don't know yet about E. Roland Madison."

"Well, enlighten me, then, Josh, 'cause once we sense this thing is on autopilot to passage, a nomination without controversy isn't news."

"I doubt the U.S. Senate really wants to be known for putting a communist on the Court."

"What? I just had a drug flashback. What year is it? A communist?"

He can tell he has Gold's attention.

Gold won't want to appear too eager, however. Eager reporters scare people. But if reporters sound like they don't give a shit, sources will try harder to impress them. It's dumb how obvious the whole thing is.

"I'm not the type to BS you, Gary. You know that. I don't play games."

"Okay," Gold says. "I'm interested, Josh."

The people who would have the most stuff on Madison would be the vetting firm. Gold has one good contact at Rena, Brooks & Toppin. He and Walt Smolonsky met when he covered the Senate and Smolo was an investigator there.

"Yo, Big Foot."

The nickname was something Smolonsky had acquired years ago when he was a D.C. Metro cop. When Smolonsky had become a Senate investigator, the nickname migrated with him, thanks to an envious former colleague from Metro turned Capitol Police officer. Gold, who had been stuck with a nickname himself, remembered the story. Using the nickname would remind the guy how far back they go.

"What you working on, Gary?"

"Me. Shit, I never know. Same as always. I'm working on whatever I can get my hands on. Just trying to avoid being caught in the next newspaper buyout. You tell me what's new."

"I'm just an ex-cop who went corporate so I could afford to have kids."

"I'm too much of a kid to ever have kids."

Smolo laughs a little.

"You remember when we climbed to the top of the Senate building and put a bra on the flagpole? Shit, what was that, like 1993? We thought since you were an ex-cop, we were protected."

"You know I was assigned by the Senate majority leader to liaison with the Capitol Police on the investigation. I was investigating myself."

"Who better?"

"It was like that movie with Kevin Costner where he is investigating a Soviet mole in the Pentagon and he's the mole."

"It wasn't that fucking good. And you didn't fall in love with Sean Young."

"Sure I did. She just never met me."

They both laugh more than the joke deserves.

"So whaddya got for me?" Gold asks.

"Very amusing, Gary. Have I ever given you any-thing?"

"Never. You're the worst old friend I have. You give old friends a bad name."

"What do you want, Gary?"

Gold can sense Smolo getting uncomfortable.

"I'm just doing rounds, man. Looking for a story."

"And what are you finding?"

"Shit, they got me on Madison duty. Background stuff. You guys are doing him, right?"

Smolonsky doesn't respond.

"So, you hear about that guy who was murdered in Rock Creek? Martin or whatever?"

Gold is using the wrong name deliberately to see if he corrects him.

"What?"

"The guy who was found in Rock Creek Park mur-dered this week. He had worked in San Francisco as a DA before coming to D.C. You think maybe Madison knew him?"

"What are you talking about?"

"Nothin'," Gold says. "Forget it. But there's another thing." Gold's voice suddenly is serious. "I hear that Roland Madison has a past."

"Yeah, the older you get, the more you have."

"No, I mean a *past*, asshole. One he wants to keep secret. From his days in Berkeley."

Smolonsky hopes he hasn't reacted audibly.

"I mean treasonous shit, Smolo. Like revolutionary stuff."

"Jesus, Gary," Smolonsky says. "Even communists are capitalists now."

"You think that kind of thing will hurt politically? You think the Common Sense movement people would get upset by shit like that?"

Smolonsky says nothing. No backhanded confirmation. Gold tries forehanded.

"So, you heard about this?"

"Nice try, Mad Dog," Smolonsky says.

"What? You're not going to say?"

"We've known each other a long time, right, Gary?"

"No shit for all the good it's doing me."

"Then you should know I am not talking about Madison, period. One way or the other."

"You can't blame a girl for trying. I also heard you guys know about this and are covering it up."

Just for a fraction of a second, Gold senses Smolonsky hesitating.

"Who's peddling this crap?" Smolonsky says. That almost seems like a confirmation, Gold thinks.

"I can't give up a source, Smolo, you know that."

"I'm not asking you to publish your source's name. I'm asking you to trade it."

"Oh, we're trading now?"

"You give me a hint, and I'll guess."

"What, are we six years old?"

"C'mon, Gary."

"Okay, I'll make you a deal," Gold says. "I'll give you a hint and you tell me if you've heard about this Berkeley stuff."

"Why would I do that?"

"Because I've got something you want—a source—and you've got something I want—a confirmation."

Smolo suddenly worries he may have gone too far.

"I'll go first," Gold continues. "My source is a guy who is at the center of the wheel, you might say."

"Give me a freaking name, Mad Dog."

"I didn't say I would tell you. I told you I would give you a hint."

"You are six years old."

"Walt."

"Yes?"

"So, you heard of this? Remember. The deal we just made?"

"No, Gary. I haven't."

When he hangs up, Smolonsky realizes his back is clammy with sweat.

Thirty-five

Lawyers don't actually call them murder boards.
They call them mock hearings. No one wants
to admit that talking to a Senate or House hearing is
actually murder.

This is the fourth mock they've held for Madison.
They have one more planned but might add another.
Madison needs to be better.

His Senate hearings open in five days.

"I'm sorry, Judge, time's up," Brooks says.

"I'm just getting to the meat of my answer."

"Yes, but that's five minutes."

"I'll be more succinct in the hearing."

"You need to be more succinct in practice. Get the meat in the first thirty seconds. Try again now."

To play the senators, Brooks has recruited mostly former Senate Judiciary chief counsels, people who know the process—and the senators they are impersonating. Brooks and her team have written most of the questions. Besides Rena and Brooks, the other observers are three people from the White House and one from the Department of Justice. Nondisclosure agreements up the yin-yang.

It is the second week of trying to teach Rollie Madison not to be interesting. They recorded the first mock so they could critique Madison's performance with him. He hasn't gotten any better. So they are recording this one, too. Rena calls it remedial video training.

Penance, Your Honor, for not learning.

"He's so brilliant, I don't know why he resists this," Brooks said.

Rena did. Madison loves to learn. He just doesn't like being taught.

Rena feels his phone vibrate.

Smolonsky. He normally emails. It must be something that needs explaining. Rena slips out of the room.

"I just got a phone call I thought you should know about."

"Okay."

"From Gary Gold at the *Tribune*."

"Okay."

"He knows about Madison's dalliance in Berkeley with the radical Left."

The feeling is always worse when your gut has warned you something will happen: Rena *knew* this would leak—and probably sink Madison. And knew he hadn't fought hard enough with the White House about it.

"What'd you tell him?" Rena asks.

"I lied. Said I didn't know a thing about it."

"You lied?"

"I'm not like you, Peter. I don't get all twitchy about that."

"People remember being lied to, Walt. Especially reporters."

"If Gary Gold never talked to me again in my life I could survive."

Smolonsky is lying right now.

"What does he know?"

"I'm not sure. He was fishing."

"Where do you think he got his tip?"

"Actually, he gave me a hint."

"He did what? Why did he do that?"

"He was trying to trade information."

Smolo may have traded more than he realizes, Rena worries.

"He said he got it from someone 'in the center of the wheel.'"

"What does that mean?"

"I don't know, Peter. But that's what he said."

If someone called Gold with this, that source is probably also ready to email talking points to bloggers like Stan Krock, talk radio hosts like Dash Zimbalist and Tom Hewitt, and to the fulminating demagogues on cable news.

"Tell me exactly what he said."

Rena tends to become calmer in moments of crisis. Things slow down, and his reactions become clearer and his mind more alert. It was a gift that, even as a kid, helped him beat more physically gifted players in soccer. They'd refined that calm for him in Special Forces. It is why they pick you for Special Forces.

He needs it now.

"He said one other thing, Peter."

"What?"

"He asked me if Madison knew Alan Martell, the guy murdered in the park."

That means two crises. Madison cannot survive two. He probably can't survive one.

"What did you say?"

"I played dumb."

"Walt," Rena says, "you need to go to California. Find out more about whatever connection there might have been between Martell and Madison."

"You really worried about that?"

"We can't afford not to worry now."

Rena can see the newspaper headline, "Supreme Court mystery: Madison knew murdered man in Rock Creek Park." Two photos, the black-robed nominee and the wooded crime scene, the grisly details of the wounded dog in a caption.

And that isn't the real problem.

The center of the wheel.

"I've got to deal with something," he texts Brooks. He violates his rule about trying to walk and takes a cab.

"Done already?" his personal assistant, Eleanor O'Brien, says when he arrives.

"No, I forgot something," he tells her. In his office, he moves quickly among the files spread out on the table. Several hours later he is gone again.

Thirty-six

6:07 P.M.
Washington, D.C.

The shot rises, peaks, begins a soft descent, then slides through the net.

Josh Albin, in a pair of gray cutoff sweatpants and a Heritage Foundation T-shirt, walks over to the ball rolling toward the fence, picks it up, and carries it, without dribbling, back to the spot from where he shot. Then he repeats his routine and shoots again. And again.

Albin feels exhilarated. The emotion is not typical for him. You work, you build, you struggle. But the moments of genuine satisfaction at what you have accomplished, those are rare. And if they come at all, it is usually on the eve of victory, not at the moment itself. The recognition of an imminent triumph—the prospect of an opponent's face two moves ahead when he sees he has been bested—is always sweeter than its arrival. This is one of those moments.

It's all the better, Albin thinks, that he is here, shooting hoops, doing something physical, alone.

He looks nothing like a basketball player—he never has. He is short and stubby. His shot is awkward. His hands are too small to launch the ball properly, so he has to use his legs more to avoid overusing his arms. He had figured all this out studying the classic shooters. And he has grooved the motion over the years into something repeatable. That is one of the satisfactions of his life, too, that he has learned to become good at this.

In his youth in West Texas, sports were a torment, and basketball was the most painful humiliation of all—for it was the sport he loved most. As an adult, when he developed the method that he believed helped transform himself into a leader, he included basketball. In his formula, you identified your weaknesses and developed a plan to strengthen them. He kept a diary of practices, and took an inventory of his progress. Basketball fit well. He could quantify how many shots he made in one hundred attempts and could chart the progress. It was good exercise, and it took his mind off work. And though he was not entirely conscious of it, he also wanted to prove something to himself. His youth might have been different. If you can shoot, people will forgive everything else. If you can shoot, you can score. You can play. If he can shoot now, he has changed himself. And if you can change, the stronger your belief in yourself.

So every Tuesday and Thursday night Albin is here, at Baskerville Park in Georgetown, on a half-court that is too small to attract many players. Practicing by himself.

He finds the spot again, goes through his routine, and shoots. The arc is right and so is the line. The ball falls through the net with a satisfying swish.

He notices a figure across the street watching him.

"I heard you could shoot like Larry Bird, and that, like Bill Bradley, you had learned to do it by sheer will."

The figure has crossed the street and entered the park. Albin puts his hands on his hips and looks at him.

"I'm Peter Rena," the man says.

Rena had seen that phrase somewhere—"the center of the wheel"—and found it in one of Wiley's background files—a profile about Albin by Gary Gold written years ago. "The upstart activist said he saw himself as the 'center of the wheel' of the conservative revolution."

Baskerville Park had been even more of a long shot. In a couple of pieces Albin had talked about his theory of working on your weaknesses, including basketball. One mentioned this park, though Rena had no idea what night. He just came.

He is not quite sure what he expects to happen. This is an improvised interrogation, with an extremely intelligent opponent, and he has one shot at it.

Rena doesn't extend a hand. No pretend friendship. Albin would sense hypocrisy and take it as fear.

"I know who you are," Albin says. "You just happen to show up to play basketball in the same park I'm at?"

"I live in this neighborhood."

"I don't believe you. You're not here by accident."

"You're right. But there are no accidents in life. Just events you don't anticipate."

The line is an Albin aphorism.

Its author smiles condescendingly. Then he turns and shoots.

Swish.

"What are you doing here?" he demands.

"I want to know what you want, Josh."

"What I want from what?"

Rena picks up the ball and tosses it softly to Albin.

"From the Madison nomination."

Albin shifts his feet, loosening his hips, bounces the ball once, then raises his hands, bends slightly, and shoots. The shot again dives through the net.

"I heard you were blunt," Albin says. The ball is rolling to the fence. "So let me ask you a blunt question. Don't you feel a bit like a whore, a Republican working for a Democratic president? Do you take any client who comes along?"

Rena had assumed Albin would be aggressive. It is his style. Going further than others are comfortable going. It is Rena's, too.

"Actually, Josh, I'm kind of picky," Rena says. "I only work for people I trust. That tends to narrow the list."

Albin retrieves his own shot this time and says to Rena, "In my experience the best test of whether someone is trustworthy is what they believe in."

He tosses the ball to Rena. "I spent most of my life in the military." Remind the tin soldier of his tin. "But in my experience ideology says nothing about character." Rena offers the interrogator's stare. "Any moron can buy a team shirt."

Rena passes the ball back to Albin. Hard.

"Ah yes, you believe in compromising and calling it progress. The middling half loaf. Don't let the perfect be the enemy of the good."

Albin shoots but misses this time.

Rena ignores the ball and walks instead to Albin. He gets his face close to the other man and speaks softly. "I've found that anyone who thinks they know what perfect is, Josh, is a fool."

Albin looks at Rena with his famous silvery blue eyes, and Rena sees fury mixed with uncertainty. It is good they are outside, Rena thinks, doing something physical. That gives Rena the advantage.

"What do you believe in, Mr. Rena?"

Time to stop screwing around. Rena ignores the question.

"What do you really want, Josh?"

Albin's eyes narrow.

"I want a better nominee."

"I thought you were different," Rena says. "I thought you were serious. But you aren't. This is just another fund-raising exercise for you, just like everybody else."

Albin steps back and raises a finger at Rena, but it isn't a steady one.

"The difference between us, Mr. Rena, is that you believe people should accept a bad result and be grateful it isn't worse. You know who also believed that? The good Germans who went along with the Nazis."

"Democrats aren't Nazis, Josh. They're just people you disagree with."

Albin turns to leave. Rena has messed this up.

"The president would listen to you," Rena tries again. "If you were willing to offer counsel."

Albin stops.

"If you were serious about making a difference."

Then Albin turns back to face Rena.

A man who likes the last word.

"Have you looked around at our country lately, Mr. Rena? Have you been to Michigan? To Ohio? These places are dying. It's crushing the people who live there. Six million manufacturing jobs lost in a decade. We don't make anything anymore. We're not an economy. We're a market. And you know why? Because the two parties compromised around economic policies like NAFTA, ideas that ignored borders and helped corporations. That's your half a loaf. Good intentions are evil if they make people's lives worse."

Contrary to the caricature his critics make of him, the man is a good deal more than the sum of his resentments, Rena thinks.

"And we don't have the will to face it, Mr. Rena.

Our enemies in the Middle East can see it more clearly than we can."

Rena realizes he likes Albin. This would be easier if he didn't.

"We are fighting for our lives. This is a war. It's a war against the delusion that greatness is free or inevitable. That is why principles matter."

Unfortunately, Rena needs to make this more personal. He steps closer and whispers.

"Don't talk about war, Josh. Politics isn't war, and I don't like civilians who confuse the two. War is about killing people. Looking through the sight of a rifle, pulling a trigger, and watching a man's brains fly out the back. No one ever died in a goddamn committee hearing. You make people laugh at you."

Their faces are inches away from each other. Is that enough, Rena wonders?

Albin steps closer, not back. "I will let you in on something," Albin says, his voice tense. "Your man Madison has a history, and I am prepared to judge it. Most Americans would be shocked at the prospect that James Nash would presume to have a man who attacked the military and preached revolution and terrorism on the Supreme Court."

Albin's face is scarlet.

"And you knew about it. You were hoping you could

sweep it under the rug. Well, when it comes out, this will be over, and you will be hurt. And not for the first time."

Rena had come here with no particular plan—other than to get under Albin's skin. He had only been guessing that Albin had been's Gold source. He has gotten lucky.

Albin's great vulnerability is being viewed as a fake. So he had run at it.

"It's too bad, Josh," Rena says.

"What is?"

"If you were serious, I think you could have a real influence on the president."

"Good night, Mr. Rena."

It takes Albin an uncomfortable minute to collect his gym bag and head off.

Rena punches in a speed dial number on his phone.

"Randi."

"Where are you? I've been looking for you."

"Someone has leaked Madison's campus radicalism to Josh Albin."

"Jesus, Peter."

"And the leak came from inside our office."

Thirty-seven

6:47 P.M.
Washington, D.C.

It will be a small needle to thread.

They have to catch Madison's opponents by complete surprise, which means being swift. And they have to knock them on their heels. Which means being thorough.

To do that, it has to be clear Madison's antiwar activities in 1970 were the actions of a bright but innocent seventeen-year-old student—not something radical or out of the mainstream.

And it has to be clear the attempts by his opponents to depict them as something else are a smear that distorts the truth.

Madison's nomination represents something new, an attempt to move beyond this kind of cartoon politics. And Madison's team is coming forward now with this information about the judge's antiwar activities to pre-empt that kind of smear. Madison long ago promised his friends to honor their desire for privacy. Given the threat to try to destroy him now, they have released him from that promise.

"Madison has to be quoted," says Brooks.

He also, they agree, should neither sound defensive nor try to trivialize what he did. He cannot repudiate being a war protestor. He has to embrace how passionate he felt about the war, and acknowledge how, with time, he sees this expression of his passion as well-meaning but naïve. A slim needle.

And he has to say something else, Rena adds into the phone, "Or I am not comfortable with this."

He has to say that "in hindsight protests that made soldiers feel ashamed for fighting were wrong." He *does* repudiate that facet of the Vietnam antiwar protests. It was a lesson hard learned for the country, and for him.

"He has to say it. And he has to mean it," says Rena.

"Agreed," Brooks answers.

"I have to hear him say it."

"Agreed, Peter."

And they have to tell everything. Especially why he had kept it a secret till now. "Nothing new can leak from anywhere else after this," Rena says.

Then let the country decide. It is their only play.

Except one thing: the rumors about the woman who spent the night on her way to Canada. Whoever she was, it was unproven, but also toxic.

"Peter, we need to coordinate this with the White House. You hear me? This is not something we do on our own." More allusions to his history.

"I'll talk to Carr," he says.

It will have to be on the phone. There is no time to meet in person.

"Call me after," Brooks says. "I'll meet you at Madison's apartment."

They had not been allowed to prepare for this. They had gathered most of the facts. But they hadn't lined up ahead of time and had ready what everyone would say. Madison's two friends, a judge and a Justice Department official, had buried themselves too deep, too long ago, to be willing to go public. It would have been exposed that they had lied and been engaged for years in a cover-up. So they are improvising more tonight than they should be.

"How do we justify holding it back till now?" Carr asks.

"We tell the truth."

Madison was always willing to acknowledge the antiwar activity. Two of the friends involved were not. He honored that. They have changed their minds now because of the attempt to attack Madison. The journalist Henry Weingarten, who was part of the group, will vouch for this.

"And they will change their minds?"

"Randi is handling it as we speak. If not, Madison may tell us he will withdraw."

"Okay, go," the chief of staff agrees.

Give the man credit. He is a decider.

"Do you want it to come from the West Wing?" asks Carr.

Rena, surprised, had expected Carr to demand they release it. Give the White House separation and let Rena and Brooks take the heat.

"No," Rena says. "We're the investigators. We found it. We released it. That makes it more direct and less political."

"We can carry this," Carr says.

"No. We'll do it. It will infuriate Albin to know he caused this. I think he doesn't play well angry."

"You a student of Josh Albin now?"

"A condition of the assignment you gave me."

"I didn't give you this assignment, Peter," Carr says.

An honest acknowledgment from a notorious liar?

"I know."

"I was opposed to Madison's nomination, Peter. A Californian doesn't get us much politically. We already have that state. And I have never been convinced one man can change the dynamics of the Court. I think you change the Court by putting more liberals there. It's math, not psychology."

They have entered new territory. Carr is leveling with him. Band-of-brothers bonding in a crisis? Or does he want something?

"To be blunt, we have a year before the president loses most of his influence. And I didn't want to use what's left of his political capital on a court nomination. If we can get a moment of bipartisanship, I want to use it for an economic package to rebuild manufacturing. Or a broad climate package that will change the course of the planet."

"You changed your mind?"

"A loss is a loss. Now that he's nominated, we need the guy confirmed."

"I will talk to Madison," Rena says.

Carr could still be lying to him. But Rena's job now is to persuade Madison to reveal everything and to make him understand it's this or nothing.

Dropping out now has all kinds of implications

Madison would hate, including suggesting that protesting the war is something to be ashamed of.

They have to find a journalist to do one story that everyone else has to follow. And do it tonight. It would be best if it breaks first thing in the morning—with a prepared statement ready. They can't risk Albin breaking this first, though Rena doubts the activist has enough information anyway.

At Madison's apartment, Brooks has already secured the judge's assent. Rena interviews him for a statement, recording it on audio, not on camera. Nominees do not appear on camera. Brooks takes care of "informing" Madison's "co-conspirators." They could now try to remain anonymous, or they could back Madison. It shouldn't take them long to realize the gratitude of the president for helping their friend get on the Supreme Court is worth more than keeping their secret.

Rena gets a statement from Madison.

"Do you think you did something wrong vilifying the soldiers who fought the war?"

"Of course," Madison answers.

"Why didn't you tell me that in California in April?"

"Doesn't it go without saying? If anything, we've overlearned that lesson. We honor our soldiers now so assiduously I wonder if we mean it."

Matt Alabama agrees this is a story about the smear tactics of Washington, not a scandal about Madison, but says he can't do the story himself. He and Rena are too close. Rena and Brooks pick Jayne Haver of the *New York Times* instead, a national affairs correspondent who, while respected, tends to be sympathetic to the Nash administration. Haver, too, sees the piece much the way Brooks explains it.

Rena and Madison collaborate on a written statement. Henry Weingarten, the journalist in Los Angeles, agrees to a statement as well. The other two men agree to be named and offer the briefest statements for now. Silence would sound like guilt, Brooks has persuaded them.

In three hours it is done.

"In 1970, when I was a seventeen-year-old sophomore in college, I, like the majority of the American public, was opposed to continuing U.S. involvement in the now decade-long war in Vietnam. Along with some other sophomores, I was deeply influenced by the writings of the American philosopher Henry David Thoreau and the idea that if you found a law or policy that you disagreed with that you had an obligation to oppose it by breaking that law. We took ourselves enormously seriously. We called ourselves the New Walden Project, in honor of Thoreau's book *Walden*. We imagined ourselves very important. We were serious, frightened, inspired, and naïve. We engaged in activities that violated the law on purpose, that were part of the theory of civil disobedience of symbolic lawbreaking as a form of free speech. At the University of California, Berkeley, we spray-painted the windows at an ROTC recruitment office and a recruiter's car. We made contact with groups trying to help people avoid the draft. I was even detained once by an army representative who caught us spray-painting an army recruitment property. We were never arrested. I think he thought we were ridiculous."

Reluctantly, Rena is quoted, too. He is the eyewitness, in effect, that Madison's team had been contacted by a reporter about this, who had told him that critics were out there peddling outrageous tales of secret communist cells and a conspiratorial cover-up. There was no cover-up.

The story will break tomorrow in the *Times* and on a network morning program. There is much to do still to make sure that what they've set in motion tonight works as planned tomorrow.

As they are finishing up the work in Madison's apartment, an exhausted Randi Brooks pulls Rena into the kitchen for some privacy. "A mole, Peter? In our office? We need to face this."

She looks at Rena, into his calm, resolute dark eyes, his delicate, sharp-angled face. He looks tired but also energized by what has happened. "I know. Starting tomorrow," he says. "Not tonight. No distractions tonight."

She gives him a worried look.

Just before 11:00 P.M., after Rena is back at his row house in the West End, Alabama calls, the nightly review.

"A prediction?"

"Been around too long for those," Alabama says. "But you've done well today.

"Then I guess we'll know tomorrow."

"It may take more like three or four days."

"Lovely."

A good deal of what Rena has learned about politics has come from listening to Alabama. The older man seems to enjoy the role.

"You know I wasn't sure whether Nash might bail out on Madison," Rena tells his friend. "I even wondered if this whole nomination was a setup."

"Oh, I didn't doubt Nash," Alabama says. "But I figured some of his people hated this pick. My guess is the ambivalence you sensed wasn't Nash, Peter. It was division around him."

Alabama has sensed all along what Rena hadn't really understood until tonight after talking with Carr. If some of Nash's people were opposed to Madison, that also explained why the president had sought outsiders to run things.

Rena mixes a martini after he and Alabama are done and slips *Moanin'* by Art Blakey and the Jazz Messengers onto a turntable. Blakey was a rare bebop leader, a drummer—a driver of the beat. Like Ellington, he led from underneath.

The vodka slides, chills, and burns. As he begins to relax, he realizes he is still wearing the basketball clothes he wore to meet Albin.

How did the conservative find out about this? Rena believes he knows the answer, though he doesn't have the evidence. It's almost the only explanation, however—they have a leak in-house. He has no idea who.

He tries to make the next three sips of the martini go slowly to appreciate them.

The doorbell is ringing.

Victoria Madison is standing in his doorway in running shorts and a sweat-soaked sleeveless T-shirt. And a shy smile.

"I was feeling nervous, so I took a late run and I . . . found myself here."

She is a charmingly bad liar.

In running rather than dress clothes, blinking perspiration from her eyes, Vic looks younger, Rena thinks, as she might have as a teenager.

He swings the door open the rest of the way for her. Her wet shoulder brushes against his as she passes.

"There anyone with you?" he asks.

"Like who?" she says with surprise. He has started this badly.

"Like reporters following you."

"Oh, no. We've become sufficiently familiar and uninteresting again." Camera crews hovered, even around the apartment, their first days in Washington.

"I'll get you a towel," he says. She follows him into the den and waits there.

"I'm having a drink," he says when he returns, seeing her looking at his. "Would you like one?"

"Oh, God, no. Water would be great, though." She looks at Rena's glass. "That looks like a martini."

"Guilty."

"A martini and jazz? Like something out of a *Playboy* ad from the 1960s," she teases. "'What kind of man reads *Playboy*?'"

Rena blushes.

"I wouldn't have guessed jazz."

"For my father, an immigrant from Italy, American

jazz was, well, the most American thing there was. He listened to it in Italy. Much more than pop music when we moved here. So that was the music in the house."

She scans the books, the picture of Katie and his father. She is reading his house, reading him.

"Peter," Vic says, suddenly serious. "Do you think Dad's nomination will survive?"

"The next couple of days will tell us."

"This bothered you from the start, didn't it? The war protests," she says.

What should he tell her?

That he lobbied against her father's nomination? That he thought her father's attitude about his anti-Vietnam protests was offensive? Why doesn't he want to tell her the truth? Why is he so afraid of disappointing her?

"What bothered me was hiding it."

That much is absolutely true.

"I think it means nothing," Vic says. "So revealing it should mean nothing."

Head tilted upward, her smoke-gray eyes are fixed on him, her expression searching his. She isn't talking about how this will play politically anymore. She is talking about what things should mean to *him*.

He holds her gaze and nods. I understand.

"Let's get you that water."

In the kitchen she measures the layout, the pots hanging above the small island, the German knives.

"Randi says you are a gourmet cook."

"I'm out of practice." He barely cooks anymore. Not since his divorce from Katie. Not for one person. "But my grandmother taught me during summers in Italy. So my father and I wouldn't starve."

He hands her the water. She downs it in a single gulp. Then she holds it out to him for more.

"You're thirsty," he says.

"You have no idea."

As he reaches for the glass, they brush against each other again. She looks at the dark spot made on his shirt.

"I've left a mark."

"Yes, you have."

A demure smile, a retreating expression, just for a moment.

"Dad and I went to another Washington dinner last night, at Senator Burke's."

His former boss Llewellyn Burke seems to be everywhere.

"The senator told me your story."

"I didn't know I had one."

She circles and moves closer. "Oh, that is very male," she says accusingly.

"Better than the alternative."

She shakes her head. "You're trying to get me to tell you what he said. Men love to hear about themselves."

"Am I?"

"I will placate your male ego, then, and tell you what Burke said. And you can tell me which parts are lies."

"All the bad parts."

She smiles in a way that suggests those are the best parts.

It bothers Rena, though, that Burke has told her this story. His personal debt to the senator is enormous—the man gave him a new career, first out of loyalty to Katie because their families knew each other, and then, after the marriage collapsed, to Rena. This particular story, however, isn't the senator's to tell, or really even Rena's.

"You were at the Pentagon in charge of a top army investigation unit. The army was about to assign a general to head Southern Command. But there was a problem. Rumors of a history of sexually harassing women under his command."

Rena gave a promise he would never tell this story. He never has. Burke learned it elsewhere.

"The general was too important to be scandalized," Vic continues. "He'd been repeatedly promoted. A scandal would tarnish the army. A sign-off from you, the top internal investigator, would give him a clean bill of health."

She pauses, waiting for Rena to say something.

"But you didn't do that. Did you?"

She moves closer to him.

He holds his ground, barely.

"You tracked down the loose ends, interviewed many of the women yourself—and became convinced that these were more than rumors."

She studies his face, more serious now, less flirtatious.

"And then, somehow, you persuaded the general to resign . . . after all those years. Senator Burke said you took the general's daughter to see him. She told him these women were daughters like she was. And you barely said a word."

She has moved so close he is leaning against the kitchen island.

"He resigned, but without a whiff of scandal. And the general actually was grateful. He began apologizing to the women, owning up to what he had done. Making amends. You got the general to resign and like it."

She pauses now, looking at him.

"But you had ruined what was a rising military career before you were thirty-five. Senator Burke offered you a job on his staff."

He can feel the heat from her body.

"You're not going to tell me whether this story is true, are you?"

"Senator Burke's a good storyteller."

"I thought the army liked initiative."

"Initiative that fulfills its objectives—not redefines them."

"You didn't know that before?"

He wants to take hold of her. He has wanted to take hold of her for months.

"The military is a paradox. It's filled with idealists trained in obedience," Rena says. "It's a difficult combination."

She touches his hand, and Rena feels an electric shot run up his arm. He closes his own over her fingers.

"Yes, contradictions. To begin with, for someone who is supposed to be such a great investigator, you really are an idiot."

"It's the core of my charm."

"Allow me to disabuse you."

She tugs at the neck of his T-shirt. "I have had to run over here, literally, for us to be alone."

She's right.

"You really know nothing about women, do you?"

"I didn't have many around much when I was young."

"That is a terrible excuse."

"Well, I know nothing about women."

Vic puts her hands around his neck and pulls him toward her.

"We'll see."

She tastes of salt and sweat and it's wonderful. They tug and pull, finding each other beneath clothes, feeling where their bodies match. She is lean and strong. Hungrily, against the island in the kitchen. Rena has imagined this moment. He knows now Vic has, too.

They are lying on the bed later, their faces close, no more pretenses. "Difficult, but not a complete idiot, perhaps," she says with a smile.

Then she props herself on her elbows. "Can I ask you another question?" she says, serious, feeling like talking.

"I think we're past seeking permission to ask questions."

"How come your father never remarried?"

She thinks his father was a widower, like her own. Or divorced.

"Because my father was still married."

"I thought . . ."

It is a night for revelations, Rena guesses.

"So did I," he says. "I was told my entire childhood that my mother was dead. But it was a lie. One my father told me, and my grandmother and my aunts in Italy, where I spent my summers, my whole family."

"Oh, Peter."

"She abandoned my father and me when I was just over a year old."

She touches her fingers on his cheek.

"I didn't figure it out completely until I was a teenager. I finally puzzled enough out to confront my father. Basically, that most of what I thought about my life was a lie."

"Where was your mother?"

"She ran off. We moved to America. My father never set foot in Italy again."

"Why?"

"We were from a small village, and though it was the 1970s for my father this was still a great shame."

"Have you ever tried to find her?"

"After my father died."

"And?"

"There was someone in Milan, it was probably her. By the time I located her, I realized I didn't care. That woman, whoever she had become, wasn't part of my life. I wasn't interested in revenge."

Vic's gray eyes hold his. "No wonder you don't like secrets."

He takes her face in his hands, and he doesn't think about Josh Albin or Roland Madison or anything else for a long time.

The lights have gone out. The figure in the Nats cap in the alley across the street drops a cigarette and steps on it.

He is not entirely sure why he followed her. Or what he plans to do next.

Boredom? The father down for the night, the daughter took off running. Who knows? An impulse. Sometimes you just go with it.

After all the months of planning, getting ready, he feels . . . pressed down, like he's using the whole of his weight to hold something up that's falling and he can feel his strength about to give out.

All day he concentrates on the judge, how he thinks, waiting. Sometimes you just have to let go.

His arm aches. But at least, he thinks, the pain's not getting worse. That's something. It means it's not infected, he hopes. That's the main thing, the woman at the farm said.

He does wish he could wear short sleeves and let the arm breath a little. It's so damn humid out here, even in June, not like home. But he has to keep the arm covered in case anyone is looking for someone with a bandage over a possible severe dog bite on their arm.

Fuck it. Everything had been so smooth until Martell. That isn't so much, one glitch, really. So he shouldn't panic now.

Maybe he will just hang around awhile. Then he starts to imagine them in there with the lights out. He feels pathetic standing here. Too easy to be noticed. He smokes another Marlboro Light. Then, he realizes, he's left trace. He isn't thinking clearly. Better take off.

Thirty-eight

Wednesday, June 17, 9:38 A.M.
Washington, D.C.

Albin looks at the shards of shattered porcelain on the floor—a piece of blue mug with the logo of the Cato Institute still visible—and the drippings of brown coffee splayed on the wall.

He is ashamed. He shouldn't have given in to his anger and thrown the mug. Then again, it's been years since he'd made a mistake as stupid as the one he made last night. Let alone seen his mistake played out in the *New York Times* in the morning.

He checks online again for updates on the story about Madison as a victim of a smear campaign by conservatives. Classic liberal media claptrap.

Unless he and his allies have something substantially new and significantly serious, any effort to push back now on the Berkeley story would only reinforce the idea that Madison is the victim of Washington's vicious political culture. His own force is being used against him. It is political jujitsu.

Albin walks over and picks up the shards. Somehow Rena figured he is the leak. How?

Worse, people know he is the source peddling the story. That has damaged his reputation as a disciplined tactician.

No one has even come close to his office this morning. Virtually no email. No calls. He looks at the coffee stain on the wall.

"How do you do the math?"

The senior staff of Fair Chance for America are gathered in Deborah Cutter's office.

"Well, I know one thing," says Todd Paulson. "Josh Albin is in an incredibly foul mood this morning."

Cutter looks up. Has Paulson really put spies in offices around town? Or does he just want her to think so?

"What, do you have a mole inside Albin's office now?" Nan Bullock, the oldest of Cutter's staff, asks Paulson.

Paulson shrugs.

Bullock can't contain herself. "You know, spies, and moles and all this idiocy isn't new," she declares. "We pulled those kinds of stunts in the seventies, when we were inventing public interest activism." Her voice tightens, her anger spiking suddenly, like a pot of pasta boiling over with foam. She knows people tend to dismiss her as old and out of touch and it enrages her. "Well, it never amounted to much. And I suspect that is all it would be worth now."

She can see she has hit a nerve with Paulson. "You see, we learned that if you try to win at all costs, you lose everything. Isn't that the point in all this? Don't we work like this so we're not shooting it out in the streets? You really can't save the village by destroying it."

She has gone too far, again, she thinks. Too much the old scold. And they will miss her point.

Cutter's eyes are on her, and the boss doesn't let the silence linger. "What we need to know, people, is whether Madison is damaged goods. Or is the White House getting out in front of this."

"It depends, I think," Bullock says, "on whether the White House has come completely clean."

"Yes," says Sylvia Blechman, Cutter's chief of staff. "They can't let this drip out."

Cutter has a thought. "Maybe we win either way."

"Careful," Blechman says slowly. "If we're seen as hurting the White House, we can get hurt, too."

Cutter notices Paulson smiling. He really is something of a weasel, she thinks, but she shouldn't underestimate him.

"Todd, I want your guys digging up whatever they can about Madison today harder than we ever have before."

Cutter's assistant, Laura Wilson, enters the room with a phone message. She hands it to Blechman to hand to Cutter.

"Well, you may need to decide quickly, Deborah," Blechman says.

"Why?"

"Because Peter Rena is on the line."

Thirty-nine

11:00 A.M.
Washington, D.C.

Rena has let Cutter pick the meeting place and she's chosen Java Green, a coffeehouse near her office, probably to annoy him.

Java Green calls itself "an organic eco café." Rena's a Republican and ex-military. He would hate it, right?

She finds him a table in the back. She looks elegantly bohemian, in flowing wheat-colored cotton pants, a silk blouse, and a dark paisley scarf.

"Not your kind of place?" she says.

"Oh, I like the food here."

"Really?"

"Our offices are nearby. Funny thing about people in the service. A lot of us are health freaks. We run. Eat carefully. Could do without the New Age attitude. I mostly get takeout." She shifts in her seat.

A waiter appears and they order. Two coffees.

"What can I do for you Mr. Rena?"

He stares at her a moment, hard and very still.

"You can tell me what you want."

"What I want from what?"

"From this nomination."

"What do I want from the Madison nomination?" she says after a pause.

One thing he had learned from the files on Deborah Cutter: She is most comfortable on the offensive. He needs her uncomfortable. She isn't that different in some ways from Albin.

"It's the president's choice," she answers vaguely. "And he didn't consult with us in advance."

"I don't know the president very well, Ms. Cutter, but he seemed to want to make a point here of making this decision alone."

"But you want to consult, now?"

"I'm not the president."

Cutter nods in a way that says, no, indeed, sir, you are not.

"But I should have called you sooner. It's my job to get this man confirmed. Knowing what you want would help."

"So why didn't you contact me sooner?"

"Not everything occurs to me when it should."

"But it did now?"

The coffees appear.

"Mr. Rena, I think what you really want is to see how we will react to this story about Judge Madison's antiwar activities. To see how much trouble Madison is in."

"Actually I want to see how much his hand was strengthened today."

Cutter laughs and tries her coffee.

"So what will you tell the press about this Berkeley business?"

Rena wants her to recognize what he's doing—that he is fixing her into a position. If she lies to Rena now, or changes her mind later, it will be as if she is lying to the president.

Cutter has to calculate that her options are more limited today than they were a day earlier. She can't possibly attack Madison for protesting Vietnam.

But he isn't sure her options will be so limited tomorrow—if anything else breaks about Madison.

That is why he needs to register her feelings now. And tell her he is reporting them to the White House.

"From the details we know so far, it seems fairly innocent. If that is all the opposition has, we would bemoan this as a witch hunt that smacks of McCarthyism."

"But not directly defend Madison."

"I think that is a defense."

"Not a strong one, but better than you've offered so far."

"You are direct, I give you that," Cutter says.

"I'm told it's my best quality."

Cutter shifts under the table, uncrossing and crossing her legs, then leans forward to steady herself.

"The wind does seem to be blowing your way. Even some of the conservative intellectual blogs this morning are dismissing this as not serious."

"It was serious. He was serious. But it is a sign of a thoughtful, searching young person in 1970, not something that disqualifies you from the Supreme Court."

Rena arguing the liberal view to Deborah Cutter?

A small smile creases her face.

"If we're being candid with each other, Mr. Rena, I want to know if that is really all there is."

Rena pauses. "I've heard you don't like me, ma'am."

That makes *her* pause. "I wouldn't say that."

"Be that as it may, you should know this about me: I'm not a fan of war protests. I served in Iraq. The second one. Plenty about the war to question. But not the bravery of the soldiers."

"Your point, Mr. Rena?"

"I'm also not a fan of spin. Roland Madison had to persuade me he's now revealed everything."

Cutter's look suggests she is trying to decide whether this little speech is itself spin.

"Tonight," Rena continues, "ABN is going to have a piece on the nightly news with interviews of two other men who were involved in this with Madison vouching for his story. One of them is a judge who is going to say that the only reason it has not come out until now is that he, not Madison, wanted it kept quiet. And there will be a long first-person story appearing in the *LA Times* website this afternoon by a journalist who was also involved, explaining the whole business in detail."

"Not just one story leaked, but several," she says. "A whole media offensive coming from various places all backing up your version of events. You've played your hand well."

"It's no play. That was the deal with Madison. Hold nothing back now."

"You've boxed in the Right pretty thoroughly."

"I don't know that."

"I do. I understand Josh Albin was furious this morning. The little general has been thwarted. By tomorrow afternoon, I suspect you will have friendly bloggers ranting about McCarthyism and how we need to change our politics and ennoble ourselves again."

Cutter leans back in her chair, takes a breath, and continues.

"When that happens, Albin and his cohort will have been weakened, and Madison will have been protected from further attack. For Madison to go down after that it will have to be something huge."

She looks pleased with her analysis and leans forward.

How would Deborah Cutter know what was going on in Josh Albin's office this morning, he wonders? It reminds him of the problem he may have in his own office of people talking.

"So, you want to know what I want from this nomination?" Cutter continues.

"Yes."

"I want a better nominee."

They are the same words Albin used.

"Which means someone who sees things the way you do?"

"What else could it mean?"

"And is that what you still want?" he asks.

"Now, Madison may be closer to being on his way," she says.

"Meaning?"

"If Madison is going to make it, we are going to do what we can to help. Is that what you wanted to hear?"

"I want to hear whatever you're thinking."

"I think I want to wait one more day. I want to know that there really is nothing else here."

Rena, who hasn't touched his coffee yet, takes a first sip. "There isn't. Not that I know of. That is the truth. A fact, in context, without spin."

Cutter smiles.

"If you want to wait a day," Rena says, "do us one favor. Don't announce you are waiting. I'm sure the president would appreciate it if the next thing you say publicly is your strong endorsement of Madison and your denunciation of the witch hunt against him."

"I hope that's what can happen," she says.

"If it isn't, then I have been lied to."

When he calls that afternoon, Gary Gold doesn't identify himself. He just starts talking.

"I know in the age of the Internet anyone can be a

journalist. But Jesus, Peter, can you at least let us write the stories so they seem like journalism?"

Is Gold calling to confirm something—the other shoe to fall? Or to fish for some remnant he thought Rena might give him?

It is the difference between this being a good call or a devastating one.

"Really, some of these media outlets should ask you to pay them. Lord knows we need a new revenue model. Is this what they mean by native advertising, where the advertisements look like stories?"

"We just decided to tell everything we knew. Once we knew it was about to be distorted."

"Oh, be careful with words like *everything*, dude. It's always the superlatives that will get you in trouble."

Rena says nothing. If Gold dangles something in front of him to comment on now, they're in trouble. If he doesn't, he doesn't have anything.

"You're not laughing, Peter. I'm told you're usually pretty droll, though some people miss it."

"I have a droll expression on my face. You just can't see it through the phone."

He hears a tight chuckle. Then silence.

Gold's voice gets serious on the other end of the line.

"You owe me now, Peter."

Gold has nothing.

"I'll remember that, Gary."

"Okay then."

Rena can check three items off the list: Albin, Cutter, and Gold. None will hurt him—for now. But the next twenty-four to thirty-six hours are critical.

Forty

Thursday, June 18, 1:30 P.M.
Washington, D.C.

The meeting with the White House is held in Spencer Carr's office. Does that signify something? Keep the president a step away from this? Avoid signaling a crisis?

When Rena and Brooks arrive, Carr is sitting with Attorney General Charles Penopopoulis, a short, round man who looks more like a corner grocer, which his father was, than the founder of the most elite law firm in the Pacific Northwest. Penopopoulis has been in and out of administrations for a generation and is the most experienced hand in Nash's cabinet. Next to him sits White House Counsel George Rawls, with whom Rena has been working since the nomination began. They are gathered around a small meeting table on the other side of the room from Carr's desk. Rawls and Penopopoulis are old friends.

And next to Rawls, legs crossed, the top foot dangling with the ease of a man completely comfortable, sits Senator Llewellyn Burke, his former political mentor.

Llewellyn Halstead Burke, who could trace his lineage to the Dodge and Ford families of Michigan as well as Martha Washington's in Virginia, is not an especially handsome man, particularly for a politician. His features are soft, his face round and boyish, but something about him, something in his confident intelligence and quiet honesty, makes virtually everyone who meets him recognize they can trust him.

Their eyes meet. Why is the senator here? He's from the other party than Nash and doesn't sit on Judiciary. But they are both scions of old political families. They are both part of a vanishing breed, independently minded moderates.

Then Rena realizes, like the tumblers clicking on a lock, how he came to be involved in the Madison affair in the first place. It all goes back to Burke. Burke persuaded Nash to hire Rena, Burke the uber-connected senator no doubt thinking he is looking out for one of his many surrogate sons. The heir of the Michigan auto establishment trying to steer the president, the heir to a Nebraska political dynasty, to a different kind of judicial nominee. It is just like Burke. A hand everywhere he thinks matters.

Further proof then that Madison's nomination can't be set to fail—at least not entirely. Burke would never do that to him. Burke sees the look on Rena's face and smiles, eyes twinkling

From a side door President Nash suddenly is inside the room. Everyone stands. So they didn't want this meeting on the president's official schedule.

"We're here as a status check. No minutes. No record of our meeting. We just wanted to look each other in the eye and see we are on the same page. In light of what's occurred. We agree we want to proceed?" Carr begins.

Rena wonders which of these men two days ago wanted Madison, other than Burke. And Nash. He has no idea.

If any of them dislike Madison because he isn't liberal enough, they could not be as critical now. The war protestor story, and the attempt to tar Madison with it, make him something of a liberal symbol. That would *not* be true if the Vietnam story had come out as a small detail in his biography in the first place.

That, Rena thinks, is politics. Context changing meaning, like a photograph conveying something different as the frame widens to reveal who else is in the picture.

"So we proceed?" Carr asks the group.

No one answers.

"Then it's agreed," the chief of staff says.

The president rises and, wordlessly, vanishes through the door by which he came.

Forty-one

Friday, June 19, 3:14 P.M.
San Francisco

Walt Smolonsky checks the two entrances again. Still nothing.

The guy is late.

Not so late that he's worrying about a no-show. But late enough that he feels a rush of anxiety about whether the day will be a bust. It's almost 3:30 on Friday afternoon, and he is running out of time.

He's been in San Francisco for the better part of two days. He's interviewed almost a dozen people—cops, DAs, former DAs, defense attorneys—and he hasn't learned much about Alan Martell that Wiley's file hasn't already told him. So you see one more guy, check one more file. Maybe the next one will break something open—like another cruise through the clues of a cross-word that's got you stumped.

Martell didn't seem like a bad guy. Someone who knew how to keep it simple. Kind of guy people relied on more than they admitted.

It isn't clear why Martell pulled up stakes for D.C., but the marriage didn't survive. He and his wife both stayed east. Maybe the children were settled.

None of it tells him what he's after—whether there is anything about Martell or his murder that might complicate Madison's nomination.

Part of the problem is he can't level with people about what he's looking for. The last thing he needs is the legal and law enforcement communities here wondering why Washington people are looking into a connection between the two. "White House Probing Link Between High Court Nominee and Murdered Lawyer." It would take exactly twenty seconds for that to get picked up by the scream-o-sphere online.

So you try hiding questions about Martell inside a supposedly general inquiry about Madison, like hiding the nut in the shell game. The flaw in this ruse is the timing. It doesn't make sense for the White House to be asking general questions about Madison this late—on the eve of his hearings.

The only excuse is the close call on Madison over Vietnam. The judge seems to have survived it—for now. But it makes sense the White House might want some double scrubbing on the man now, even last minute.

The guy he's waiting for is a former San Francisco assistant district attorney named Creighton Ashe, a partner at one of the firms out here that handle Silicon Valley work, intellectual property, patents, and the rest. Corporations fighting other corporations. Money about money.

He sees someone heading his way looking straight at him. He gets close, his eyes searching against the description. "Mr. Smolonsky?" The man extends a hand and professional smile. Smolonsky stands.

"Creighton Ashe?"

"Please, Tate."

Smolo runs through the preliminaries—working for the White House, checking last-minute facts on Madison. Due diligence, blah, blah, blah.

"What kind of judge was Madison?"

"Superb. But he was at Superior Court less than two years. He was parked, so to speak, on his way to better things. Yet even in those few months he showed flashes of brilliance."

"People resent that? That he was just parked, I mean, on his way up?"

"No. He was already a famous legal scholar. Hell, he was a professor of mine at Harvard."

Smolonsky nods sympathetically.

"Look, you really should talk to his clerks. Frankly, I'm surprised you're doing this now. You say you're working with the White House? Wasn't he vetted thoroughly before being nominated?"

"We're just anticipating some specific testimony now that we have the witness list for the hearings next week. It's pro forma, really."

"Why? Is someone testifying about his tenure as a Superior Court judge?" Ashe asks.

Ashe is sharp. Smolonsky doesn't want to give him any more time than necessary to become suspicious. "I've been talking to a bunch of folks from the DA's office." He takes a long pull on his coffee, to break the flow of questions. He lets a little dribble on his chin and makes a show of using napkins to dab the mess. Make him doubt me, Smolo thinks, and take his mind off Madison.

"Um, hey, did you know, by the way, that guy who was murdered the other day in Washington? Alan Martell, the former assistant DA?" He hopes it sounds like a digression.

Ashe's expression stiffens. "Terrible," he says.

"Yes. That was Rollie's, uh Judge Madison's, reaction, too. They had cases together?"

"We all did. It's a small community at Superior. The city and county of San Francisco are not that big."

"Same in D.C.," Smolonsky says. "I was a police officer there, a long time ago."

Ashe nods, registering that into his assessment of Smolonsky.

"You knew Martell?"

"Of course."

"Nice guy?"

"Sure," Ashe says, noncommittally.

"Why'd he leave?"

"Most do, eventually. The DA's office is good training, but it's not a good living."

"Martell a good lawyer?"

"He was fine," Ashe says in the clipped diction of someone being deposed.

"If I were still a cop, I'd wonder if there was anyone who would want to kill him."

Ashe doesn't respond. Smolo hasn't asked a question. More deposition training.

"Any theories?"

"I haven't seen Alan in years."

"Yeah, of course."

"What does that have to do with Judge Madison?"

"Nothing. Old reflexes is all. I worked homicide. Even now, someone gets murdered, you get curious."

Ashe looks at Smolonsky with growing disapproval, which is fine. If you want to hide something in your questioning, distract the guy by making him dislike you.

"Back to Judge Madison. Any controversial cases that could bite us in the ass?"

"You mean did Judge Madison have any controversial cases in Superior Court?"

"Yeah, that's what I mean."

Ashe leans back, relaxing again. "I wouldn't say so. It's not a place where you often encounter knotty constitutional issues."

"You miss it, the DA's office?"

Ashe smiles distantly. "Do you know how much money an assistant DA makes?"

"More than policemen."

"The average partner working for a firm like mine makes six times an assistant DA," Ashe says. "Maybe eight. And a rainmaker can make half again more than that."

"You didn't tell me whether you missed it."

"I don't miss living in an apartment, worrying about paying off my law school loans, and wondering if my kids could ever go to college."

"But."

Ashe looks like he wished he hadn't brought it up.

"You know what I do, Tate?" Smolo says. "I help sports teams find out whether their athletes are criminals and wife beaters before they sign them to huge contracts, or whether CEOs dress up like little girls and demand to be spanked by prostitutes."

"Yes, well, corporations will pay millions to fight over things that don't matter even to the lawyers doing the work. But we won't pay for lawyers to prosecute criminals to protect us from evil. There are two legal systems in this country. One is lucrative, works well, and uses up precious resources. The other is what we call the justice system."

In a minute, Ashe is heading back to his office upstairs. Smolonsky feels himself tiring. It's closing time in Washington for the week, and he still has nada.

A weird vibe, though, from Ashe just now about Martell, not dissimilar to ones he had sensed in snippets from others, or is he just imagining it because he wants to?

Smolonsky checks his watch. Rena will expect him to work through the weekend, but it's hard to be motivated. This is a butt-covering exercise.

Who's left on his list of old Martell contacts to track down?

Next up is a lawyer named Rochelle Navatsky. She'd been in the public defender's office when Madison was at Superior Court. Case went to trial. Murder.

Smolonsky opens his laptop. Maybe she's still in the office or he can get a home number and see her tomorrow, Saturday.

The public defender's office doesn't list her. She's probably moved on. Check Martindale.com, the listing of attorneys. It's better for private practice than government lawyers and not perfectly up to date. But you never know.

Nothing. Maybe she's left the city. Google? It says she's with a law firm now in Oakland. But the firm's website doesn't list her.

What about the archives of the local legal newspaper? There's usually one in a big town. He sets the search parameters for the last year. Maybe there's something from a trial she had in front of Madison. He sees nothing.

But there's an obit.

Navatsky has died? Then the headline registers and Smolonsky's hands go cold.

Not just died. Murdered. Three months ago.

"Peter," Smolo says when Rena picks up. "We've got another problem."

Forty-two

7:04 P.M.
Washington, D.C.

Rena needs to find Wiley. Half an hour from now he's supposed to join the Madisons and Brooks to celebrate the completion of murder boards. Confirmation hearings begin Monday.

He calls Brooks.

"I'm going to be late. You should pick up the Madisons. I'll meet you there."

"What is it?"

"I'll tell you when I get there."

As brilliant as his partner is, she sometimes is too open with people, Rena thinks. She might not manage to wait for Rena before telling Madison. Rena wants be there when they tell him another lawyer in a case he presided over has been murdered. He wants to see Madison's face.

"I'll be there as soon as I can."

Wiley isn't answering her cell, email, or text. The woman who can track down anything about anyone knows how to get off the grid. Finally she calls.

"Meet me at the office in ten minutes."

He tries to plumb what he can from the Web about Rochelle Navatsky and Alan Martell while waiting. He doesn't get far. In between, he mulls who in his office may have become an enemy—or a fool. Who might have talked to someone who knew Josh Albin—the source of Albin's knowledge about Madison's war protests at Berkeley and their silence about it? Who in his office had either knowingly or unknowingly become part of the little man's network of spies? One of the young lawyers who work for Brooks? One of his ex-military colleagues he had brought in? Who might be a secret believer in Albin's agenda? Or secretly dissatisfied with Rena's? Or did Rena and Brooks no longer have an agenda—other than new clients? Had they become what their critics said about them?

He had taken steps to check on everyone in the firm—an outside, covert play. Not even Brooks knew. Her own movements had to be monitored, in case she had accidentally been part of the leak. Rena had called on old friend, Carter White, a mentor from army investigation days. Cart was not from politics, not from Washington. He was discreet in a way that almost no one in political Washington could fathom. Rena had no idea what the man would find. It might unravel his whole life. And Rena didn't have time to think about it.

He hears the front door unlock, the sound of footsteps upstairs, and Wiley appears in his door.

"I owe you for this," he tells her.

"Friday I have folk dancing at the Y."

In five minutes, she has the case records and cross-references Martell and Navatsky. They had twenty-one cases together over the years. Seven before Edmund R. Madison during his short tenure at Superior Court. Three went to trial. The others pled out before trial.

"Print everything you can about those cases. And the others in front of Madison, too. And put whatever links you have in the protected file on the server."

He calls Smolonsky back in California. "Find whoever you can who might know about Navatsky and Martell, whether they knew each other, whether they were friends. Tell them you're a private investigator looking into Martell's murder. So no doubling back on anyone you have already talked to."

"I'll do what I can."

"The three cases we care most about are the ones that went to trial. Two drug cases. And a murder," Rena says, looking over what Wiley has unearthed so far and put in front of him. She is tapping away on her magic investigative machine looking for more, the black and gold chain on her reading glasses dancing as she types.

One of the drug cases was major, a defendant named Randall Fulmer, who sounds like he was a member of some crew in town that controlled crack in a part of the city. The murder trial involved a defendant named Robert Walsh Johnson, a high school kid. He was convicted of murdering a girl from school.

"Okay, but it's Friday night," Smolonsky says.

"And the hearings start Monday," Rena says coolly. "Walt, you've done great work. But it's just the start."

"I get it."

Rena's late. He navigates his ancient Camaro toward Georgetown and onto Canal Road toward the restaurant, a place called the Old Angler's Inn, outside the city.

Does he really imagine these murders are linked? He cannot assume anything. Isn't that what James Nash went to him for? No surprises.

Rena has always had a love-hate relationship with hunches. Intuition is the unconscious mind seeing things before the conscious mind does. His father had called it "the little voice." His soccer coach called it "unconscious anticipation." The key is to be alive to the inferential mind but not fall in love with your hypotheses. If the facts begin to disprove them, you have to move on. That is the mistake bad or lazy investigators usually make. They "like" someone, a theory of who done it, and never see anything else.

Is he in love with a hunch that Madison isn't telling him something? So two people who know each other and know Madison are both murdered. They happen three thousand miles apart. Maybe he is overreacting.

His little voice tells him something else. Madison knowing one person who'd been murdered is a tragedy. Two is a coincidence. And coincidences are rarely that.

Madison had implied he barely remembered Martell. In fact they had had more than a dozen cases in eighteen months. Madison is holding something back. What could it be they don't already know? Or is Rena—because he suspects Madison isn't telling him something—turning this into a witch hunt about the judge?

The Old Angler's Inn in Potomac, Maryland, sits next to a tiny waterway called the Chesapeake & Ohio Canal. The C&O had been the brainstorm of George Washington, who feared the young American nation wouldn't survive unless the new states in the East were linked economically with the Ohio Territories in the West. The general imagined the canal, running alongside the Potomac River for almost two hundred miles, as that link. An almost impossible engineering feat, it wasn't finished for two generations after Washington's death. But he had been right about the economics. The canal operated for almost two hundred years.

Old Anger's Inn was built during the Civil War, midway through the canal's history, as a way station for passengers. The restaurant, a favorite of Rena's, features a magnificent bar, a garden, dark wood and fireplaces, and an upstairs dining room, the walls and floor bent with a century and a half of settling, otherwise unchanged. Before Smolonsky's call, it had seemed a good place to celebrate.

Brooks and the Madisons, already seated, are having wine. There is an empty glass for him. Everyone is laughing.

Madison stands. Vic smiles a secret, welcoming smile—and Rena feels a great weight suddenly, as if something were pressing down on his heart. He is so focused on her father, he hasn't thought about her feelings. And what he is about to do will hurt her.

"Now we can toast properly," Brooks says after they resettle. She fills his glass. "To the honorable Judge

Edmund Roland Madison, who killed in his final murder board today.

"And if I may," she adds before taking a drink, "I would like to read an email from Richard Attinger, the former deputy attorney general, who sat in today for the final session." She looks down at her phone and reads the email: "'Judge Madison was brilliant today. Superbly prepared. Charming. The single greatest performance I have seen in a mock hearing for any post.'"

Vic looks proudly at her father, eyes moistening, daughterly and maternal. Madison bows his head sheepishly, pleased, gracious, embarrassed.

"You all right?" Vic asks Rena.

He sips the wine, but the taste, or maybe it's his mood, is bitter. He isn't sure how to start.

"Remember the first meal we had together?" Brooks says. "At the place up on the mountain."

"Alice's," Vic says.

"Where there is no one named Alice," Brooks says.

"Just as I'm sure there are no old anglers here," Vic says.

"To misnomers," Madison says, raising his glass in another toast.

"To justice," Vic says to her father. Then she looks at Rena. His silence leaves her quizzical.

He takes another drink. When the food comes, he can barely taste it.

When the dinner plates are removed, he can contain himself no longer.

"Judge, I need to speak to you. May we go outside?"

Rena glances at Brooks. She nods, just slightly. He hasn't managed a way to tell her what he's found, but each of them knows that when the other has something important to raise, their job is to cover the other's back.

"Maybe you should take Vic home. I'll call you later," he says. "I'll take the judge home."

Vic looks angry and hurt and Rena realizes this is a mistake. Vic deserves to be part of this, whatever it is.

Madison is harder to read—he always has been.

"Let's finish dinner and then take a walk together," Brooks says, bailing him out.

"Then we better get the check," Rena says.

They walk over to the tow path, a gravel road alongside the canal from which mules would pull the barges by rope. The heat of the day has released and the summer humidity has broken. The June night is pleasantly cool.

"What is so urgent?" Vic demands.

"Judge, if you lie to us, if you hold something back, you will get found out, and at this point that will sink your nomination."

"Peter, what are you talking about?" Vic says.

"I sent Walt Smolonsky to California two days ago. He called me tonight. Alan Martell is not the first attorney who had cases before you who's been murdered. So has a woman named Rochelle Navatsky. Both were killed recently. Both cases are unsolved."

"And you think there is some connection between these killings and me?"

"I don't know, Judge. Is there?"

"Peter!" Vic exclaims.

"Did you know Navatsky had been murdered?"

"Yes, I did."

"And it didn't occur to you to tell us?"

"Tell you what exactly, Peter?" Madison says, his voice rising. "That there had been a terrible coincidence?"

"That you are connected to two people who have been murdered?"

"Connected? You sound like a tabloid TV program. Do you know how many lawyers I've met across the bench? How many trials? It's like saying that if two of the thousands of law students I have had in class had both died of the same disease that I was somehow connected."

"I don't care about all those trials. I care about the three involving these two lawyers."

"What do you want to know?" Madison asks.

"Was there anything special about them?"

"Special? As best as I can remember, one was a drug trial, another a robbery, and I think one was a rape and murder. Were they special? In America, sadly, no."

"Peter, you can't possibly think that there is some connection here between these people being killed," Vic says.

"I can't possibly assume there isn't."

"I would be grateful, Randi, if you could take both of us home," Madison says, looking at Rena.

"That's a good idea," Rena says. "I'm going to California."

Brooks's expression tells him she has his back, even though he has caught her off guard. "Hearings in three days," she says.

"I'll call you tomorrow from San Francisco."

PART FOUR

Hearings

June 22 to July 1

Forty-three

Monday, June 22, 1:13 P.M.
Washington, D.C.

Virtually no one hears Senator Furman Morgan bang the gavel. The old man's gaunt, speckled hand cannot swing the wooden hammer hard enough anymore to silence the cavernous Senate Judiciary Committee room in the Hart Senate Office Building. His voice, however—reedier than it once was and marked now by a higher timbre and a slow, appealing vibrato—still resonates.

"I'd like to call the committee back to order. Judge Madison, if you would please return to the witness table." The southern drawl is more pronounced when he speaks in public.

Madison, standing with his daughter and Brooks, turns, nods and heads toward his seat.

"Judge Madison, I also want to thank you for your patience. Our protocol in this body calls for members of the committee to make opening statements before the nominee testifies for him or herself. So I want to congratulate you for having already sat this morning through twenty-one speeches."

Room 216 of the Hart Senate Office Building fills with laughter.

"Now, if you would please stand and raise your right hand, I will swear you in."

On the floor photographers scramble for position.

"And keep your hand up for a few extra moments, Judge. This being a representative democracy, we have eighteen photographers who want to take your picture. And that particular image of you swearing the oath, I have learned, is what they call, I believe, the 'money shot.'"

More laughter.

"Do you solemnly swear that the testimony you will give before this Committee on the Judiciary of the United States Senate will be the truth, the whole truth, and nothing but the truth, so help you God?"

"I do."

"Thank you. Now, Judge, you may be seated. And the floor is yours."

From her seat in the row behind the witness table, Brooks takes a deep breath, trying to calm brittle nerves, and silently prays: Please, Rollie, say it as written.

Madison had procrastinated about writing his opening statement, agreed to a draft last week, torn it up Saturday—the morning after the argument with Rena—and recrafted something yesterday morning. Brooks thinks it's good, better than good. She just doesn't know if he will deliver it now or start ad-libbing again.

She wishes Rena were here. Not off in San Francisco with Smolo "running down leads." She had to handle the weekend chaos without him.

They had survived last week's crisis over Madison's antiwar background. But he wasn't strengthened by it. It was still a scare. And even scares you survive add up. That is Washington math. Reagan called it "blood in the water."

Madison at least looks the part he plays now. They brought the president's tailor to a room at the Hay-Adams, and she, Vic, and Rena had picked out a new charcoal gray Hickey Freeman suit and a black and silver dotted tie. The clothes transformed the judge from university intellectual into someone with whom senators could better relate, like a CEO or a head of state.

He's starting.

"Senator, first, I want to thank all the members of the committee for the many courtesies you've extended to me and my daughter over the last month. I have found these meetings to be invaluable in better understanding the concerns of the committee as it undertakes its constitutional responsibility of advise and consent."

They had battled over that line all weekend. She wanted him to thank the senators. He had argued it sounded like pandering.

She breathes.

He also recognizes, Madison continues, how thoroughly the senators and their aides have prepared for these hearings—reading the books, articles, and opinions he has written. "It strikes me that consuming these writings of mine, particularly the scholarly literature, may constitute some new form of cruel and unusual punishment."

Several senators nod their appreciation at Madison's attempt at levity, but there is no laughter.

Don't try to be funny, she had warned, especially not ironic. But the line had remained.

He also thanks the two home state California senators who formally introduced him to the committee this morning. "And I owe a debt I can never repay, most of all, to my daughter, Victoria, to my colleagues at the court in California, at the Stanford and Harvard law schools, and across the country. And finally I want to thank President James Nash for the honor of his nomination. I'm humbled by his confidence."

The photographers are still moving. Senator Morgan coughs disapprovingly, and Brooks recalls a nun from her Sunday school who used to cough in warning that way.

Now Madison gets to the meat of it. Brooks's heart is pounding.

"In America, we are taught that we live in a land of laws, not men—and I would add to that, women. That concept, so central to the Founders' idea of the new country, says something, I think, about the role of judges, and the role I imagine I would play on the Supreme Court. We must be as dispassionate as possible, for we are there to interpret the laws, to the best of our ability, not to make them. We are the law's servants, not the other way around.

"The question is how best to do that. My view is that this is best done with an open mind, with humility, and without dogma, platform, or agenda. While everyone is shaped by his or her own life experience, judges must more than match that with the gift of empathy and the intelligence to imagine experiences beyond their own. In other words, in addition to knowing the law, a wise jurist must listen—really listen—and have the ability to put himself or herself into the shoes of those who might be affected by the Court's decisions on all sides of a matter."

Senator Morgan is leaning back in his chair, his eyes nearly closed. Senator Stevens of Rhode Island, the ranking Democrat, is leaning forward, peering over reading glasses. Senator Tucker of Texas is staring at Madison. Senator Upton, their top swing vote, is watching Madison but stealing glances at other senators. Most of the rest of the panel appear to be listening intently.

"Finally, there is another question that fundamentally shapes how a judge will rule. What does that judge think is the purpose underlying our system of law? What is the law for? I believe the underlying purpose of the vast web of law we have built—our Constitution, our statutes, our rules, regulations, practices, and procedures—is to help the many live together productively, harmoniously, and in freedom. In other words, the key concept of our Constitution and our laws is to promote liberty.

"It has been said that the law is those wise restraints that make us free. That sounds right to me.

"So my promise to you is this: I will listen. I will try to read the law with humility and in accordance with its basic purposes. And I will do my utmost to see that decisions I help make reflect the letter and the spirit of the law that belongs to everyone."

Brooks feels a rush of adrenaline. Rollie, you goddamn, lovable, petulant, genius pain in the ass. Thank you.

He has even used the phrase "to read the law." Madison had written "interpret," and they had quarreled over it. Say "read," she said. *Interpret* is a hot word.

"Hot," he had said with quizzical dismissal. "Judges are not simply reading. Is it controversial now to suggest they think, too?"

Yes, Rollie, it is. Say "read."

His reaction was something between disgust and horror, but today, bless his contrary ass, he has said "read."

Then she realizes the silence around her.

They had wanted a statement to be brief, cogent, to give senators as little as possible to find objectionable. What Madison finally wrote was so succinct, the audience doesn't realize he has finished.

Senator Morgan leans back and to one side to hear

an aide whisper in his ear. In the momentary awkward silence, Senator Stevens coughs and then mumbles something to Senator Fuller sitting next to him.

During the pause, Brooks feels a tap on her shoulder. Spencer Carr has slipped into the hearing room and taken a seat behind her. You rarely see the chief of staff in public other than at White House photo ops.

"Good start, Randi."

"Thank you."

"Where's Peter?"

What had her partner told the White House about going to California?

"Running down a loose end."

Forty-four

10:30 A.M.
San Francisco

"This is like looking for a dead rat in a closet full of snakes."

That is Smolonsky's phrase for a hopeless task.

He might be right, Rena thinks.

He and Smolo are trying to solve two murders three thousand miles and three months apart. They have no leads, no knowledge of the cases, and no formal law enforcement authority in the jurisdictions involved. And they have twenty-four hours.

They also need to do it without raising the suspicions of the people they're interviewing.

Yeah, a dead rat in a closet of snakes.

They're testing just one theory: Is there reason to think the two murders are related? That narrows the list of potential killers. But it also might be a bogus theory.

"We have to be able to rule it out."

"Meaning we have to be able to prove a negative," Smolonsky had said.

"That's not as hard as people think. If the facts aren't there, it's ruled out."

That's when Smolonsky mentioned the dead rat.

Rochelle Navatsky's killing is a blank slate. She was bringing groceries home. Someone grabbed her and suffocated her. There were virtually no clues, no fingerprints, no forensics, no suspects. The killer apparently wore gloves, left nothing behind. Police suspect a robbery gone wrong.

The Martell murder is different. Whoever killed him seemed out of control. The wounded dog is weird. It happened three thousand miles away.

Hard to think it is the same killer.

Rena looks back at the lawyer he is interviewing and tries to focus.

Drew Kimmel had sat second chair for Rochelle Navatsky eight years ago at the murder trial of Robert Johnson, the kid convicted of killing the cheerleader.

He now works at a private law firm. Rena has told him he is here as a special investigator from Washington looking into the Martell death.

They are sitting in a twenty-fifth-floor conference room of Kimmel's law firm, a space designed to inspire or intimidate—depending on whether the firm represents you or the other guy. Rena can see Alcatraz Island and the Bay Bridge to the east out the enormous windows, the bridge almost in silhouette from the morning sun reflected off the shimmering bay. The land here seems energized by the convergence of sun and sea, the light brightened by it, the air cleansed.

"Why were you second chair?" Rena asks. "You were the more experienced lawyer."

"Rochelle was good, and we wanted her to get experience. You have to start somewhere."

"How'd she do?"

"Mr. Rena, how exactly can I help you?"

"Frankly, I'm fishing, Mr. Kimmel. I'm trying to find out if there is anything that might link the deaths of Rochelle Navatsky and Alan Martell."

"You can't be serious."

"I've flown out here from Washington. I am pretty serious."

"So where do we start?" Kimmel asks.

"With the trial of Robert Johnson."

"What I remember most was the case was circumstantial."

"But enough to convict?"

"Obviously yes," Kimmel says.

He's defensive. Too defensive.

"What was the evidence?"

"Johnson was obsessed with the girl, Regina Morrison. He had taken a lot of pictures of her and had sort of a shrine at his house."

"What else?"

"He and Morrison were seen having some kind of argument in the parking lot of a fast-food place. A lot of people had seen it. And, of course, there was the chrome pipe."

"The chrome pipe?"

"That was key. Johnson was cited for speeding later that night. The officer noticed a chrome pipe on the floor of the car. When they found Morrison's body a couple of days later, the officer remembered the pipe and the white car. Johnson couldn't explain why the pipe was there. The car was borrowed. He said the pipe wasn't his."

As he recalls details, Kimmel is becoming calmer.

"And Johnson had no alibi. He had this job as a pizza delivery guy, but he wasn't working yet that day at the approximate time of death. He said he was out driving around and thinking."

"No physical evidence?"

"That was our argument. The police had woven together the story of an obsessed young man who snapped after rejection. But a story was all they had. No forensic evidence. No trace to prove that the chrome bar was the murder weapon. Not even clear the white car Morrison got into that night was the same white car Johnson was driving."

"Did he kill her?"

Kimmel runs his hand through his sandy hair again, which falls back exactly into place each time.

"Honestly, I didn't know."

Kimmel wants to tell him something.

"Look, Mr. Rena, if the client pleads not guilty, you need to assume he's not. That's how it works."

"Rochelle Navatsky couldn't poke holes in all that?"

Kimmel's eyes move to Alcatraz in the distance.

"I don't know where to begin."

"Begin with the fact that you feel guilty about the quality of the defense you two gave Robert Johnson."

Kimmel tries angry but his heart isn't in it.

"Rochelle became an excellent trial lawyer. But this was her first murder trial . . . she took the loss hard."

"Harder than she should have?"

"I think most people in jail think they got incompetent representation and spend their time in prison blaming their lawyer."

"Is that what Johnson did?"

"Actually, he just seemed to be in shock. Or more like shattered. Like he expected bad luck to happen."

"So she wasn't to blame for him being convicted?"

The question seems to jar Kimmel.

"Mr. Rena, this was an awful crime. A rape-murder of a beautiful, beautiful young girl. In those kinds of cases, juries tend to want to find justice for the victim, not the accused."

"And Johnson died in jail?"

Wiley's file on this was slim.

"Stabbed. There aren't a lot of details."

They weren't known, or Kimmel hadn't taken the trouble to learn them?

"What did you make of Alan Martell?"

Kimmel sighs.

"I knew him fairly well in those days. And I didn't like him. He was arrogant and shouldn't have been."

"But he won?"

"Oh, juries loved him. He thought trying cases was easy. Just tell a story. Focused more on that than the law."

"Don't a lot of lawyers?"

"Let's just say DAs have a lot of advantages. Police, forensics experts. The defendants are often sketchy. Their lawyers usually have no time to prepare." Kimmel is making a speech.

"Look, being a public defender is the toughest job in law. We averaged five hundred criminal cases a year. That's about four hours per client. I once handled twenty-three arraignments in a morning. And you know what the average pay is?"

Rena lets him get it out.

"Forty-six thousand a year. And in the last five years, the public defenders' budget was cut thirteen percent while the workload grew twenty-nine percent."

He seems done.

"Were Martell and Navatsky friends?" Rena asks.

Kimmel laughs. "I think Rochelle despised Martell. He was the kind of lawyer she didn't want to become. And he beat her at trial."

Forty-five

This is out of the blue.

Senator William Stevens, the ranking Democrat, has just thrown a horrible curve.

As the senior member of the minority, Stevens should go second in questioning the nominee after Chairman Morgan, whose own opening questions were respectful and vague, a series of ritualistic queries about precedent and original intent, simply laying down a line of inquiry for his GOP colleagues to follow.

Then he turned to Stevens: "Senator, you have five minutes to question the nominee."

"Mr. Chairman, I'd like to pass and reserve my time," Stevens said.

What?

This is most decidedly *not* the plan—a plan worked out meticulously over the last several weeks. Stevens is supposed to be their foundation, building Madison up, insulating him from the inevitable attacks to come. Without that, the other Democrats would be putting drywall up without a frame.

Stevens is also the most experienced Democrat on the panel, the one with the most prestige among liberals, and the most friends among the old-guard conservatives.

What is Stevens up to? And why hasn't he tipped them off? God damn it.

You can prepare these things within an inch of their life. But U.S. senators are demigods. They've reached the highest point most of them are likely to go. They are impossible to control. Even harder to predict.

The room is buzzing. Camera motors clicking.

Damn it to hell.

Up to this moment, Stevens has been coy about Madison in public. He hasn't praised him, but he hasn't criticized him, either—and that is good given how harsh Stevens has been privately. Stevens also hadn't said a bad word in his opening statement earlier this morning. Actually, come to think of it, he virtually ignored Madison, offering a paean to liberal traditions on the Court.

Is it possible Stevens is considering the unthinkable? Did he pass on questioning because he wants to hear Madison answer questions before he has to take a stand on him? Is that why he has reserved his time?

That would be too goddamn terrible to contemplate, Brooks thinks.

She can feel her cell phone vibrating with multiple messages. Various people no doubt asking her what is going on. Including the White House. A quick scan of the messages and emails confirms it. This is a mess.

Stevens passing means the malicious and savvy Aggie Tucker is up.

Craggy Aggie. The feral boy senator of Texas. At age fifty-one, he already has close to a decade and a half in the body and still no friends to tell from it, though there are scores who fear him. Tucker has a fierce look and canny catlike eyes that can light up in a way that says, "I am going to screw with you and enjoy it."

For all that people dismiss Aggie as crazy or just mean, the man is in touch with a part of the American psyche, and a feeling about politics that is only growing. He was the first real Senate champion of the Common Sense movement, before any Common Sensers themselves had been elected there. He is also smarter than he pretends—Princeton and Harvard Law School—and possesses something many other sharper but less intuitive senators like Wendy Upton lack: He has no fear of living on the edge, where no one else would go. He loves it when people say, "Did you see what Aggie did?"

If Aggie can draw blood now, some of his colleagues—the people her old boss used to call "weather-vane senators"—might be swayed.

Brooks can feel the hush in the room behind her, people leaning forward—waiting for Tucker.

He stares down at Madison with his cat eyes. Then begins.

"Judge, throughout your career, you have set forth what you have called in your writings a 'pragmatic, nonideological vision of law.'"

"Yes, sir."

"If I may, I'd like to quote you:

"'The law is a human institution serving human needs. To advance the cause of justice, therefore, judges should approach it pragmatically, finding how it fits for the way that people actually behave, not the way we wish they might.'

"If you would, Judge, could you expand on what you mean by this so-called pragmatic vision? How did you put it? Make the law 'fit'? What do you mean, 'fit'?"

If Madison thinks this is a setup for an attack, he doesn't show it.

"I often have been struck, Senator," he begins, "by why judges wear black robes. I've always thought it was to signify that a judge is not speaking as an individual. Judges look alike because when they speak, they do so for a body of rules and institutions and precedents, not for themselves. For the judge, the robe is a reminder to try to interpret the law for everyone, not enunciate a subjective belief or preference. This is no less true for a jurist on the Supreme Court."

"Well, that is fine, Judge. Mighty fine. Would you agree, then, that a judge's authority derives entirely from the fact that he or she is applying the law? It's not anything personal?"

"Of course."

"Then would you also agree, Judge, that the meaning of the law is found in the understanding of the law by those who enacted it, by what some call original intent?"

"Whenever possible."

Careful, Rollie, Brooks thinks.

"Whenever possible? I'm sorry. When is it, exactly, that you think the meaning of the law is not ascertained from the understanding of those who enacted it?"

"In those instances, Senator, when it is unclear what the authors of the Constitution intended."

"Why should a federal judge do anything when it is not clear what the Constitution intends?"

"The Framers of the Constitution were writing and debating about life in eighteenth-century America. And they were writing a document that would win votes at a constitutional convention and then across the colonies, a political as well as legal document. In my opening statement I talked about humility. To me, humility includes admitting we do not always know what the Founders had in mind. Or if they agreed on a single intent."

"If you don't know what they had in mind, why do anything? If the Constitution doesn't address it, then it doesn't address it."

"Well, it might be easier to say the court can't go there, because it's not clear what the Framers wanted. But maybe they intended the court to act in this area and they just weren't explicit about it. There is ample scholarship and history to suggest this is the case."

"Well, sir . . ." Aggie tries to get in.

Rollie is still answering. "And then there are all the elements of modern life that the Framers naturally never envisioned. Are we to conclude that these aspects of our life are not covered by the Constitution because the Founders couldn't imagine the future? Finally, what of those parts of the Constitution that contradict each other, or that require the right in one amendment to be balanced against those in another? Are we not to try to balance them because it is unclear or unstated how do so?"

Aggie is leaning back happily.

"So what do you think judges should do about these areas of doubt?"

"I think they must infer from what we know about the Framers. And they must not extend beyond what can reasonably be inferred. But there is some subjectivity to this. And reasonable people may disagree. This is not a matter of making new law. It is a matter of understanding old law for new times. And there is no doubt that the Framers did have in mind that the court would do that."

"Well, Judge, seems to me you have just made for yourself three mighty convenient loopholes. And you could do anything you want there."

"Not loopholes, Senator. Judicial obligations."

Aggie has a hateful gleam in his eyes now.

Madison's not wrong. But he has just committed the first sin of testifying. He has answered the question honestly and given doubters a reason to vote against him.

Aggie has made sure of it.

Aggie is fumbling for some paper now. He finds the sheet he wants and says with a new coldness: "Judge, did you say the following words?

What do I think of the theory of strict construction-ism? I think it is more of a political argument than a legal one. And it collapses under scholarly scrutiny. The Constitution was the work of people, not gods. Judges who claim the mantle of strict construction-ism don't strictly adhere to the text, either. All judges live in the real world, apply the law in the real world, and as such they have an obligation to push against the politicization of our legal theories. The idea that the constitution is complete and omniscient, almost biblical, and that judges need do nothing more than apply the facts in the cases against the magic text to arrive at their decisions, well, it is doesn't meet the test of intellectual honesty.

Shit. Brooks does not know where this quotation comes from.

And that is probably the worst thing that can happen. They knew Tucker would pull something. They'd gone through all the documents and cases and quotes predicting what it would be. They didn't have this.

Aggie's team has out-investigated them.

"Judge Madison, do you remember these words, sir?"

Madison looks uncertain.

"To refresh your memory, it is from a seminar lecture you gave on August 2005 at Stanford University, before you became a judge."

Madison looks lost.

"What year, Senator?"

"Two thousand five."

"Yes, senator, I do remember the lecture," Rollie says. "I believe, Senator, that must be from an extemporaneous conversation with students. So I cannot tell if you that is a verbatim quote. But I recall the seminar."

"Well, Judge, if you need something to help your recollection, I have an audio recording of it. Made by one of the students present, who was frankly shocked by your words, and it was obtained by my office. Would you like me to play it, sir?"

Someone in the back of the room, melodramatically gasps, probably a plant acting on cue.

The quotation doesn't reveal anything Madison

hasn't said before. But the idea of a covert recording revealed in a hearing is different.

An audio means replays on cable TV, endlessly, with a transcript scrawling across the bottom. With pictures of Madison looking surprised. It means this will be the moment that people take from the first day of the hearing. It means they have lost the first day. Badly. And it is her fault. This is what she was paid for. To find everything and prepare for it. She has failed.

"No, Senator. That is not necessary. My belief that the academic theory of strict constructionism cannot hold up against the experience of being a judge is well documented. It is not a secret. You needn't have unearthed an audio recording to learn it."

"Needn't I? It seems to me, Judge, you go further here, in this unearthed recording as you put it, than suggest the theory isn't practical. You call judges who believe it intellectually dishonest and political. You accuse them of being ideologues. That group would include, I believe, at least four members of the current Supreme Court, including the chief justice. Do you consider these men intellectually dishonest?"

"With all due respect, Senator . . ."

"Oh, please don't insult me by trying to say that isn't what you said. I can hear as well as you can. You're a smart man, Judge Madison. No doubt about that. But,

when I take these two things together, your denunciation of adherence to the text of the Constitution, and
your theories about how we need to interpret the old law
in new times, it sounds to me that what you have outlined here is a clever excuse for judges doin' just about
anything they want. Now, Judge Madison, I myself was
just a country lawyer. You know, trials for murder, and
robbery, and such, everyday kinds of things. Real-life
law, I think is how you described it. But it sounds like
what you just outlined, in my experience, is the most
astonishing justification of radical judicial activism I
have ever heard, one that that would allow judges to
use courts to extend government into every aspect of
American life. I think this is a revelatory moment. And
I hope our media take note of it. And replay this statement. And replay it again so every American can hear it.
You know, people complain about how Court nominees
come up here and don't level with this committee anymore. They just dodge and weave. Well, you have been
candid over the years. And I admire you for it, sir. Because it reveals who you really are. And I think the only
the difference between you and the most radical activist,
socialist-style judge, is that, being a scholar, a Harvard/
Stanford law professor and all, you've developed a nice
theory to justify your radical judicial activism."

"Senator . . ."

"I think you've answered the question, Judge, thank you."

"Senator Tucker, would you let Judge Madison finish?" interrupts Senator Jonathan Kaplan of New Jersey, the freshman senator who has emerged as a serious new voice, but who used to be a host of a program on Comedy Central.

"He had plenty of time, sir, and I believe you are out of order and that this is my time. You're new here, Senator Kaplan, so perhaps you didn't know."

"Senator, I find . . ." Kaplan tries again.

Chairman Morgan bangs his gavel. "There will be order now. We aren't going down that road, gentlemen. Are you through, Senator Tucker? You have one minute more."

After a pause drawn out longer than necessary for dramatic effect, Tucker says, "Ah, Mr. Chairman. I think I will reserve the remainder of my time and at this moment simply ponder what the judge has said. My mama taught me it was always when you have heard something upsetting to think on it."

The room erupts in laughs and jeers in equal measure.

Brooks looks at Tucker. The senator looks as if he were upset by what Judge Madison has said. Not triumphant. He's a good actor.

Forty-six

5:23 P.M.
Washington, D.C.

Brooks feels repelled by the demagoguery. Of the day, the city, the whole damn system. The feeling has gone in waves, at times replaced by concentration as she has tried to listen, assess the political fallout, and cope with the panic of Democrats and the White House.

In the four hours since Senator Tucker pulled his stunt, they've moved through every senator once except one, and Republicans can smell blood. The questioning of Madison has gotten progressively more malevolent. No one has laid much of a hand on him. They don't have to. Aggie Tucker's stunt took care of that.

And rather than uncovering something meaningful—or tricking Madison into some dreadful utterance—the damn bastard has just done theater, a fabricated pseudo-event, revealing a supposedly covert audio recording, the accompanying charge of hidden radicalism. It's the irony of it that she keeps being struck by, such serious people over such serious things engaging in such fiction. The purity of it makes her feel as if she were new to Washington and watching a hearing for the first time.

Roland Madison's critique of strict construction is a reason for him to be *on* the Court—not kept from it— Brooks thinks. His arguments are an important effort to replace the polarization in public legal arguments with a better approach, she is persuaded. And his ideas have taken root in legal scholarship among conservatives and liberals alike. It is the next big idea. And now a mockery of it is being used against him.

Tucker is not a man who can be dismissed. Not anymore. Not with the way his party has moved. He is a bellwether now, not a crank. He is also a lawyer and former Supreme Court clerk himself.

Chairman Morgan has made things worse, too, by refusing to take an afternoon break. So she and the White House and Madison's Senate backers have had no opportunity to confer except by email and text. There is outrage and worry, and in some quarters self-serving panic. Brooks has reached out to groups supporting Madison and asked them to check in with key senators but not heard much back yet. Everyone is waiting to see how others will react.

A glance between the panicked emails and messages tells her social media is out of control, too, filled equally by people panicked that Madison is doomed and those charging that he is guilty of treason.

Spencer Carr, who left after Madison's opening statement, sent a chilling email: "We need to talk."

Christ, why isn't Rena answering his phone or email?

Only one senator remains to ask questions.

William Stevens. The old liberal, the veteran of more Judiciary hearings than anyone other than Chairman Morgan, who had passed on questioning Madison this morning.

Brooks has frantically been shooting texts and emails to Stevens's staff ever since that happened. They claim they were caught off guard, too. She is sure they are lying.

Stevens, now in his late seventies, can be pretty bad on a bad day. And he seems to be operating on his own agenda.

2:33 P.M.
San Francisco

Focus on the person in front of you, Rena tells himself.
Ignore the constantly vibrating cell phone.

"You said you had questions about Alan Martell's
murder?" William Wellman says.

Bill Wellman had been acting district attorney
during the murder trial of Robert Johnson. Wellman
had worked at the DA's office only briefly, eleven
months. The place had been rocked by a scandal when
the former district attorney got caught in an affair with
one of his lawyers. There were headlines, charges of fa-
voritism, a messy resignation, an even messier divorce.
The mayor asked Wellman to take a leave from private
practice and step in as interim DA.

Wellman is apparently a rare bird—a man with more
political friends than ambitions. After settling things
down at the DA's office, he simply returned to private
practice—seemingly without reward or demand. From
the size of the law offices of Wellington, Knight LLP,
the rewards might be less political, but they were obvious enough.

In slacks and a well-worn sweater, Wellman looks
more gentle and professorial than rich and connected.

Rena would put him near sixty, with dark, intelligent eyes in the middle of a kindly face. There is a mustache, losing a battle from red to gray, that he wears in the shaggy style popular in the 1970s. Rena guesses he grew it in college and hasn't changed it since—a man who finds things and sticks with them. Wellman projects trust.

"This might seem far-fetched. We're checking to see if there's a possible connection between the murders of Alan Martell and Rochelle Navatsky."

Wellman's expression reveals nothing.

"I want to ask you about one case in particular that Navatsky and Martell had together when you were acting DA. The murder trial of Robert Johnson. Martell convicted him of killing a classmate from their high school. You remember the case?"

Rena places a copy of the transcript in front of him.

"Not really." Wellman glances at the document.

"Then tell me what you thought of Alan Martell."

"He was a victim of a bad situation."

"What does that mean?"

"When things are running properly, Mr. Rena, the prosecutors in a city should push the police to be more scrupulous. Attorneys are officers of the court and thereby operate according to more restrictive rules than police. That means they should act as a gravitational pull toward more conscientious police work."

"That wasn't happening?"

"The main pressure at the time was for quick results."

"Doesn't everyone want quick results?"

"This was different. The DA I succeeded had a theory that any case that didn't close in seventy-eight hours would never close."

Wellman picks up a baseball from his desk and tosses it in the air.

"This became a kind of dogma, which led both prosecutors and police to very simple approaches. It was the definition of quick and dirty: Pick the suspect you like most and build the case."

"How does that connect to Alan Martell?"

"Are you a baseball fan, Mr. Rena?"

"A little. I grew up in a town that didn't have a team for a long time."

"In baseball, if you have a young hitter with power, you can ruin him by asking him to hit too many home runs too soon. Better to teach him how to read pitchers and hit to the opposite field. When he has mastered that, his power will be magnified."

"What are you telling me, Mr. Wellman?"

"Alan was a likable guy, with a lot of potential as

a trial lawyer, but he learned too many shortcuts. He learned to rely too much on his likability and the power of the DA's office, the presumption that someone who was arraigned was probably a bad person."

"Is that what happened in this case?"

"I don't remember what happened in this case. You asked me what I thought of Alan Martell."

An idea he cannot quite identify begins to form in Rena's mind.

"What are you looking for, Mr. Rena?"

He's out of time. Out of options. How much is he willing to bet on Wellman? What choice does he have?

"I'm going to level with you. I trust, on behalf of the attorney general and the president, that you will not repeat what I am about to tell you. Hell, I'll hire you so you can't repeat it."

"You don't need to do that, Mr. Rena. I know why you're here. You're working for the White House. You're in charge of Roland Madison's nomination."

Rena takes a breath.

"It wasn't very hard to figure out. A few moments on the Web." Wellman gives Rena a grave look. "What are you really looking for?"

"I need to rule out the possibility that these two murders could be linked," Rena says, "and, if they are, whether it involves anything that pertains to Judge Madison."

Wellman's expression betrays only curiosity, not surprise. A veteran lawyer.

"Do you have reason to think there's some connection?"

"I have to make sure there isn't. And I don't like coincidences."

Wellman picks up the trial transcript and begins to flip through it.

"Who was the lead investigator on the case?"

Watching the lawyer trying to remember even the most basic facts, Rena is struck at how far-fetched it is to think he can resolve this in a day. He should fly home tonight. He needs to be with Madison. He needs to see Vic, who hasn't returned his calls. He could catch the red-eye home.

"Here it is, Calvin P. Smith," Wellman says. He turns to his computer and begins to type. "I don't remember him, but I know who would." He picks up the phone and dials a number he reads out of his computer address book.

"John, Bill Wellman here. I was wondering if you could do me a favor. I am trying to locate a detective, or former detective. He might be retired. He was involved in a case when I was the acting district attorney a few years ago. His name is Calvin Smith. Calvin P."

Rena glances out the window at the Bay Bridge. This view is even better than the one he had seen in Kimmel's office this morning.

"Ah . . . too bad. Okay, thanks, John . . . I'm sorry. . . . Excuse me?"

Wellman's eyes narrow. "Yes, I appreciate it," he says. "Bye, John. Thanks." Wellman ends the call by pushing a button and then slowly hangs up the phone.

"If you don't like coincidences," Wellman says in a dry voice, "you are going to hate this."

"What is it?"

"The lead police investigator was murdered two and a half months ago, the same week, I believe as Rochelle Navatsky. In San Mateo County, just south of the city."

Wellman sees the expression on Rena's face. "If you want to make a phone call, Mr. Rena, feel free to use the conference room next door."

Forty-seven

6:07 P.M.
Washington, D.C.

Senator Stevens begins by fumbling with his reading glasses. "Judge, I want to go back to your exchanges with Senator Tucker concerning how to interpret what is less than clear in the Constitution. Senator Tucker said he found your comments extraordinary and appealed to the media to replay them and he said we should all ponder them. So I'd like to take him up on his offer to do that."

"Yes, sir."

"The Ninth Amendment of the Constitution contains the following statement: 'The enumeration in the Constitution of certain rights shall not be construed to deny or disparage others retained by the people.' What do you think that means?"

"The authors of the Constitution were saying that Americans have rights not mentioned in the Constitution, Senator."

"And when it talks about 'unenumerated' rights," Stevens continues, "how would you, as a Supreme Court justice, determine what those rights are? How do you know what isn't there?"

"That's a critical question. What did the Framers mean by the word *others*? And why were they so vague? I think they used this word *others* purposefully— because they wanted to be expansive, not limiting. I think, at least in this regard, their intent was clear: They wanted the government to inhibit people's lives as little as possible, and they wanted no one to think that the rights named in the Constitution were any more important than, or by implication disparaged, the ones that were not named."

"Ah," Senator Stevens says. "So they are saying that the Constitution is not meant as an all-inclusive document?"

"Correct."

"Because if it were all-inclusive, omniscient, perfect, that would make it limiting?"

"I think there is no other conclusion," Madison

says. "They were worried that people would read the Constitution too literally. They knew they were fallible, that there were things missing. They were even worried about it."

"So, what are judges to do, then, about these other rights that are not enumerated?"

"I think the Framers here are making it clear that judges have to imagine what those 'others' might be."

"And how do judges do that? I mean how do you apply or infer words that aren't there?" Senator Stevens asks.

"You start with the text, for after all, there are many phrases in the text of the Constitution, as in the Fourth Amendment, that suggest that privacy is important, even though privacy isn't mentioned."

"Is that all?"

"You then go back to history and the values that the Framers articulated. And you look to the precedents that have emerged over time. You also look at what life is like at the present as well as in the past. Finally, you think about what a holding one way or the other will mean for the future. Text, history, tradition, precedent, the conditions of life in the past, the present, and a little bit of projection into the future. That, I think, is what the Court has done, and virtually every justice has done, through history. That's not meant to unleash subjective opinions. It's how you search for original intent, which broadly is what all judges must do."

"Is that what you mean by your skepticism of strict constructionism? That you cannot simply apply the text, because, as the text itself says, the Constitution is not all-inclusive?"

"Senator, I think most Americans can understand this from their own lives. Theory is one thing. Real life is another. When we are young, we imagine what it will be like to grow up. And when we grow up, we discover adulthood is different from what we imagined. And your theories have to give way to common sense, to experience, to actually performing a task. I was a scholar for many years. We are paid to theorize, and we do it at universities, at some remove from the problems of everyday life. When you become a judge, you no longer operate at that remove. You have real cases involving real people. That is where the law lives. In real life. The law is designed to help us live. It has no other justification. If it cannot do that, if it operates only theoretically, the law will fail us."

Senator Stevens stares over his half glasses at the nominee, pausing a long time. Why, Brooks wonders? Is he trying to come up with another question? Or is the man trying to decide whether he is done? With Stevens, it is always hard to know what he is thinking.

"You aren't a radical, Judge, are you? You're just the opposite. Calling you a radical is a gimmick, a label, made to scare people or to give ammunition to opinionmongers on TV. You may be one of the most nonpolitical court nominees we've ever had. And one of the most candid. That, I think is what scares some people in this town. I think you are owed an apology today, Judge. And I think you are owed a confirmation by this committee and by the Senate. Senator Upton said you don't have to agree with everything a nominee believes to support him. Well, I don't agree with you on everything, Judge. But sitting here today, I came to the realization that good people shouldn't be destroyed because of disagreements. We are a better country than that. In fact, the ability to disagree and coexist is what our country is all about. Sometimes people in this town just lose their common sense. But, as you say, you have to be practical and forgive them."

Stevens then removes his reading glasses and leans back in his big leather chair.

Brooks sees Aggie Tucker looking at Stevens. Stevens turns, looks over at Tucker, and with a boyish grin, winks at him.

In return, to Brooks's astonishment, Tucker offers Stevens what she could swear looks like a small salute.

Forty-eight

3:55 P.M.
San Francisco

"You got it?"

"I understand," Smolo answers.

Now Smolonsky knows about Calvin Smith. And the fact that they are now trying to triangulate three murders. So Rena can check at least that task off the growing list of disasters.

Did Martell, Navatsky, and Smith have any other cases in common? If not, then whoever killed them probably had some connection to the trial of Robert Johnson.

"Lean on the police," Rena tells Smolonsky. "They

haven't looked at these cases together before. But don't mention who the judge was."

"There comes a point, Peter, when we won't be able to keep that lid on."

"We don't have to lift it off, Walt."

Rena hangs up and checks the time. Almost 7:00 P.M. on the East Coast. Madison's confirmation hearings may be over for the day.

He should call Brooks. And probably Spencer Carr. But not yet.

He could tell people don't feel good about Johnson's murder trial. It isn't clear to him, though, whether Johnson was guilty—or innocent.

"You okay?" Wellman asks when Rena returns.

"We still off the record?"

Wellman waves his hand: Stop worrying.

"If someone were systematically killing people involved in the Robert Johnson case, someone who thought Johnson was innocent, who might that be?"

"While you were making that phone call, I made a couple of calls of my own. Discreetly," Wellman adds.

There isn't anything Rena can do about it now. "Find anything?"

"Johnson had friends who were gang members. It could be one of them. He had uncles who were involved in crime. It could be one of them. He also had a brother who was in prison."

"I need to find out more about Calvin Smith's murder."

"I still have friends in the police department."

Wellman hands Rena some documents sent to him in the last few minutes. Police files.

"You wouldn't have been able to get these so easily on your own."

"Why are you helping?"

"This case was under my charge. If we got it wrong, I'm responsible, too."

"What makes you think it was wrong?"

"I don't know that it was. But if someone is trying to kill the people involved, I'd like to know. And I know Rollie Madison," Wellman adds. "If anyone deserves to be on the Supreme Court . . ."

Another Madison admirer.

In the cab to his hotel, Rena turns on his phone. He has 317 messages and 43 phone calls.

What has happened?

Brooks isn't answering her phone. She must be in post-hearing meetings with the White House and Madison.

But the text messages from her are clear enough: You need to come home.

Rena finds his assistant O'Brien, who books him on the red-eye at 10:30. He can eat at the airport, read the file on Smith, call Brooks, maybe Carr, and check in again with Smolonsky before boarding.

He tries to sort out what's occurred by checking websites via his phone. There are accounts of questioning by Aggie Tucker and an audio recording by a Stanford student. And some counter-questions by Senator Stevens. The stories are fragmented. Whatever had occurred in the hearing apparently is proving hard for reporters to process in real time.

At the airport, Rena finds a place to eat with a television turned to news. Deborah Cutter is debating Josh Albin. They're on the cable channel with a largely Republican audience.

"He talked about the rule of law. He talked about precedent. He talked about humility," Cutter says.

"This man is a radical, a secret member of a terrorist cell in college who engaged in crimes against the military, who is on the record holding the Court's most esteemed members in contempt as intellectually dishonest. This is the most dangerous man to be nominated to the Supreme Court since William O. Douglas, who was a socialist."

"Josh, I've known you a long time, but you're becoming unhinged."

"I would expect nothing less from you, Deborah, than challenging my sanity. That is what the Soviets used to do to dissidents."

People seem to be fraying.

Rena orders something to eat, a bad taco salad, and as much water as he can drink. A vodka martini would not go well with a plane ride.

Finally Brooks calls back. "You picked today to be off the grid? Where are you?"

"The airport. Flying home. I'll be back in the morning."

"I need you here. We messed up. Tucker's people found an audio recording of a Madison lecture at Stanford we didn't have."

"Was there anything new in it?"

"No. Another denunciation of strict constructionism. But that doesn't matter. Tucker made it seem like a revelation."

"How much are we hurt?"

"That's what I'm trying to sort out. The Left is in an uproar, maybe because they think they can dump Madison. And the Right thinks they might have hurt Nash.

"The only person who had his wits about him was William Stevens," she says. "He helped repair some of the damage. And he endorsed Madison today. Strongly."

The old senator knows the fundamentals, Rena thinks: All political battles are symbolic. He couldn't leave Madison undefended on the issue.

"Peter, I don't know if we're going to make it," Brooks says. "I need you back here."

"We have another problem," he says.

"Sure. Bring it on," she says, sounding punch drunk. "I'll solve everyone's problems."

"Randi."

He wonders for a moment if he should wait to tell her about Calvin Smith. Does he really think someone is out there killing people? And that it might be over a case that Madison adjudicated and possibly muffed? She sounds like she is on the edge, trying to hold everything together.

"Tell me, Peter," she says. He walks through how there are three people dead. And he needs to talk to Madison.

"Christ. Get back here," she commands.

"I'm on my way."

Then his phone is ringing again. The lawyer Bill Wellman.

"I just received a phone call about the Johnson case from a reporter. Someone named Gary Gold. He is onto the same question you are, Mr. Rena. I did not share information with him."

Everywhere he turns Gold is there.

They'd barely thwarted him on the Berkeley story. He must have pivoted to Martell. He's got to be at least a day behind them, or they'd have picked up more sign of his trail.

Gold would also call for comment if he were ready to write. And he hasn't. Nor is the reporter among the 317 emails.

But Gold's presence represents another level of threat. If something *did* connect the murders of three people involved in the Johnson murder trial, Gold would connect it just as he and Smolo have. And he would look at the case in the most negative light.

That is one concern, a practical one.

The other is more obscure, but in some ways it bothers Rena more. Something about this case haunts Madison. Rena had sensed it a week ago in Madison's reaction to Martell being killed. It's why he had sent Smolo out here. He saw it again Friday night. It's why Rena had come to California, too. Now three murders.

He has to talk to Madison. Face-to-face.

A weary older couple next to him paw wordlessly at airport hamburgers. Their exhaustion makes him feel his own.

Should he call Carr? No, there is apparently enough anxiety in the White House about whatever happened in the hearings. He wonders what Carter White may have unearthed about rot inside Rena and Brooks's office.

He dials another number.

Senator Llewellyn Burke answers on the second ring. Only a few people have the number to his cell.

"I need a favor, Senator. I need to have tomorrow's hearings postponed. It's critical that the hearing not resume first thing tomorrow morning. At a minimum, not until the afternoon."

Burke is not on Judiciary, but he and Senator Morgan are friends. He could ask the chairman for this and get it. But it couldn't come from the White House. Politically that would be too damaging.

"Peter, today was a difficult day for Judge Madison. A postponement would not benefit his chances. Why do you want this?"

Whatever he tells Burke, the senator would have to share with Senator Morgan. Which means it could leak.

"It's not a political matter, sir."

"You're not going to tell me?"

"No, sir."

Burke is silent on the other end for what seems like minutes.

"Peter, you can't postpone these hearings more than a couple of hours," the senator says at last. "Not after today."

"Even a few hours would help."

"I will see what I can do."

Rena hangs up, closes his eyes, and takes a deep breath. The tired couple has left.

He calls Smolonsky. He needs to tell his investigator that he's returning to Washington. "Have you seen Johnson's mother?"

"Tomorrow morning."

Like old police, they slide into comparing notes on Calvin Smith's murder. He'd been bludgeoned with a rock while fishing. Police had nothing. No DNA. The trail went cold right away. Smith had become something of a bitter drunk in retirement.

"All three of these murders share one thing: no clues," Rena says.

"Which could be a coincidence."

"Or a sign of a skillful killer," Rena says.

"Who did these victims know in common who was a skillful killer?"

"That's one place to look," Rena answers.

"Pete, there's another thing."

"What?"

"If it is one killer, he's changing. Getting more violent."

"He's starting to like it," Rena says.

Rena wakes to the sound of the pilot announcing final approach. The red-eye from San Francisco arrives at Washington Dulles International Airport in Virginia at 6:15 A.M.

The airport is a waking village, workers pulling up store grates, turning on grills for cooking breakfasts, filling bakery displays. Rena waits till 6:30 to call Madison.

"Did I wake you?"

"I was going for a run."

"Not this morning. Meet me at my house in an hour."

He calls Brooks from the cab. Morgan had postponed the start of the hearings until 11:00 A.M., she says, which is helpful. The White House had scheduled a strategy meeting in the Old EOB at 8:00. Can he be there?

So Burke succeeded, and the delay wasn't so long that it might signify panic.

"I'll probably be late," he says. He needs to see Madison first, he explains. So the Judge will be late, too.

"Tell me about this other killing," Brooks says.

He fills her in with more details about the murder of Calvin Smith.

"Jesus, you think someone is killing people involved in this case?"

"It's a possibility."

"Have you told Carr?"

"I want to talk to Madison first."

"I'll take care of talking to Spencer," she says. "He's already so angry with me I think it's better if I absorb the fury for both of us."

"I'm sorry I wasn't here yesterday."

"We've got more important things to worry about at the moment than my feelings," she says. "But thanks."

At home Rena intends to shower but lies down for a moment. Ten minutes later the doorbell wakes him. He is asleep in the clothes he put on yesterday morning. At the door, Madison holds a large coffee in each hand.

"A peace offering," the judge says with a wan smile.

They sit at the small breakfast table in Rena's kitchen, a nook bathed in light overlooking a small patio. Madison makes uncharacteristic small talk about the weather back home in California, whether Rena saw the hearings.

"No, but I talked with Randi."

"She's worried," Madison says, more a question than a statement.

"That's why she's so good, Judge."

"Yes, she is the methodical one," Madison jokes.

Rena's stomach isn't ready for the coffee.

"Aren't you curious why I called?"

"I was waiting for you to tell me."

There is no preparation for this. No long interrogation path.

"Alan Martell and Rochelle Navatsky are not the only ones you know who have been murdered. So was the chief police investigator in one of the cases they had before you, the murder trial of Robert Johnson. The police officer was named Calvin Smith. All three murders are unsolved."

Madison lifts his head back and closes his eyes.

"My God."

"Judge," Rena says after a moment, "I think you'd better tell me about the trial of Robert Johnson."

Forty-nine

Madison's recall is almost photographic. Rena feels as if he is seeing for the first time how the famous scholar's mind really works.

"I had been a judge six months, and it was already my third murder trial. I was discovering, after decades of being a law professor and a law school dean, just how different criminal law was in theory than in practice. And how ugly that difference was."

Madison's eyes are fixed past Rena on something in the patio outside.

"Whenever I think of the trial, I think of the third day. There was a moment, when Rochelle Navatsky was thumbing through papers looking for some lost document. Two large dark stains of perspiration began to spread out on her silk blouse. She mumbled something about begging the 'court's indulgence.' I knew at that moment Johnson had no chance."

"What had happened?"

"Nothing in particular. She'd simply lost her place for a moment. She reminded me of a first-year law student, someone who is talented but too nervous to stay out of her own way. She'd probably be a fine lawyer someday. But right then she was panicking. It annoyed and confused the jury."

Madison's eyes find Rena's.

"She was also very self-conscious of her looks, and she compensated by dressing like a prison matron. The jury hated her."

"And Martell?"

"He was winning and he knew it. He was a mediocre lawyer, but he had a kind of everyman charm that connected with the jury. That seemed to make Navatsky even more panicky."

"Was Johnson guilty?"

"Robbie Johnson?"

Madison leans his head back.

"He was not sympathetic. He was a sullen eighteen-year-old, physically awkward. He had a kind of twisted mouth, some mild disfigurement. Mostly he was in shock. He looked at his own lawyer as if they were strangers."

Madison's expression melts into sadness. "He wore the same polyester suit to court every day. It was the wrong size. He looked like a sinner dressed for church."

"And was he guilty?" Rena asks again.

Madison shakes his head as if the question were irrelevant.

"The prosecution had two things going for it. A theory that fit the facts: Morrison was a cheerleader, vivacious, good student, social, popular, pretty. Johnson was a loner, quiet, on the edge of trouble. The evidence was clear he had become obsessed with her, wrote about her in diaries, had a collection on his computer of pictures of her. All of which might well have been innocent, but could have been stalking. And Johnson had no alibi.

"The other thing Martell had going for him was confidence. He didn't care about the weaknesses in his case. He didn't think they mattered to the jury. So he laid it on thick, like slopping paint over a crack to make it look as if it's disappeared."

"Why didn't Navatsky plead out?"

"I wondered. There could be lots of reasons. A skilled defense lawyer could have shredded Martell. She was trying. She didn't know how."

"And why didn't you do something?" Rena asks.

Madison pauses.

"You know what I learned during this trial? I discovered how common a problem it is for judges to oversee two bad lawyers. Bench judges talk about it constantly."

Madison's gaze is fixed on something outside again.

"I even raised it during a monthly lunch we had of the judges. What did they do when both lawyers were bad?"

"What did they say?"

"Bromides mostly. That 'it's the worst.' That 'you can't try the case for both sides.' 'Take two Advil.'"

"Not very helpful," Rena says. This story is leading somewhere. Rena needs to let Madison get there.

"Some of the advice was more thoughtful. They told me that there's a lot judges can't know. Lawyers have strategies in mind that a judge may not recognize. What might look like a mistake may be a lawyer trying to avoid exposing some other, more damaging hole in their case. A judge intervening can actually make things worse.

"Someone even told the old joke about a lawyer asking to see a judge in chambers and saying, 'I don't mind if you try my case, Judge, just don't lose it for me.'"

"So bad lawyers are a joke?"

"No," Madison says, almost in a whisper. "They're a bruise, a flaw in the system, a source of contention. At the lunch, it turned into argument. Someone said that judges presiding over bad lawyering should lean more toward protecting the rights of defendants, because the power of the state was always stacked against them. He was shot down by someone more senior who said judges are there to protect the law, not the defendant or the prosecution. Which, of course, is the textbook answer."

"Is that what you did with Robbie Johnson? Protect the law?"

Madison doesn't answer. He isn't finished with the story.

"My closest friend among the judges was a woman named Elizabeth Labow. She was a bright star on that bench. She didn't offer an opinion, but she asked the senior judge, a man named Sam Weiss, what he thought."

"And what did he say?"

"He said he wasn't sure you *could* protect the law. But he thought you could protect the trial process. Like a boxing referee, you can try to make sure it's a fair fight, even with bad lawyers, but you can't guarantee it will be a good one."

"You don't think this was a fair fight, though, do you? Or a good one?"

Madison looks at Rena.

"A judge's hands are supposed to be tied. You can set aside a guilty verdict and let the boy go free, available for retrial if the police find new evidence. But almost no judge would. It would be extraordinary. The only way a judge could overturn a guilty verdict in a case like this is if he knew with certainty the boy was innocent."

"Rollie, what did you do wrong?"

Fifty

No one gets to Senate confirmation without every minute detail of his or her life scrutinized. Everything public is found—every trial, every press clipping, every public statement. And nothing untoward had surfaced in the Johnson trial transcript. If there were anything there, Brooks's team or the White House—or conservative groups opposing the nomination—would have found it.

They had not found anything.

Yet someone might be engaging in revenge killings over Robert Johnson's conviction. That means eventually somebody else, probably Gary Gold, is going to take another look at that trial.

And something about this case nags at the judge.

Whatever Madison is hiding, Rena has to find it now before the hearings go any further.

"Do you think Johnson was innocent?" Rena says again.

"What I thought didn't matter. It was a jury trial. The judge doesn't determine guilt."

Rena stands up.

"Well, that's great. You may have presided over an innocent man going to jail because it wasn't your job to worry about it. You were only the judge."

"That's the way the system works, Peter."

"Most Americans don't know that."

Rena stops pacing.

"Rollie, there is a reporter a half step behind me on this. If he connects these murders and starts to wonder why someone is taking revenge for Johnson, the nuances about jurist prudence and the role of judges won't much matter. The story will be how an embattled Supreme Court nominee presided over the conviction of an innocent man."

The two men match stares.

"It's the most frustrating thing a judge faces," Madison says, looking away. "A terrible crime and a weak case. Both lawyers were bad, for different reasons."

"Whatever happened to 'better to let a thousand guilty men go free rather than send an innocent one to jail'?"

Madison smiles wearily. "Blackstone's Ratio."

"What?"

"That's Blackstone's Ratio. And the line is better that 'ten guilty persons escape than that one innocent suffer.'"

"God damn it, Rollie! Did you send an innocent man to jail?"

Madison stands up. "Do you know how many innocent people are convicted each year in the United States, Peter? Even if it's just one percent—and that *is* the academic estimate—that's more than ten thousand a year. Each year. A hundred thousand every decade."

Rena moves to the table and tries a swallow of coffee, but he's still not ready for it.

"Ten thousand people, Peter, wrongly convicted annually. And, of course, most of them are poor and most of them are people of color. I didn't mention that in the hearings yesterday, by the way."

Madison is pacing now.

"Oh, and, of course, let's not mention that the problem is getting worse, because we lock up about triple the number we did thirty years ago."

Rena feels the weight of his exhaustion begin to

make him dizzy. He rubs his face, trying to massage the tingling sensation away.

"What happened during that trial, Rollie?"

"What happens in most trials? The forensics is vague. The police work is imperfect. The eyewitness testimony is weak. The people who can't afford good lawyers suffer most. If you think rich people get better medical care, multiply it by ten for the legal system."

Rena is certain none of this made it into the idealized depiction of the American legal system Madison offered the Judiciary Committee yesterday, either.

"Probably every bench judge in America has overseen sending an innocent person to jail, and most don't even know it."

Suddenly Rena knows what Madison is hiding.

It isn't that Johnson was innocent or that Madison suspects some connection between the Martell and Navatsky murders.

It is something *Madison* had done.

"You think you mishandled the trial. Something haunts you."

Madison opens the patio door and walks outside. Rena follows him.

"I've never said this to anyone before, not even Vic," Madison says, turning to face Rena.

"Said what, Rollie?"

"I did everything a judge is supposed to do and a man who *clearly had not* been proven guilty by law went to prison anyway. And then died there."

"I don't understand."

"What bothered me is that this was entirely acceptable. No, not acceptable, expected. Demanded. The jury decides. The judge presides. Almost every bench judge would have done exactly as I did. Except I knew Robbie Johnson was not guilty as a matter of law."

"What does that mean?"

"It means that I couldn't see a way to act as a judge is expected to and worry about justice at the same time. And, you're right, that haunts me. It means that what we tell our judges to do struck me then and strikes me now as inadequate. And this wasn't theoretical. I saw those people in front of me. A car wreck of a trial. And I have never figured out entirely how to reconcile that."

Madison sits down on a patio chair. He looks utterly weary.

Rena sits down next to him.

"I've pondered it many times, just to myself. But if I were a bench judge now, that trial would have been different. I would push the limits. Not simply ensure the fight is fair. I would do everything I could to see that the treatment of the victim and the defendant both were just."

"You would have directed the verdict?"

"No. The system won't allow that. But I would have made the lawyers better. Made the trial better. I would find a way to tell that prosecutor that his case was weak, to scare him into not being lazy. I would bring the defense counsel in with her co-counsel and tell them that they couldn't train Navatsky at Johnson's expense. It means I would find some cracker-jack defense attorney in town and force that lawyer to help out on the case. It means I would do whatever the system allowed me to do, not just what it expected me to do. Seven years ago I was learning how judges and police and prosecutors and defense attorneys behaved. I hadn't learned how they could behave."

Madison looks down at the ground, as if he were praying.

"I didn't know about Calvin Smith. And it never occurred to me that Alan Martell's murder or Rochelle Navatsky's might have anything to do with the Johnson trial."

But they almost certainly do, Rena thinks. The only thing Navatsky, Martell, and Smith had in common was Robbie Johnson.

And now someone is killing them. Killing everyone involved.

The thought of it jars Rena. He pulls out his phone and calls Hallie Jobe, the ex–FBI agent from his firm. She could be there sooner.

Fifty-one

Vic has come to love the C&O Canal. She can run
north along the Potomac into Maryland one way,
or downriver toward the city and the Kennedy Center
the other. Either is one of the most beautiful spots in
the city. The terrain is flatter than the hilly trails back
home and makes for a more liberating run.

She slows down at Thirty-First Street. She always
walks the last two blocks to cool down, then does some
stretches before heading back inside.

She has run well today, her body loose, the run
easy—a day when you imagine you could run for
hours.

She hadn't begun that way. But in the first mile, she felt a kind of elation, the tension of the day before melting away like snow after a storm. She isn't just worried about her dad's nomination. She is angry—with her father for keeping things from Peter, with Peter for the way he has acted, and with herself, for not doing more to help Randi and Peter help her father.

She has stronger feelings for Peter than she expected. She isn't entirely clear what they are.

"M . . . m . . . mornin', ma'am."

Hubert, the utility man who works at the Elmwood Apartments, where she and her father are staying, is pulling tools out of his van. They exchange pleasantries, as they do most mornings. He has become something of an unexpected pal. He has a slow, courtly manner, seems undaunted by his slight stutter, and takes pleasure in being kind—a southern thing, she thinks. She has spent so little time around the rest of the country.

"S . . . s . . . s . . . aw your dad on TV. He looked good. Tell him I . . . I . . . I'm rooting for him."

"Hubert, if he has won you over, he has nothing to worry about."

"Well, he's the o . . . o . . . only judge I know. So course I'm for him."

Vic climbs the stairs to the second-floor apartment, walks through the living room to the kitchen, and towels off. She could use some water, and needs to cool down for a few minutes before she showers.

She has no idea when her father will be back, and she's apprehensive about him being gone. Peter calling her dad after taking a red-eye, needing to see him right away—everything in Washington seems urgent. Maybe it is. Everything you do seems to be on C-SPAN.

The doorbell rings. Maybe Dad is back. Did he forget his keys?

"Hi, Hubert."

"'Scuse me, ma'am. You, uh, you know how I said I had to check the water usage? I know it's mornin'. But, well, I've got to leave early today. I wonder if I could do it now. Just get it done. The m . . . m . . . meter is in the closet in the hall."

She was planning to shower, but she can have breakfast first.

"Of course, come in."

The legs of Hubert's baggy overalls rubbing against each other make a swooshing sound as he heads down the hall to the meter near the bathroom. Vic begins to make coffee and assemble fruit for breakfast.

"Where's your father?"

"Hubert? Excuse me?"

"When's he coming back?"

Hubert is in the kitchen. His voice is strange.

"I don't know. Why?"

Hubert moves toward her, closer than she is comfortable with. She begins to think she should say something.

His expression hardens. Before she can decide how to react, he brings his right hand up behind her head and grabs her hair at the back of her neck. He pulls her hair down, forcing her face upward.

The surprise of it doesn't quite register in her mind. Hubert, this friendly man she has known every day for almost a month, has her by the hair. She can feel it pulling underneath his leather work gloves.

"When's he coming back?" The stutter is gone.

"I don't know!" she says.

"Come on," he commands.

Come on where? He is dragging her down the hall by her hair. She can feel hair pulling out of her scalp.

Then fear jolts into awareness and she kicks her legs out wide, trying to catch something along the hallway wall. The more she kicks, the harder he pulls and the more she feels her scalp tearing.

It takes forever to reach the bathroom at the end of the hall. He is filling the tub. He is going to drown her in it. Drown her in the bath. She is going to die here.

"Hubert, don't."

"Shut up."

On the sink, four neatly torn pieces of duct tape are hanging in a row.

With his free hand, he puts one piece of tape over her eyes, a second one over her mouth. The sudden blackness makes her heart feel as if it were tightening in her chest.

What she felt before, in the hall—in her whole life up to now—is not fear like this. This is something tangible, something liquid.

"Do you feel this?" he says.

It's a knife against her neck. She nods.

"You struggle, I'll slit your throat."

She feels the blade move away. Then he lets go of her hair, takes hold of her wrists, and yanks her arms back behind her—hard. She feels duct tape winding around her wrists.

She pictures the scene in her mind, as if she were floating above it. She sees herself, in her running shorts and tank top, standing in the corner, her back against the towel rack in the bathroom facing the sink. He has pushed her there, against the wall, to steady her. She is blindfolded, muzzled, and tied at the wrists.

"Who's in charge now?" he says. "Who's the judge now?"

She begins to cry and can feel the tears leaking underneath the duct tape. He pushes her down, so she is now sitting on the bathroom floor. Oh, God, she thinks, don't kill me.

Then he stops.

She can sense him still standing over her. But she can hear nothing. What's happening?

Something has distracted him. A sound? She isn't sure.

But an opportunity. She tries to kick.

"Don't do that," he says. His voice doesn't sound panicked, merely irritated.

He puts his hands on her throat and pushes down. He has put the knife down somewhere.

"Stop it now and I won't kill you."

She starts to kick him harder, pummeling bicycle kicks.

What happens next occurs slowly, as if she were underwater. He punches her very hard in the face. And she feels everything that comes next perfectly: The push of his fist against her flesh down to her bone. The back of her head hitting the tile floor. The recoil of her neck bouncing up from the tile.

She can't believe how slowly time begins to move. It would be wonderful if things seemed to move this way all the time. You can appreciate everything so much more. At this speed life is experienced in a heightened, adrenal consciousness—as if, at last, for the first time, she were using her whole mind. She hears a pounding and wonders if it is the sound of her own heart. She hears a voice, but she does not know whose or where it's from, or whether it's even real. She sees a scene surrounded by dark, like a movie. Is she dreaming? Is she sleeping? If it were a dream, wouldn't recognizing the dream mean you are waking up?

A thick, dark veil begins to slide over her mind. It is heavy and at the same time weightless. And the dark seems absolute.

"Victoria! Vic!"

She shoulders the door open, smashing the doorjamb.

"Vic, it's Hallie Jobe!"

It had taken Jobe only minutes to get here since Rena called. Her town house is a few blocks away.

No one in is the kitchen, but the milk is out on the counter. Someone making breakfast interrupted.

"Vic!"

Gun drawn.

Living room?

Hallway?

Bedroom?

Another bedroom?

At the end of the hall is a bathroom door that's closed. "Vic!"

Jobe looks down the hall and her training tells her she has limited options. If someone were going to shoot her through the door they might have fired already. The hallway is too narrow for her to come at it from an angle. She just needs to move quickly. And create some distraction. She screams a banshee yell and kicks full force near the door handle.

Vic is lying on the floor, bound, gagged, and not moving.

She moves to her. "Vic?"

Look for a wound or signs of strangulation.

Then, vaguely, she senses motion behind her. Her mind registers an indistinct object.

Someone hiding in the shower. Swinging something.

Not one body now, but two. He looks down at the woman who came down the hall. Blood trickling from the scalp.

Truth is he was lucky. Woman had a gun. Could have gone differently.

Time to go. If this one came so could others.

Pick up the tools and walk to the van like there was nothing going on. Clear head.

The walk is an eternity.

And he is limping. When the daughter started kicking she caught him once in the thigh.

He sees no one.

He opens the back door, puts the tools in, and takes a breath. His mind seems locked in fourth gear. Breathing too fast.

Take a couple of long inhales.

Then he realizes: This is the end of it.

After more than a year of planning and then doing it. The longest he's ever worked on anything in his life.

Done and done. Can't come back. Can't do the judge. Whatever he thought he was gonna do, he's done it.

One thing he knows for sure: He is never going to prison again.

He's imagined plenty about what comes next. That he will disappear to Mexico or someplace before anyone pieces together that the killings are connected, then write his mother and tell her the truth. Then people would know that Robbie was really innocent. Because if someone has done all this for him, well, then he must be.

And maybe they would think on vengeance and justice. And think he is not the disappointment everyone always said.

Other times he's imagined telling no one anything. He will just disappear and no one will connect it all. Just three killings. Or five. Just more mystery. No meaning to it. And he'll be free.

Mostly he's wondered what Mama will think. If she knew the truth, she would say she doesn't understand. You can't make a wrong thing right with another wrong thing. Quote the Bible. But in time? With people talking? Some would quote other parts of the Bible. Say, it is really something, isn't it, what he did?

Either way, he can't get caught. Then she would only be more unhappy.

When Robbie was arrested, then convicted, then killed, Mama just dried up. She had always been the one talking about hope. And after he died, she didn't do it anymore. Because she hadn't any hope left. She had poured it all into Peanut and then it was used up.

It isn't like he and Peanut were close. They were so different it was hard to believe they were brothers. But he loved him. And now he has proven it.

One moment kept coming back to him all those years when he was inside. The first time he was arrested, when he was seventeen and Peanut was eleven. When he finally got home, after being arraigned and spending a night in jail, Peanut just cried. Momma was there, too, looking like he had stabbed her or something. And he looked at Peanut, so small and weak, it made him angry. Whimpering, like a girl. Weaker than a girl. It made him boil.

"Stop crying."

Robbie turned away from him and kept whimpering.

"Stop crying, damn it."

Robbie's crying only made it worse. It only made their mother feel worse. It only made James look worse.

So he hit Robbie.

The boy went down and lay there in the fetal position.

"Get up."

But he kept crying and kept lying there.

"If I end up in prison, you've got to be the man. Understand?"

Mama ran to him and grabbed him. "Oh, please, please, please stop." Wailing, tears, holding his arms. "Please! Jimmy James, please." Her wailing and Robbie whimpering. He had stomped out that night and not come back for three days.

The memory haunts him. Of all his regrets, of all the bad things he's done, all the ways he has disappointed people, that one picture, that moment, keeps coming back.

He closes the back doors of the van and takes another deep breath. Once he's behind the wheel, he stops for a second and closes his eyes. Too much gone down. Too much to take in. Then he turns the motor over, puts the van in gear, and drives.

Fifty-two

R ena sees Jobe's car and pulls the Camaro in next to it.

Jobe could get here sooner. That's why he'd called her.

In the passenger seat next to him, Madison is silent. Rena has said nothing other than that they had to get back here. He didn't need to. He swings open his door and is about to move at a run when he stops.

"Go into the apartment, Rollie," Rena says coolly. "And be ready to call 911."

"You're not coming?"

"Check the apartment. And be ready to call 911. Go!"

Rena switches the Camaro back on and watches Madison run toward the apartment.

As they had pulled in, he'd recognized the face, behind the wheel of a white van. A face from the file Wiley and Lupsa had given him. A police photo, side and front. The face in the photo was younger, and angrier, but the same face now. Robert Johnson's brother, James.

The two men had locked eyes a moment as the van was pulling out, and Rena sensed James Johnson had recognized him, too—though Rena had no memory of ever seeing Johnson before.

He had a look Rena had seen in combat. Mortal rage mixed with fear.

In the weeks he's been pretending to be Hubert, he has thought a lot about what to do if he had to run. The white van stolen in California would be a liability, slow, poor handling. So he worked something out, an escape plan.

He needs it now. Especially, he thinks, because the guy in the car recognized him.

The streets in the oldest part of Georgetown by the river are a maze. Some are just a block or two long. He has walked them all, looking at every angle, until he could see them in his mind, draw a map from memory.

He will head right into the maze, with all the short turns, and try to get out of sight of any car tracking him. He's even figured a route, the way out, like Bird taught him.

He pulls out of the parking lot behind the apartment onto Jefferson and makes a right, down the hill to K Street under the freeway.

K is so old it has rail tracks and cobblestones peeking through the blacktop. He goes just one block and makes a right, glancing in the rearview mirror as he slows. He sees the tip of the Camaro getting to K Street one block behind him. Did the Camaro see him turn?

Now his maze begins.

Just a few feet up there is a little alley, South Street or something. A left there.

If he can get through the alley unseen, he is out to another street, a main street, sometimes jammed with cars, Wisconsin Avenue. If it's crowded, that would screw him up. But if it's clear, he only needs to travel on it about thirty feet and then he can cut right onto another alley, take it for a block, and turn again. He would be making a circle. By then, he should have lost the Camaro if he hasn't already. And he could head out on K toward the bridges and Virginia and be gone.

It's early in the morning. Streets should be pretty clear. A glance back for the Camaro. Nothing.

But there is a guy in the alley dumping garbage, and he has to slow down for him.

C'mon. To the corner. Get to the corner.

The big street is clear.

He pushes it and is able to make a hard right onto the second alley, head back, and circle around.

He is through the second alley, right on Thirty-First Street, then down to K Street. If he has lost the guy, he is only two blocks from a freeway.

As he gets to K, left or right? Is he clear? Can he make the left? He glances back.

And sees the tip of the Camaro. He veers the van to the right.

The van swerves a little as it enters K Street, as if the driver intended to turn left and then changed his mind and turned right. Away from the freeway. Back to the river. Down K street is a dead end.

Rena presses the Camaro, double footing, racing technique, left foot on the brake, right on the accelerator, to power around the corner to get onto K Street. He can see the white van bouncing down the last vestiges of K Street underneath the Key Bridge.

The van is going to run out of road. It disappears through a small tunnel underneath the old bridge. He points the Camaro down the cobbled road and the big engine pushes the car forward with a rush.

At the end of the road the van is stopped. Beyond it,

a figure in work overalls is running. Rena stops behind the van to block its escape, jumps out, and begins to chase.

Beyond the end of the road are docks on the Potomac used by the crew teams from local colleges and high schools. Past the boathouses is a path that runs alongside the river. At a certain point the path diverges from the river and hugs the road. Though they are still in the city, if the guy in the overalls manages to get to the river at that point he could get away.

In a few hundred feet, the man in front of him turns off the path into the bush toward the river. The bush is thick and Rena can see only a few feet ahead. But he can hear the brush of the legs of the cotton overalls chafing against each other as Johnson runs.

He is bashing through the thicket to the river.

Fifty-three

Rena stopped loving guns a long time ago. There is only one reason to have one. And he had left that part of his life behind.

Something in the man's motion makes him wish he had one now. A slowing, then a reaching into the pocket of his overalls. A handgun comes out. A Glock 22. The kind of gun Jobe owns. The man is changing from pursued to pursuer.

Before the motion is complete, Rena dives into him and they tumble into the river.

The Potomac here is only two or three feet deep but frigid, even in June.

They thrash at each other from their knees, slowed by the wet and the cold and made clumsy by the mud.

They grope for control of the dark metal in Johnson's hand.

Then they pull each other down. They are on their sides, facing each other, their noses and mouths submerged, their legs tangled, a cold, stinging, slow-motion wrestling. They are drowning each other.

Johnson has hold of the gun, but Rena has both the man's wrists in his grip. He extends his leg and finds Johnson's foot and pushes, splaying Johnson's legs. He lifts himself and pins Johnson under him beneath the water.

Johnson bends his head up for the air, and when he cannot hold it there he begins to thrash, shaking his head back and forth.

Rena stares into his eyes, and the two men exchange a moment of strange, frightful intimacy: one man watching another decide his mortality.

Then Rena thinks a terrible thought. If Johnson is alive, so is his story. He isn't just a killer. He is also in his own mind at least an avenger of injustice, or so he could claim.

Rena begins to push Johnson beneath the water. His mouth. Then his nose. Then his face disappears into the dark.

No one would know.

Beneath him, Johnson begins to buck, kicking, twisting, panicking. And finally weakening.

Rena watches. And then slowly loosens the pressure on Johnson's wrists and releases him.

Johnson pushes himself up just enough to breathe. He begins to cough. He lifts himself onto his elbows.

The mud droplets on his face look like tears.

Then he lifts Jobe's Glock 22 from the dark water and points it at Rena's head.

Fifty-four

The door of the apartment is open, the doorjamb broken.

He doesn't yell out. But in the hall, after checking the small living room, Roland Madison sees Hallie Jobe's legs sticking out of the bathroom.

Oh, God. Victoria?

Halfway down the hall he sees her body behind Jobe's on the bathroom floor, lying next to the tub.

Oh, my God. No. No!

What have I done?

There is blood coming from a wound on the back of Jobe's head.

Madison steps past the still figure of Jobe to check his daughter. She isn't moving.

Please, he thinks, please.

He will need to check now for signs of life. This is the first question they will ask when he calls 911.

He kneels, his knees on the cold porcelain tile, and leans over to feel for a pulse. Whatever he finds, he must do it for Jobe as well.

Brooks wonders why Rena hasn't called. What did Madison have to say? She is sitting in a conference room in the Old EOB listening to the metallic voices of worried White House staffers. Eleven people in suits trying to create a strategy for events they cannot control. They are grateful the hearings were delayed this morning. The White House is under the impression the postponement was at Chairman Morgan's request.

No one on the White House team seems to be giving up on Rollie, she is relieved to hear. But the White House thinks he is wounded. "He needs to have a good second day," the White House counsel, George Rawls, warns. "We need to pick up where Senator Stevens left off."

What Morgan did was a cheap trick. "But what matters is what happens today," Rawls says.

Where is Judge Madison? Why isn't he here?

If unarmed and facing a gun in close combat, Rena had been trained, always charge. Toward the weapon, not away from it. The shooter's reflex will be to pull the weapon back and turn the barrel slightly to the outside.

Rena propels himself, angling his arm at the gun hand, almost reaching it when the shot goes off.

He feels his flesh tear and his shoulder burn. But his momentum carries him into Johnson's body and knocks the man backward into the river.

The fatal, ironic reflex in drowning is panic. When a person submerged underwater begins to experience it, they gasp for air. The gasp allows water to begin to fill the lungs. A drowning person loses consciousness prior to death. Unless a heart attack occurs first.

When Johnson begins to lose consciousness, Rena thinks, he will submit, and Rena can subdue him.

Not this, not dark, *not like this.*

Johnson wants to scream; he needs to breathe. His mind careers across faces—Navatsky, Smith, Martell, Victoria Madison—then Peanut, so young, and he wonders whether he is grateful it is ending, whether it was worth it.

Then his right arm is free.

And the tip of the Glock emerges again from the water.

Rena sees it and once more they go under.

Rena feels the explosion

And slowly, one limb and then another, Johnson's body goes limp.

From the boathouses, people have come running up the path and through the bush, a man and a group of teenagers. They keep their distance, unsure whether he is a threat or needs their help.

"Call 911," Rena says hoarsely. "Tell them, a man police are looking for has been killed. And there is a second man with a gunshot wound."

Fifty-five

Rena sits nearby on the riverbank waiting for the ambulance. He is soaked in mud, river water, and blood, mostly his own. It takes him several minutes to catch his breath. The shoulder where he has been shot burns.

A Good Samaritan from the gathering crowd helped him drag the body to shore to keep it from drifting downriver. They tried resuscitation but it was too late. The corpse's mouth and eyes were open, as if in a permanent scream. Then the man covered it with a bandanna.

Rena can hear sirens in the distance.

He digs his phone out of his pocket, but it's soaked and dead. "Does anyone have a phone?" Faces turn his way, and the expressions tell him his request is viewed as macabre. The crowd is made up mostly of teenage girls from the women's crew team and their coach, who called 911. The crew coach hands him a phone.

Rena dials the private number he memorized six weeks ago and leaves a message to call back, adding that the situation is an emergency.

The second call is to Spencer Carr. Rena tries to keep it simple: The man who killed a Justice Department attorney named Alan Martell had also stalked Madison; he may have attacked Madison's daughter, too, and Rena's colleague Hallie Jobe; the killer is the deranged relative of a man whose murder trial Madison had presided over; he had shot Rena; Rena in turn has killed him. "I understand," Carr keeps saying, prodding Rena to finish.

"How are you?" Carr asks.

"All right. I'm probably in shock."

Rena sees a man and woman in matching blue T-shirts moving through the crowd, carrying red equipment bags and pulling a gurney. EMS, arriving before the police.

"I have to go."

"Who can I call for you?" asks Carr.

Randi. He hasn't called Randi.

"She's here at the White House," Carr says. "I'll take care of it. What hospital are they taking you to?"

Rena asks one of the two paramedics, a man in his twenties, a weight lifter bursting from his EMS shirt.

"Put the phone down, sir."

"Just tell me where you are going to take me."

The muscular paramedic glances at his female partner.

"Georgetown University Hospital," she answers.

"Georgetown."

Another call is coming in. Rena recognizes the number.

"I've got to go," he says, trying to manipulate the phone buttons without losing the incoming call.

"Peter?" President James Nash says on the other end of the line.

Nash is returning the call Rena had left a moment earlier.

The paramedic grabs the phone out of his hand. "Buddy," the guy says into the phone, "your friend has been shot. He has to hang up now."

Whatever the president of the United States says on the other end of the line apparently isn't persuasive.

"Yeah, right, and I'm George Clooney."

The president's next words must be more convincing. The EMS guy looks unsteady, says, "Yes, sir," and returns the phone to Rena.

"Peter, we're taking over from here," Nash says. "Our doctors will meet you at the hospital. You're going to get the best care there is."

"Find out about Vic and Jobe," Rena hears himself say.

Everything is beginning to sound farther away.

At some point in the ambulance Rena loses consciousness.

Everyone seems to have arrived at once.

The small apartment is filled with uniforms. EMS technicians have turned the hallway into a triage space. It doesn't all quite seem real. Madison can't get the picture out of his mind of Vic lying there on the bathroom floor.

He is standing in the living room and a patrolman who looks about twenty years old is asking him questions. The kid, the name tag says Schmidt, has a flat top and a thin blond mustache that fails to make him look older. He seems confused.

"You escaped?"

"No," Madison says. "I got here afterward. But I think we saw him leaving, or at least we saw a man who we think is responsible."

"'We'? Sir, you are alone. There is no we. Are you sure you're all right? Were you attacked?"

"I already told you, I arrived with a friend, who went off in pursuit of the man who we think might have done this."

"So there were two of you? Did he come into the apartment?"

The paramedics are beginning to move Jobe out of the apartment on a gurney. They must be ready to take Vic, too.

"I have to go," Madison tells the officer. "I have to go with my daughter."

All Madison knows is that Vic was breathing, barely. Jobe, too.

The patrolman gets a hard look on his face.

"You aren't going anywhere until I am done with you, sir," Patrolman Schmidt says with practiced menace.

"Gotta move her," Madison hears one of the paramedics call out.

"I have to go," Madison insists.

"Sir."

"Officer Schmidt, if you persist in this, I should tell you I am a federal judge. You can arrest me, for no reason, a decision you will spend weeks trying to untangle, or you can let me go to the hospital. I will be happy to answer any questions you have there."

More people are arriving, not all of them uniforms, too many people. It's obvious that there is something about this situation that is out of the ordinary. Even Patrolman Schmidt senses it. Madison slips behind Schmidt to follow the second EMS unit that is now carrying Vic out of the apartment.

"I'm going, Patrolman."

Schmidt looks at him in silence, an uncertain expression on his face. As Madison heads out, a man with close-cropped hair and a dark suit moves in step with him. "Judge Madison? I'm Alan Gentry, FBI. May I ride with you in the ambulance to the hospital?"

The first thing Rena sees when he wakes is Randi Brooks.

He is in a bed, in a room, with a curtain.

"Hey," she says with a relieved grin.

"I just told Spencer Carr to call you. How did you get here so fast?" He realizes he doesn't know where he is. Brooks laughs.

"Peter, I've been here for hours. You've had surgery. You're in recovery in the hospital."

Rena tries to process what she has said.

"It's three in the afternoon."

He feels great. He wishes he could sleep like this all the time. Brooks strokes his head. Suddenly Rena is aware of everything. He feels overwhelmingly grateful to see her. "Thanks for being here."

"Where else would I be, you idiot?"

She could be all *kinds* of places, Rena thinks.

"I'm not the only one. There is a whole team in the waiting room. Matt Alabama, Wiley, Lupsa, O'Brien."

His mouth is crusty. "Can I get some water?"

She hands him a cup with ice chips. He isn't sure he has ever had anything so tremendously refreshing.

"Vic? Hallie?"

"They're alive." Her voice is grave.

"Hallie had surgery. They're sleeping."

"I want to see them."

"Peter, you just got out of surgery yourself."

"I need to see them. Call the president if you have to. Call Spencer Carr."

Brooks laughs. "I don't think we need to go that far, Peter. We have FBI crawling all over the place. You guys are VIPs. I think we can arrange almost anything."

"Do it."

"Do you want to know if you're going to die first?"

"Am I?"

"Apparently not. The bullet has been taken out. A shoulder wound. You won't be lifting anything for a while."

"Then you'll have to serve me."

"But no more of this cowboy bullshit, okay?"

"I want to see Vic and Hallie."

"Hold your horses, Deputy Dawg. I'll see what I can do."

Brooks disappears. He would like another cup of ice chips; yes, that would be really nice; he really needs them; he is beginning to feel a little desperate about it.

The drugs have made him stupid.

A nurse enters. Rena pretends to sleep. Brooks returns. "They're ready to move him to a room, as soon as he's awake," the nurse tells her.

"I'm up," he says, opening his eyes.

"Good," the nurse says. "How are you feeling?"

He persuades her that he feels better than he does and in a minute she leaves.

"It's all arranged, Peter. As soon as you're out of recovery in your own room, we can get you into a wheelchair and you can pay a visit."

"Then let's do it," Rena says.

Ten minutes later, Brooks is rolling him and all his tubes out of his new room to Vic's, a few doors down the hall. His left arm is in a sling to immobilize his shoulder. The three conditions are he cannot push himself in the wheelchair, get in the wheelchair by himself, or walk anywhere.

Vic is asleep. Roland Madison is sitting by her bedside. Vic's face is bruised and swollen. Rena feels guilt and remorse wash over him. Madison stands, walks over, and takes Rena's one good hand in both of his.

"Peter."

"How is she?"

"We hope okay. Facial bruising. A severe concussion. That's the diagnosis for now."

Rena foggily tries to process what that means.

"She was unconscious for more than a half hour. They did a CT brain scan, but they found nothing abnormal. Her vision was fine. No serious amnesia. But she remembers nothing from today."

"What happens now?"

"We just observe and hope nothing shows up."

Rena's feelings come in great waves. Relief. Worry. Self-reproach. He is struggling to not be upended by them. The drugs again.

"It's okay for her to sleep?"

"Apparently it's good. The only concern would be if she began to sleep for prolonged periods and had difficulty waking up."

"The gang's all here," the voice from the bed says with a thin smile. Vic is awake.

Rena forgets his shoulder and tries to wheel himself to the bed and winces.

"You are the shittiest patient in this hospital," Brooks tells him.

Rena is relieved to see Vic laugh.

"I'm so sorry," he says to her.

"Don't," Vic says.

Rena feels overwhelmed by all he wants to say.

"I heard you got him," Vic says.

It's the first time anyone's mentioned Johnson; the thought of him jumbles Rena's feelings even more.

Vic takes his hand weakly. She smiles and closes her eyes.

"Have you seen Hallie?" she asks without opening her eyes.

She has more presence of mind than he does, Rena thinks, even now, half-asleep with a concussion. He realizes how she has gently managed things well all along.

"Not yet," he says. "I'm so sorry."

Vic is asleep suddenly.

They aren't allowed to enter Jobe's room in intensive care, but outside they find her mother and sister keeping vigil; the two women explain what they've been told about her condition. Jobe has suffered a skull fracture and an intracranial hemorrhage, or bleeding in the brain. She's had surgery to relieve the bleeding and to check for clots. They won't know much for a while. Problems might not show up for months, perhaps a year. All this is his fault, Rena thinks. A nurse finally shoos Brooks to take Rena back to his room. "Now. And get some sleep," she commands.

Rena spends the next hours in a state of dozy incompetence. At one point two FBI agents interview him, assuring him it's simply protocol.

The night is endless. Nurses enter at all hours to poke and prod him and fiddle with his IV; the hallways are full of light and noise. The next day goes on and on, full of visitors and boredom.

In the afternoon, Rollie Madison comes down the hall to visit.

"How is Vic?"

Madison hesitates before answering. "Tired. Scared. Vulnerable. But more herself than before."

The judge looks pale and drawn, as if he had been locked indoors for months. "Peter, I intend to withdraw."

Rena isn't sure he has heard him right. "What?"

"I think it best."

"Why?"

"Because of what's happened. Because of Vic. Because of James Johnson. Because of everything."

Rena props himself up; the effort sends pain shooting up his arm and across his neck. "You are not responsible for this," he says. It comes out with a passion that surprises him. "James Johnson is. And I am responsible for not protecting you. And the police are responsible for not catching him sooner. But you are not responsible for James Johnson."

Madison smiles sadly. "You are a good man, Peter."

"Rollie." There is bile in Rena's throat.

"James Johnson is not the point, Peter. You can only control your own conduct."

On top of everything, now this. Rena would be angry, but he is too spent.

"We've had our ups and downs, Peter. I know I may not have been the easiest nominee to have managed. But I respect what you have done."

Madison stands up to leave.

"I was wrong about you," Rena says.

Madison turns to look back. "Thank you. Yes, you were."

Rena feels another wave of emotion sweeping over him.

Fifty-six

Saturday, June 27, 9:48 A.M.
Washington, D.C.

Three days later the White House calls.

The hospital had sent Rena home after two endless days. It would have done so after one had the White House not intervened. The media could be kept away more easily in the hospital.

Alabama took the day off to bring him home. Reporters surrounded them at the hospital exit.

"C'mon, guys, give the man a break," Alabama told the scrum. "When he's ready, he'll say something."

"So you can have the exclusive and we can have nothing?" some kid from a cable channel demanded.

Alabama gave the young producer a look, and something in it conveyed the decades, all the stories, all the evil that Alabama had covered over forty years: genocide, war, pandemics, being shot at, jailed, and beaten. Not doing paparazzi stakeouts in Washington.

"Don't make a goddamn fool of yourself out here, son."

The cable guy froze, the crowd parted, and they moved to the car where Eleanor O'Brien was waiting behind the wheel.

Now the White House has summoned him. President Nash would like Rena and Brooks to come for a meeting. It will be Rena's first outing.

Brooks comes to the town house to fetch him, and O'Brien drives them to the White House. In the anteroom, the president's secretary, Sally Swanson, tells them to go right into the Oval Office. The president is waiting.

Nash is sitting with Attorney General Penopopoulis, Senator Burke, and Senator Stevens. Vice President Philip Moreland, a tall former governor from Tennessee whose good looks seem to have turned gaunt from attending funerals for five years, is with them.

Nash rises and takes Rena's hand, his one good arm, in both of his, and leans his head close to Rena's, an intimate shug. "Peter," the president whispers, "I put you in an impossible position. Thank you."

What does Nash mean?

Brooks gets a full hug. The president looks at her sympathetically. "And you? Holding up?"

"Yes, thank you, sir."

A door opens, and Spencer Carr enters from his adjoining office, followed by the White House counsel, George Rawls.

"I think everyone is here. Let's get started," Nash says.

Get started with what, exactly? From his one day home, Rena had deduced that the White House had once again succeeded in portraying the story of James Johnson the way it wanted. The media narrative of the last three days was unambiguous and almost unanimous.

Johnson was a convicted felon with a long history of criminal activity; he'd engaged in a series of cold-blooded murders over two months across the country in some attempt at vengeance for his brother Robbie, himself a convicted rapist and murderer, who was killed in jail. Johnson's killing rampage included his brother's own defense attorney, the policeman who investigated the case, and the prosecutor. In his frenzy, Johnson considered everyone on all sides responsible for his brother's death in prison. Roland Madison, the president's nominee for the Supreme Court, had presided over the jury trial at which Robert Johnson had been convicted.

Johnson had apparently then begun stalking Madison, and eventually tried to murder Madison's daughter, Victoria, who was staying with him in Washington, D.C., during his Senate confirmation hearings. The attack was interrupted by a former federal agent working with the White House to help prepare Madison for the hearings. Johnson attacked the former agent, Hallie Jobe, and then fled, leaving both Victoria Madison and Jobe gravely hurt. Johnson was then chased down by another man working for the White House, a military veteran named Peter Rena. During the chase, Johnson shot Rena with a gun he had stolen from Jobe, and in the ensuing struggle, Johnson died as he and Rena wrestled for the weapon in the waters of the Potomac River near Georgetown.

Judge Madison, not at the scene of the attacks, found his daughter unconscious in his apartment, along with the former federal agent sent there to protect them. Both Madison's daughter and Jobe remain hospitalized, having both suffered head trauma. Rena, recovering from his gunshot wounds, has been released from the hospital.

Profiles of Johnson, his criminal record, and his brutal background have run widely.

The White House has handled Nash's response with the usual delicacy. Every action the president takes is symbolic and to some extent a president must behave as the public expects, or at least that expectation must be taken into account if the president decides to do something unexpected. Hence a president always walks a fine line between recognizing the symbolism of his own life and never trying to appear as if he were exploiting it. Nash had visited the hospital to see Rena, Vic, and Jobe without cameras. The visits reinforced the notion that they were people to be honored, victims of a deranged murderer, were lucky to be alive, and that Rena and Jobe were heroic, but the absence of cameras made it look sincere rather than political. There was a single picture of one moment, the visit with Vic, a still photo taken by the president's personal photographer.

Others had visited, too, not always as sensitively, including Aggie Tucker, who seemed to want to make a show of his concern. Senator Morgan, the chairman of the Judiciary Committee, had visited Vic and Hallie also, the day after Rena was released but entirely privately. One young aide. No cameras. He prayed and held Jobe's hand. No one in Washington knew of that visit.

Belinda Cartwright had showed up, too. Flown from Utah to visit Rena. He hadn't expected it.

All of it reinforced an uncomfortable realization: Their little band had become briefly famous, public figures of a certain kind, which meant people had opinions about them, and expectations about how others in the Madison nomination drama should treat them. It was uncomfortable. Rena had gained more appreciation for the loss of freedom Nash, Morgan, and the others endured.

Privately, Nash and Carr had also met with "the groups," including Deborah Cutter, asking them to affirm their support for Madison. It had been a major push, done proactively, a sign of no White House hesitation about Madison.

The attacks had proven to have another effect on the administration's potential critics. Madison was now a crime victim, not the nominee of a Democratic president presumptively or at least possibly soft on crime. There was no way Josh Albin, already defensive after being accused of trying to tar Madison for his antiwar sentiments, could oppose him publicly now.

Though Rena was sleeping when it happened, he also found out that Albin had visited him in the hospital. Sat with him for a half hour while he was sleeping. Brooks was there. She couldn't believe it. Rena could.

The Senate hearings were suspended. When they resumed, yesterday, the ritual excoriation of Madison by

critics or deification by supporters—still for the benefit of the culture wars and the groups that financed
the parties—had, if not ceased entirely, become more
restrained—an expression of constitutional responsibility rather than mock outrage that such a bizarre and
dangerous character might be considered for a judgeship rather than flogging.

One thing had not happened. So far at least, no
story had appeared raising questions about the Johnson
murder trial. There had been plenty of stories that dis-
cussed James Johnson's criminal life, some mentioning
his brother's conviction and death in jail. But none had
raised doubts about Robert Johnson's guilt or the quality of the trial Madison oversaw that convicted him.
Johnson's mother had gone to ground. A family friend
had told local TV stations in San Francisco she had had
enough pain.

That didn't mean a story couldn't still appear about
Madison presiding over the conviction of a possibly
innocent man. Gary Gold had even written a version
of it, Brooks had heard from friends at the *Tribune*.
Gold's editors had refused to publish it. They weren't
interested in a speculative story that implied without
hard proof that the murderous rampage of James Johnson might be somehow misguided revenge for a mis-
carriage of justice. But that didn't mean the story was

dead. That someone else might not put the pieces together and write it. Or that Gold would stop trying. Or not leak what he had to a blogger who could get it out there. These days virtually everything gets published somewhere eventually.

"Thank you all for coming," President Nash says, taking a seat in an armchair about midway in the semicircle the group formed.

"In my experience, people find it particularly hard to lie to the president of the United States," he says grinning. "I am counting on that today."

Then Nash picks up the phone and tells his secretary, "Please send him in."

Through one of the doors, into the Oval Office enters Rollie Madison.

"Judge, thank you for coming. Please sit," President Nash says.

Madison moves to the chair where Nash has directed him.

"What am I doing here, Mr. President?" Madison asks.

"I want to ask you something," Nash answers. "I would like you to tell me about the murder trial of Robert Johnson."

Madison's eyes fall on Rena. Rena answers with an almost imperceptible shake of his head: *I don't know more than you do.* The judge takes a breath and then, unfolding his long legs, looks at President Nash.

Madison holds nothing back.

He recites the facts of the Johnson murder trial, the weakness of the lawyers, the limits of the case. He describes what he saw, what he did, and how it altered his sense of judging. It had taken months for Rena to see him this open. Now Madison was sharing with strangers.

Nash pauses with theatrical timing before asking the judge, "Did you help send an innocent man to jail?"

It's not the right question, Rena thinks. Madison has taught him that.

"I don't know," Madison answers.

The president nods. Apparently satisfied. Apparently finished.

"If I may, Mr. President. I would like to say one more thing," Madison says. Nash gives a look of interested permission.

"Judges learn on the bench; they grow, or they should. Sometimes they become embittered or timid. But the best of them become more assertive, while also more humbled by the enormity of the process in which they are engaged. At least I have. I was more cautious back then, more uncertain, and I regret it. If you believe that what's happened because of that trial and my conduct during it merits reconsidering my nomination, I understand. That is why I have written my letter of withdrawal. I know you will choose what you think best for the Court and the country."

The president, impish but cool, answers: "The longer we live, the more ironic life becomes. Most judges on the Supreme Court have never been trial judges. They have never faced any of this."

Madison looks back grimly, tired—not the cadaverous figure he appeared to Rena two days ago—but different from the man he met in April.

"Thank you, Judge," Nash says, rising. Everyone stands. The president puts a hand on Madison's shoulder and escorts him to the door, which opens to reveal the president's secretary, Sally Swanson, waiting outside. "Sally will take you back to Spence's office. We'll be with you in a few minutes."

Nash takes off his suit jacket and sits down in his favorite spot, the corner of the sofa. "There are a lot of options here," he begins.

He surveys the faces in the room. "We could, I believe, end this and move on, without any stigma attached to Judge Madison. He has told me in a letter yesterday what he indicated here today, that if I prefer it, he is offering to withdraw because of the trauma to his daughter. No one would doubt him."

"You have his withdrawal letter in hand?" Stevens clarifies.

"Yes." Nash pauses to let the group absorb this and then says, "On the other hand, if we continue I believe Judge Madison would win overwhelming, possibly unanimous confirmation. He has the country's complete sympathy, and I don't know of a single senator at this moment who has signaled an intention now to challenge him either publicly or privately. This morning, I got a call from Furman Morgan. He gave me the courtesy of telling me that he believed there were sufficient votes to move Judge Madison's nomination to the floor and that he was personally inclined to approve as well."

Nash scans the faces in the room.

"I want to know each of your thoughts. Charlie?"

The attorney general, Charles Penopopoulis, says in a charcoal baritone, "As far as I'm concerned, Mr. President, Judge Madison has done nothing to warrant any loss of confidence. This Robert Johnson matter was a jury trial. The determination of guilt or innocence was not Judge Madison's to make. Nothing in the case was overturned on appeal."

"G?" Nash says next. G is short for "G Man," the president's nickname for George Rawls. An old Washington hand and top Washington litigator, Rawls has worked more closely with Rena and Brooks through this than anyone. He is also a staunch liberal.

"I see a lot of advantages to moving in a new direction, Mr. President. Our obligation is to the American people, not Judge Madison. If you have any doubts over this matter, I don't want to think we are papering something over. You have complete freedom now to move on."

"Lewis?" Nash says, turning to Senator Burke.

Llewellyn Burke is not only the sole Republican in the room besides Rena, he is also the most pragmatic tactician Rena had ever seen, a quality that has made people from many quarters seek his counsel. That, Rena thinks, also gives Burke a good deal of latitude to change course here. If he thought it was better to switch now, Burke would not hesitate.

"I appreciate the concern about not wanting to hide anything. This is a big choice, important to get right, a lifetime appointment," Burke says, in his gentle, unhurried, informal way. "But there is something unusual about our court system today at the appellate level and at the highest court. Our judicial system has become hijacked by politics, often extreme politics. This is an invisible constitutional crisis. Do presidents respond by escalating these political and cultural wars by picking even more extreme judges? Or by trying to defuse and end the politicization? Maybe I am a dreamer. But I worry about the stability of the center. That is our common ground. Our spine. It's still mine. I think these wars are divisive for our courts. I would like the polarization and politicization of judges to stop. It's bad for our judiciary. It's bad for our country."

They're almost the same words Nash used to hire Rena in the first place.

"And I would say this about Judge Madison: I don't believe we are papering over anything here. What we do know is that Judge Madison did what he was supposed to do. The fact that he is worried about it now is proof of the kind of man he is, not proof that he did something wrong. I would hate to think that we would do anything to raise questions about him as well, out of political expediency or protectiveness."

Nash turns to Senator Stevens. "Bill?"

Stevens folds his hands atop his formidable stomach. If Stevens signs off on this after having been included in the decision making, the groups on the Left will be more inclined to go along. And the Stevens mafia, the huge network of his former aides who populate powerful positions in town, would send the word out to make it happen.

"I offer no opinion other than this, Mr. President: Go with your gut. You will have my support, publicly and privately."

"Randi?" Nash says, turning to Rena's partner. She and Rena are just hired hands here, not advisors. He has no responsibility to ask their opinion. But he is.

"I've scrubbed this man's background, read his opinions, spent days with him under the most stressful circumstances. I've learned nothing to change my view of your selection of him, sir."

Nash now turns to Rena and lifts his eyebrows in invitation.

Rena's arm suddenly aches. His mind casts back over the last few months: disliking Madison, arguing against him, regretting he hadn't been more forceful.

"Mr. President, when you first asked me about Roland Madison a few months ago I said I worried he was too theoretical, too remote, and that his famous legal theories might be more intellectual than real. From what you heard from Judge Madison today, it should be obvious that I was wrong."

Nash looks as if he expects more. There is none.

Then Nash turns to Spencer Carr. The chief of staff usually reserves his counsel only for the president. If he ever gave it publicly and it were ignored, his power in town would evaporate. But Carr answers now.

"I agree with the White House counsel that it's time for a fresh start. Even if Madison is confirmed, we don't want a story six months from now saying he let an innocent man go to jail, even if it isn't true."

Carr has flipped again.

"But he's confirmed for life," Nash says.

"I'm not worried about how that affects him, Mr. President," Carr says. "I'm worried about how that affects you."

Only one person is left.

"Philip?" Nash says, turning to the vice president of the United States. If everyone else has offered advice, and the vice president isn't even asked, the already diminished former rival of Nash would look even smaller.

"Honestly, Mr. President, I've been skeptical all along of the so-called third way that Judge Madison espouses. I don't think there is a third way. Once conservatives cast everything they don't like as liberal and activist and began to groom and advance ideological judges, they set us on a path that there would be a fairly distinct line between Republican judges and Democratic ones. The parties have polarized. And so have the judges. This is an arms race. To win it, we need bodies, not middle-ground arguments."

The vice president uncrosses his legs. This is a

speech he clearly has wanted to make for some time to someone other than Nash.

"The way to do that is with a strong liberal voice. The interests of the country, I believe, are served by moving on."

However neutered the emotional Tennessee Democrat has been in the cool Nash administration, Moreland has thrived as a southern Democrat by seeing things in black and white—the way a lot of voters do.

"Thank you, everyone." The president stands.

"Thank you, Mr. President," the group answers in a staccato chorus.

"Randi, please take Peter home to recuperate."

Brooks smiles.

"Spence, Phil, mind staying?"

As they head in the car back to Rena's town house, he feels his phone receive a text. A glance while Brooks is looking at the road. The number is unfamiliar.

"Call me. C.W."

The sneaky old army cop, Carter White, whom Rena has asked to investigate his friends and partners, the man Rena has asked to find their mole.

Fifty-seven

Wednesday, July 1, 9:30 A.M.
Washington, D.C.

Rena decides he should come into the office four days later. He has gotten thoroughly bored at home, watched too much TV, done too little reading, and found himself sitting in the kitchen answering work email anyway—many of them from people worried because he was still at home. Brooks picks him up and drives him in.

The staff is gathered in the lobby.

"We wanted to say, well, how much we were worried," Ellen Wiley announces. "How brave we think you are. And how glad we are that you're okay. And, of course, that we are praying for Hallie."

Some people are crying.

"Thank you. Everyone," he says.

"How are you feeling?" asks Arvid Lupsa.

"I'm fine. Sore," Rena says.

They are expecting more.

"Now back to work."

There is a smattering of nervous laughter. They had sent him balloons at home, and most of them had visited at the hospital. He should say more.

"We're not ready to go back to work yet and you're in no shape to make us," Smolonsky says. The laughter this time is genuine.

Maureen O'Conner comes up to him with an odd look. "I'm just going to kiss you," she says, standing on her tiptoes, and she gives him a peck on the cheek. "And I'm not even going to ask if I may." A tear forming, she turns on her heels.

More greetings and gingerly given hugs and people crossing that line between work friendship and their personal feelings.

Then Rena turns to his partner. "You got a minute?"

"Be there in a second."

In Rena's office, Eleanor O'Brien has arranged the morning papers on the coffee table for him. Rena has already read them electronically.

The front page of the *Tribune* is upside down on the table.

"Madison Wins Unanimous Approval in Committee. Confirmation Now All But Assured. Judge Wins Vote While at Hospital with Daughter."

"We have that other thing to take care of," Brooks says, entering the office. "You ready?"

Rena scratches his wounded shoulder.

"How did he figure it out, anyway?" he asks her.

"Carter White found a family connection, an uncle, that had been the tip-off, someone connected to Albin."

Brooks hands a file to Rena, who takes a minute to read it.

"You want to do it?" he asks her.

"I thought you would."

"Gee, thanks," Rena says.

"You're welcome."

Rena dials the number and hits speakerphone.

"Hey, can you come in, please."

He and Brooks look at each other. Brooks takes a deep breath. O'Brien appears in the doorway.

"Hi," she says.

"Hi," Rena says back. "You'd better sit down."

She settles uncomfortably on the sofa.

Rena tosses the file with the name of her uncle and his connection to Albin on the coffee table in front of her.

When she looks up, she has tears in her eyes.

"We know you were the leak about Madison to Albin. Walt Smolonsky is going through your desk right now and putting your things in a box. Ellen has your computer. I will take your phone," he says, holding out his hand.

O'Brien looks terrified.

"Here is what is going to happen, Eleanor."

Rena is standing over her, leaning against the side of his desk. "You've been badly misused in this. People being sent to be spies in each other's offices. But you're young. Too young. So no one will ever hear about this from anyone here. If anyone ever finds out, it will be because Albin bragged."

O'Brien is crying harder.

Rena looks over at Brooks to see if she has something she wants to add.

She speaks to the young woman with a hard edge people rarely see in his partner. "Eleanor, you know what we do here. We investigate things. So we're going to keep track of you. We will know where you work from now on. And if it's someplace fishy, where we think you may be acting like some kind of spy, we will make the call. From now on, for the rest of your fucking life, we are watching."

O'Brien's expression freezes.

"If you want a life in politics, we want you to have that chance. But you have to do it right, Eleanor," Brooks says.

"Why are you doing this?" O'Brien manages through her sobs.

"Because this wasn't your idea. And because at your age you should have a second chance," Rena says.

O'Brien wipes her eyes with the bottom of her palms, then looks at Brooks.

"You think I didn't know what I was doing?" she says.

"Not in the slightest, even if you thought you did."

O'Brien smiles grimly. "You two are such hypocrites. You dig up dirt on people for a living and tell yourselves if you behave well and just tell the truth, things will turn out right," O'Brien says. "Well, that is why everything in the world is going to hell. Because things don't just turn out all right by themselves. We have to save this country."

Rena's shoulder starts to throb.

"I'll escort you to the ladies' room, Eleanor," Brooks says. "You can wash your face. And then get your scrawny little butt out of here."

O'Brien looks defiantly back at her. "I'm fine," she says, rising from the sofa and marching, quickly, self-consciously, out of his office. Brooks follows her.

Rena sinks into an armchair and closes his eyes. He feels bent and rattly—like an old car with too many miles. They'd won, hadn't they? Or is that only because they trained the nominee not to answer questions, withheld the truth about his antiwar history, and used the discovery of a mole in their office to flip it against their opponents? Then they had skirted over Madison's biggest regret, presiding over the conviction of a possibly innocent man.

What was Nash's old campaign slogan? "Get it done"?

He gets up and walks to the window. Down on Nineteenth Street, he sees a young couple about O'Brien's age walking toward M Street, both in suits, starting their Washington day, hair still wet from showering. They are holding hands. They are coming from the metro station a block away. Behind them the street begins to fill with other people pouring out of the subway, most of them young, serious-looking, full of hope and purpose, mature for their age. That part of the city hasn't changed. Every year another wave, like another subway car. He and Katie and all their friends had that shining look. A city of the exceptional, the best of their generation, come to give back, to make a difference. It is one of his favorite things about the city, and one of the things that makes it feel tragic.

The phone is ringing.

He wonders if it might be Vic.

The receptionist's voice crackles through the phone intercom: "Peter, it's Gary Gold calling from the *Tribune*."

Rena looks back out the window at more people flowing out from the subway. Then, slowly, he heads to his desk.

Acknowledgments

There are more people to thank than I can count. The list begins with my parents, who had different tastes in fiction from each other but who both passed on their passion. I owe an enormous debt to Antonella Iannarino. She believed in this journey and made the manuscript immeasurably better. And, like Peter Rena, she was always blunt.

Thanks also goes to David Black, who is no less candid and always has my back. I am ever in his hands. Thanks, as well, to many others at the Black Agency who have helped me over the years, now including Jennifer Herrera.

I am grateful to many friends in politics, left and right, who inhabit this story. That list includes elected officials whom I have covered and who shared time with me, many gifted and dedicated staff who make up so much of government—consultants, lobbyists, communications experts, and interest group activists. It is popular today to see such work in the most cynical light. The facts, I find, are different.

Thanks to countless friends in journalism; a few in particular will see parts of themselves here. The irrepressible Gary Cohn, a long-ago friend, may be surprised to be here. The gentle Jim Wooten, a teacher and good man, may also be. Many in the law contributed to this story. Thanks especially to the Honorable Beth Freeman, who shared the story of her own nomination, and the no-less-honorable Bill Freeman, who shared many thoughts about the law.

Drew Littman helped the manuscript with wonderful and encouraging suggestions at just the right time and with many insights from inside the game. Katherine Klein made Peter Rena better. Craig Buck showed me the power of the keepin' on. Martha Toll continually inspires me by her example, and Dan Becker has been her supporter and mine.

I owe special gratitude to two people: John Gomperts not only read nearly every version of this book but also debated every plot turn with me. Forty-five years of friendship and we're just getting started, pal. Zachary Wagman, my editor at Ecco, found this story and these characters and believed in them. With a deft hand, Zack, you made this book much better. I couldn't be luckier. Thanks, as well, to many others at Ecco, including Emma Janaskie who believed in this story—my team.

I am grateful above all, and as always, to my three special women: my girls, Leah and Kira, who have always believed in their dad; and my bride, Rima, who has put up with me and also lived this dream.

Last, to those who write, not the oldest profession but the best.

HARPER LUXE

THE NEW LUXURY IN READING

We hope you enjoyed reading
our new, comfortable print size and found it
an experience you would like to repeat.

Well – you're in luck!

HarperLuxe offers the finest in fiction and
nonfiction books in this same larger print size and
paperback format. Light and easy to read, HarperLuxe
paperbacks are for book lovers who want to see
what they are reading without the strain.

For a full listing of titles and
new releases to come, please visit our website:

www.HarperLuxe.com